AGED FOR MAYHEM

AGED FOR MAYHEM

(A Tuscan Vineyard Cozy Mystery-Book 3)

FIONA GRACE

FIONA GRACE

Debut author Fiona Grace is author of the LACEY DOYLE COZY MYSTERY series, comprising nine books (and counting); of the TUSCAN VINEYARD COZY MYSTERY series, comprising four books (and counting); of the DUBIOUS WITCH COZY MYSTERY series, comprising three books (and counting); and of the BEACHFRONT BAKERY COZY MYSTERY series, comprising three books (and counting).

MURDER IN THE MANOR (A Lacey Doyle Cozy Mystery—Book 1) is available as a free download on Amazon!

Fiona would love to hear from you, so please visit www.fionagrace-author.com to receive free ebooks, hear the latest news, and stay in touch.

TABLE OF CONTENTS

CHAPTER ONE

"Dear Marcello," Olivia Glass began her email, "I am so sorry about what has happened."

She was working on her apology while seated in a comfy armchair in her Tuscan farmhouse's cozy living room. Hoping for inspiration, she looked up and stared at the rain drumming the darkened windowpane.

This wasn't the way she'd expected her first-ever letter to her handsome, blue-eyed, winery-owner boss to begin.

She'd nursed a secret fantasy that a note to him might start with, "Thank you for a wonderful time on our first date last night! The dinner and wine—and, of course, your company—were amazing."

Olivia sighed in frustration. After the terrible mistake she'd made, there wouldn't be any possibility of a date. She'd be lucky if there was the prospect of a job!

Also, it hadn't been a mistake. That was downplaying the severity of her actions. She'd deliberately caused a disaster, and she needed to own up to it before Marcello found out.

Pushing aside a lock of blond hair, she bent to her task again.

"I realize that I have cost you much-needed money, as well as wasted valuable grapes which you can never get back. It was irresponsible of me to have done this."

What should she say next?

Olivia clutched her forehead. At this critical time, she had writer's block.

Writer's block wouldn't have been allowed in her previous life as an ad agency account manager in Chicago. Campaigns had to be launched on deadline, no matter how many cups of coffee, late nights, and hysterical tears it took.

At the beginning of summer, Olivia had quit her high-pressure but well-paid job after her boyfriend Matt had broken up with her. She'd joined her friend Charlotte on vacation, and had impulsively applied for the position of sommelier at La Leggenda, one of Tuscany's most famous wineries. To her amazement, Marcello had hired her, and Olivia had taken a wild leap into a new life.

Acting with even more reckless abandon, she'd sold her cozy Chicago apartment and plunged her life savings into this hilly farm, hoping that she could fulfill her dream of making her own wine one day.

She was thirty-four, and, as her mother never stopped telling her, she was far too old to make such a drastic life change. Olivia kept reminding her mother that she'd already *made* the change, but Mrs. Glass seemed convinced that if she repeated her words often enough, she could rewind time and undo the folly of her daughter's actions.

Rewind time! Olivia groaned, reminded again of her terrible misdemeanor. How was she ever going to make things right with Marcello? Would he trust her again? She wished she could backtrack a few weeks to reverse the damage she had done.

With time on her mind, Olivia glanced at the clock on the wall. Appalled, she jumped to her feet. She'd been so focused on her work predicament, she'd forgotten about her evening chores. She needed to check whether her baby grapevines were weathering this gale-force wind. And she had a goat to care for—an unpredictable goat who could have roamed anywhere by now in search of a nighttime snack! In the worsening storm, Olivia would have no hope of finding Erba if she'd gotten impatient while waiting to be fed, and decided to go adventuring.

Hurrying to the array of clothing draped over the hall table, she pulled a rain jacket over a thick, water-resistant coat. After some thought, she stepped into Wellington boots and pulled on ski gloves.

Finally, with some difficulty—she should have done it before the gloves—she wedged a rain hat onto her head, forcing the hat as far down as it would go.

"Ready," she said, glancing apprehensively at the pitch-dark window.

The downpour hadn't abated. In fact, it was worsening.

Olivia hadn't expected rainstorms in Tuscany to be so dramatic. So tempestuous. So—so horizontal. Every storm was accompanied by gusting winds that threatened to sweep her off her feet. She wished there had been some warning about this. She'd bought the farmhouse in the height of summer, and there had been nothing in the purchase contract that hinted at the apocalypse to come as fall set in.

Olivia thought back to her Chicago apartment with a pang of regret. The modern place was well insulated, with double glazing, and the front door opened into the corridor. You could go the whole way downstairs and climb into a cab without getting as much as a drop of rain on your shoes. There had been years where she'd barely noticed it was winter. Weather had been an abstract concept, something that happened on the other side of the windows.

Those days were over. She was committed to becoming a wine farmer now, whatever it took.

Olivia glanced sadly at the ruined umbrella that lay in the corner. It had taken just two seconds of a Mediterranean storm to turn it inside out.

"Well, it's not getting any better," she said aloud. The sooner she embarked on her mission, the sooner she'd be back inside.

She pushed open the front door.

Straight away, the wind slammed it in her face again.

"Damn," Olivia said. The task was harder the second time around, because rain had blown inside and her shoes were skidding in the puddles.

She managed to wedge the door open a crack and shoved her boot through it, spitting and blinking the water away from her face.

"Okay, here we go!"

She was out, the door banging behind her, shunted sideward by the gale as she headed on her important—in fact, critical—errand.

Slipping and skidding down the stony slope, the pathway invisible in the dark, Olivia somehow managed to end up in the vicinity of her closest grapevine plantation.

She removed one of her gloves and delved in her inside jacket pocket for her phone, turning on the flashlight with fingers that were already numb.

Olivia felt her heart swell with relief and pride.

The hardy grapevine saplings were withstanding the torrential rains. In fact, they looked to be thriving, swaying in the gale, their baby leaves vivid green in the flashlight's glow. It was rewarding to think that the compost and fertilizer she'd so carefully added to the seed beds was now soaking into the ground, ready to nourish the spreading roots.

Unlike herself, her first ever crop of grapes looked superbly adapted to survive the upcoming Tuscan winter.

Sighing—or rather, spluttering—with relief, Olivia put her phone back in her pocket and turned away. The second part of her outdoor quest was even more important than the first. Gritting her teeth, she plowed through the maelstrom, heading for the almost invisible outline of the large barn.

By the time she reached it, she was drenched and shivering. Stepping through the barn's open doorway into the quiet, musty-smelling interior was a relief. Even though Olivia had not yet procured doors for the huge, open doorway in the old but solidly constructed building, she was surprised by how dry the barn remained. Whoever had built it had known where the prevailing winds blew, and had ensured that the barn's entrance was protected.

Long ago, this high-roofed barn had been a winemaking building, and Olivia was determined that it would be again—as soon as she'd cleared the huge pile of rubble out of it and invested in a tall, strong pair of doors to secure it.

For now, though, it had another function.

With numb fingers, Olivia turned on her phone flashlight again.

The beam danced over a pile of straw placed in the corner of the barn to provide a dry, warm, and sheltered bed.

Which was empty.

Where was Erba?

Olivia bit her lip. She had no idea where to begin looking for the independent-minded goat. She might have to search the whole farm!

Then, out of the corner of her eye, she glimpsed movement above her head.

Looking up, she saw Erba peering down at her from the top of the stack of bales. Clearly, she'd decided that this lofty, uncomfortable-looking perch was far more appealing than her lovingly made nest of straw.

"Erba! What are you doing up there?" Olivia shifted from foot to foot, her teeth chattering. Erba regarded her calmly while Olivia's drenched clothing formed puddles as it dripped.

"You must come down. Dinner's late, I know, but it's time now!"

Next to the bales stood a pink water bucket and a large steel chest which Olivia had purchased. She checked Erba's water before opening the chest and tugging a chunk of alfalfa from the bale concealed inside. She'd had to buy the chest because Erba was greedy about alfalfa. Olivia had been amused to learn that the Italian translation of alfalfa was, in fact, *erba medica*. How appropriate!

She placed the deep green, leafy wedge in the bed of straw and watched in admiration as Erba leaped nimbly down the stack, heading eagerly toward her dinner, and began to munch.

Olivia leaned forward and scratched the goat's head. Her fur felt soft, warm, and dry.

Olivia had to admit that her nonexistent winemaking facility had been successfully repurposed as a goat stable. She wasn't sure if she had what it took to be a vineyard owner, but she was doing a phenomenal job as a one-goat farmer. Erba wanted for nothing.

At that moment, her phone rang.

"Hello, Olivia! It's Bianca. How are you doing over there?"

Olivia's numb lips curved into a smile.

Bianca had been her assistant at the ad agency, and was still working there. In fact, she'd emailed Olivia a while ago to say she'd been promoted to junior account manager.

"It's great to speak to you." She was thrilled that Bianca had found a moment to call her. She guessed it was mid-morning in Chicago, so Bianca must be at work.

There was only one problem. If Olivia continued speaking to Bianca out here, she would perish from exposure before the call ended.

"Can you give me a moment? I've got to run back to the farmhouse. I'm in the barn right now."

"The barn!" Bianca echoed admiringly, as if this was the most exotic destination she'd ever imagined.

"There's a rainstorm, and it's freezing, so I need to get back inside."

"Gee, is it winter there?" Bianca sounded confused, as if she'd thought it was always summer in Tuscany. Well, to be fair, so had Olivia, for a while.

"Late fall, but there's been an unseasonal cold snap. The weather must be changing where you are, too?"

Bianca paused.

"I don't know. My office blinds are closed."

If she hadn't been shivering so violently, Olivia would have laughed.

"Give me a minute," she said. "Night, Erba," she called to the goat.

Then Olivia powered her way out of the barn, ducking her head as the rain hit her.

She blasted through the front door, skidded in the puddle she'd forgotten about, and aquaplaned across the hallway floor, arms windmilling.

Luckily, she'd slowed down by the time she reached the kitchen, and was able to grab hold of the doorframe and stumble inside.

She breathed a sigh of relief to be back in her happy place.

It was toasty warm thanks to the fire burning in the grate. The curtains, made of thick green and white plaid fabric, were drawn against the storm. Olivia had put a lot of thought into the countertops, and had eventually chosen a pale lime Caesarstone. She was thrilled by the bright, fresh ambience this gave the room. When the curtains were open, the green of her countertops seemed to echo the color of the faraway hills, making Olivia feel connected with the outside environment.

She pulled off her jacket and gloves, stepped out of her boots, and headed to the fluffy rug in front of the fireplace. She sat down cross-legged next to her semi-tame black-and-white cat, Pirate, who was curled up on a corner of the rug, fast asleep.

"I'm inside," she told Bianca.

"How's your wine farming progressing?" her ex-assistant asked. "Are your wines available yet? Can I order a bottle?"

"Well, the vines I planted are still babies," Olivia explained. "They'll only produce grapes next year at the earliest. I'm lucky they even sprouted before winter! There are wild vines on the property, and I discover more of them every time I take a walk, but I haven't picked any of those grapes yet."

Olivia remembered the thrill of joy when she'd discovered the first vine growing wild on her farm. That was the moment she had realized that grapes could, in fact, thrive in the stony soil. Since then she had learned that her property had been a wine farm long ago, before it had fallen into disrepair. A few of the vines had survived, but she knew it would take a full day of adventuring around the hilly twenty acres to find all the randomly located plants, which were now laden with ripe grapes. She hadn't had a chance to set the time aside yet, but foraging among her wild vines was the only way she would be able to make a small batch of wine this year.

"And your job?" Bianca asked. "Are you still working for the winery?"

Olivia shifted uneasily on the rug.

Bianca's words provided an uncomfortable reminder of her predicament.

"I'm actually in a spot of trouble at work," she confessed, imagining how Bianca's forehead would furrow in consternation at her words.

"What happened?" she asked. Now Olivia could visualize her starting to chew at her fingernails. It was her nervous habit whenever she was under stress.

Olivia decided to unburden to her former assistant. This was her chance to confess the folly of what she'd done.

Chapter Two

"I was left unsupervised in the winemaking building, and I misunderstood what I was allowed to do there. I used a whole lot of grapes that weren't meant for me at all," Olivia confessed to Bianca.

She reddened in shame as she remembered the confidence—no, arrogance, with which she'd danced into the building, her beginner's brain abuzz with idiotic and unworkable ideas for undrinkable wines.

"That's terrible! Why did they leave you unsupervised? They know you're not experienced," Bianca said in an awestruck tone, which didn't make Olivia feel any better at all.

"It was the end of the growing season, and Nadia, the vintner, was working at our other winery for a few weeks before going on vacation. She said there was excess wine left in some of the barrels, and I could experiment with it and try my hand at blending."

"Okay. Then what happened?" Bianca sounded intrigued.

"Then the last few harvests came in. They were intended for specific wines that were part of the vineyard's yearly production plan. Everyone knew what to do with them, but because I was there, they thought I was in charge and listened to me instead."

Olivia remembered her gleeful delight when the freshly picked grapes—the last of the autumn harvest—were delivered. She'd thought in her ignorance that they were available for her to use, too, and she'd had a brainwave.

A brain fart, in fact, she acknowledged. Those grapes had each been intended for a specialized purpose. Merlot grapes to make merlot. The final, precious harvest of sangiovese, which had been in short supply, to make sangiovese. Nebbiolo grapes to make barolo.

And so on. She buried her face in her hands as she remembered the audacity of her actions. What an idiot she'd been.

"I did a stupid thing. I used them all. I wasted grapes that were meant for hundreds of expensive bottles of wine, on my ridiculous experiment."

"Oh dear!" Bianca sounded worried.

"I only realized this afternoon, when Antonio—he's the youngest of the three Vescovis—came in to compile a report for Nadia before leaving on his vacation. He was horrified. He practically ran away when he found out what I'd done. Nadia has a terrible temper, and she's his older sister."

"I would be scared, too," Bianca agreed.

"I've been trying to compose an email to Marcello, but while I've been speaking to you, I've started wondering if a personal apology would be better."

"I agree. Definitely better. Talk it through with him. That sounds like a good plan," Bianca said.

"How are things going at work?"

Olivia hoped that being regaled by the latest shenanigans at the advertising agency would be entertaining enough to distract her from the worrying task ahead, but as she and Bianca chatted, she found her mind returning again and again to the scary face-to-face meeting that now dominated her future.

She dreaded to see the disappointment in Marcello's eyes as she confessed her reckless actions to him.

The following morning, the storm had blown over. Cool, bright sunshine streamed in through Olivia's bedroom window. She climbed out of bed carefully so as not to disturb Pirate, who was sleeping next to her feet, and stared at the view.

The last of the gray clouds were dissipating, and the early morning sky looked blue and friendly again. Olivia loved the way the lower rays made the landscape seem more dramatic, the shadows of the trees darker and longer, and the hills and fields a deeper and more vivid green. It was only now that she realized how parched the landscape had been at the end of summer, dusty and golden-brown, thirsty for the nourishment of the rains that winter would bring.

Olivia resolved to get to work early, so she could meet with Marcello before Nadia arrived. That way, he'd understand how sorry she was, and how urgently she wanted to make amends.

Perhaps, once Nadia had calmed down, Olivia would get away with a final warning and a salary cut to make up for the financial damage she'd caused.

She checked the weather forecast. No rain was expected today, which meant that she and Erba could walk to work, and not have to use her elderly gray Fiat pickup parked by the side of the farmhouse.

Olivia opened the wooden wardrobe which she'd bought from a second-hand store and spent a weekend sanding and varnishing. The warm tones of the natural wood paired perfectly with the cream shade she'd chosen for the bedroom walls, and the yellow curtains. The color scheme made the bedroom cheerful and homely, which suited the atmosphere of the farmhouse, too.

She chose a stylish yet practical outfit for her day's work, opting for beige pants, brown boots, and a long-sleeved top in a gorgeous shade of lime. Then she grabbed her pretty green and gold jacket from the wardrobe and headed downstairs.

Erba was already perched on the kitchen windowsill, expecting her morning carrots. After serving them to the goat in the courtyard, which was lined with beds of herbs she'd planted herself, Olivia made a quick cup of coffee. Then it was time for her to head to work, with Erba trotting enthusiastically behind.

La Leggenda's elegant stone buildings, washed clean by the rain and free from summer dust, glowed golden-bronze in the morning sun. As she headed up the paved driveway, Olivia admired the closest vine plantation on the sloping hillside. She felt proud to think she'd been working here when they had been planted. Now, the fast-growing, sturdy-looking vines were healthy and strong. They, too, seemed to have thrived and in fact had shot up after yesterday's storm.

Before she approached the tasting room's arched entrance, Olivia risked a glance at the winemaking building.

There was no sign of Nadia.

Perhaps she was only back at work tomorrow. Miracles happened—didn't they?

More worryingly, Marcello's car was not in the parking lot. That meant he might be inspecting the vineyards, or even working at the other winery near Pisa this morning. She'd have to wait and watch out for him, and be ready with her apology the moment he appeared.

As Olivia headed into the tasting room, her eyes widened. It sounded as if there was a stand-up fight in progress.

"*Non, non, non!*" an impassioned, French-accented voice shouted. "How can you allow such a thing? It is wrong, wrong, so very wrong. Unacceptable!"

Olivia recognized the distinctive tones of Jean-Pierre Pelletier, her brand new assistant sommelier.

Who was he fighting with so early in the day? she wondered.

Hurrying inside to try and manage Jean-Pierre's tirade, Olivia stopped in her tracks as she heard the screeched reply.

"I will allow whatever I want. I am in charge here, and I will not be told what to do by someone who is young and ignorant and still has water behind their ears!"

Olivia recognized the irate, Italian-accented tones of Gabriella, the restaurant manager.

Gabriella also happened to be Marcello's ex-girlfriend. Since Olivia had felt an immediate spark of attraction toward Marcello when she met him, and sensed he felt the same way, she guessed this was why Gabriella had disliked her from the start. In fact, it wasn't dislike, it was venomous antipathy. Gabriella had tried her best to sabotage Olivia's job, and her future at the winery.

Well, if Jean-Pierre was annoying her, that was a shame, wasn't it?

Olivia slowed her hurried pace to a casual stroll and moseyed inside, listening with a flicker of glee as the shouted argument continued.

"Ignorant? My father worked in one of Paris's most famous Michelin-starred restaurants for ten years, and he taught me that the red wine glass is placed to the left of the white wine glass in a formal table setting."

Jean-Pierre didn't sound aggressive, Olivia realized, as she stopped mid-saunter to straighten one of the tasting sheets placed on the long wooden counter. He just sounded passionate, as if he couldn't bear that Gabriella was getting it so wrong.

"We do it differently in our restaurant," Gabriella snapped back at him, and Olivia could hear the defensiveness in her voice. She knew this meant Gabriella had lost the argument and was only retaliating to have the last word.

"Well, you do it incorrectly!" Jean-Pierre cried, and Olivia heard real exasperation in his tone.

"Good morning, Jean-Pierre. Are we ready to start our day?" she called, deciding that intervention at this moment would allow Jean-Pierre to have the final say, and ruin Gabriella's day completely.

Jean-Pierre ran back into the tasting room, leaving Gabriella frustrated and open-mouthed as she searched for a suitable retort.

Lean, dark-haired, and just twenty-one years old, Jean-Pierre had been the candidate she'd hired out of the five hopefuls eager to start a career in the world of wine.

She'd chosen the young man because of his evident passion and his expressive nature. The way he'd waved his arms when he got excited during the interview reminded her of Nadia. She thought he would fit in with the Italian spirit at the winery, and that his enthusiasm would take him far.

So far, Olivia's instincts had been right, but she hadn't realized she would have to spend quite so much time managing his tempestuous outbursts.

"Good morning, Olivia. Everything is prepared for the tourists to arrive. I was trying to assist with the table settings next door," he explained, giving her an anxious glance.

"The tasting room looks perfect," Olivia praised him. She felt a surge of pride as she gazed around the spacious room. The long tasting counter gleamed, and the display of wooden barrels under the winery's logo provided the perfect backdrop for guests. The glowing warmth of the gold lettering symbolized the friendliness of the welcome and the tasting experience that guests enjoyed.

Framed posters displaying La Leggenda's history and wines lined the walls, and there were brand new glossy pamphlets on the tables with more detailed information, ready for guests to browse.

Olivia was proud of these because they were her creation. She'd recently taken on the winery's marketing in addition to her tasting room work, and the brochures were one of the ways in which she was enhancing La Leggenda's brand presence.

"Any time you notice anything wrong in the restaurant, make sure to let Gabriella know. After all, we need to uphold the highest standards in every part of the business," she added. She raised her voice as she spoke, just in case Gabriella was listening in. She was sure she would be, and Olivia felt pleased to be one up on her again. It had taken a while.

When Marcello had asked her to hire a new assistant sommelier, Olivia's first suggestion had been Paolo, a waiter in the restaurant who enjoyed helping in the tasting room during busy times.

Gabriella had outmaneuvered her by immediately promoting Paolo to head waiter. That was a great opportunity for the handsome young student, as it meant a bigger paycheck, and that he no longer had to polish the glasses, which was a job he resented.

Olivia had been disappointed, correctly inferring that Gabriella had done this just to spite her.

Now, she was pleased that Jean-Pierre, who had been appointed because Paolo was no longer available, seemed to have an uncanny knack for annoying Gabriella. This wasn't the first time they had clashed. Olivia couldn't help a warm feeling of satisfaction every time she heard their raised voices. She hoped it showed Gabriella that mean-spirited actions could have unintended consequences.

"We have a special treat for guests over the next few weeks," she told Jean-Pierre. "If they take the full tasting menu, they can sample La Leggenda's first-ever Metodo Classico sparkling wine."

Jean-Pierre's eyes lit up. Olivia had already discovered that sparkling wine, and particularly French champagne, was his favorite drink.

"I am pleased. I think that this sparkling wine is exceptional," he enthused. "I know the guests will enjoy it."

"It's a triumph of winemaking," Olivia agreed.

The mention of winemaking gave her a chill in the pit of her stomach, reminding her that a whole world of trouble lay ahead.

And, at that moment, a piercing shout rang from outside the tasting room.

"Olivia! Where is Olivia? I want to speak with her immediately."

Olivia's stomach dropped all the way to the gleaming tiled floor. Out of the corner of her eye she saw Gabriella hovering at the restaurant's entrance with an eager expression, as if sensing that trouble was coming Olivia's way.

Nadia had arrived.

She hadn't had a chance to apologize to Marcello and now the moment had been lost. She would have to face the full brunt of Nadia's fury, and her dreadful mistake would be exposed for the whole winery to see.

CHAPTER THREE

"Olivia! There you are!"

Nadia burst into the tasting room.

She held a carafe of glowing pink liquid in her right hand. She was gesticulating wildly with her left.

Olivia felt a pang of anguish. The wine was a beautiful, almost jewel-like color. It was a tragedy that something so bright and pretty looking was going to be her downfall.

"Where is Marcello? Is he here?" Nadia demanded.

Olivia swallowed. This was worse than she'd thought. If Nadia was demanding Marcello's presence, it meant that Olivia's actions were unforgivable.

"I don't know where he is. I've been looking out for him because—er—"

Her voice tailed off. The heartfelt apology she'd been planning was now redundant.

Nadia grimaced. "What a shame. Well, I guess you and I will have to discuss this, then. And Jean-Pierre, of course." Her face brightened, as if she was pleased to find a bigger audience.

Olivia gawped at her in consternation.

Jean-Pierre? Why was he being brought into this? Was Nadia going to send her home and ask Jean-Pierre to take her place?

Risking a glance toward the restaurant, she saw Gabriella's expression of evil glee. The restaurateur was peeking around the door, reveling in Olivia's predicament.

"Jean-Pierre, *mon beau cheri*." Nadia beamed at him. She had taken an immediate liking to the gangly, outspoken Frenchman. The two of them seemed twin souls who had instantly recognized their key personality traits in the other. "Get us some glasses, *merci beaucoup, jeune petit beau grand homme.*"

What was she calling him? A young, small, beautiful, tall man? With Olivia's basic knowledge of French, she couldn't tell whether this mishmash of words was even correctly conjugated. She didn't think Nadia knew, either. The vintner seemed to enjoy practicing her execrable French in conversation and, apart from the occasional wince at her accent, Jean-Pierre was good-humored about hearing his language inadvertently mangled.

Even though Olivia was working hard on her Italian and her grasp of it was improving every day, she was far too shy to speak it yet, and could only admire Nadia's bravado at attempting to converse in a foreign language.

Olivia watched in confusion as Jean-Pierre reached across the counter and produced three tasting glasses with a flourish.

Nadia smiled proudly as she poured a portion of the wine into each.

"Jean-Pierre, taste this. It is La Leggenda's first ever rosé wine, and your boss made it!"

She beamed at Olivia, who nearly dropped her glass in shock. This wasn't turning out the way she had expected.

"It is still a very young wine, but perfectly made for its purpose, which is to be sold and enjoyed next summer. So it will not require much more maturation before being bottled. As you can taste, it is an absolute triumph. This is more than excellent, it is superb. Olivia, I believe that through your experiment, you have created another Miracolo—a wine that should not have worked, but did, and which will bring our winery extraordinary success and accolades."

Nadia sipped, looking infatuated.

Olivia leaned against the counter. She was grateful for its support, because her legs felt like jelly.

Nadia loved her wine? Where was the trouble she'd anticipated? The vintner didn't seem angry about the grapes at all. For a moment she wondered if she was still asleep in bed and this was all a weird dream.

She wiggled her foot to check.

Nope, not asleep. If she was, Pirate would have clawed her toe and woken her up. And, in any case, Jean-Pierre and Nadia were still discussing her creation.

"It is delicious," Jean-Pierre agreed. "I love a good rosé. Such a modern wine. And this is a fine example. A subtle, complex, and very drinkable taste."

"Exactly." Nadia slammed her palm on the counter. "In terms of sales, rosé is the fastest growing type of wine, particularly in the American market."

"Why is that?" Jean-Pierre asked. Olivia could see he was ready to take mental notes and improve his wine knowledge.

"Some people think this is because it appeals to millennials—they love it—while others believe it's because there are so many good quality rosé wines being produced today," Nadia explained. "Thirty years ago, they were sickly sweet rubbish, nothing more than lurid cough mixture. Today, most rosés are dry or off-dry, and far better quality. Plus, the beautiful color is an additional selling point."

Finally, Olivia dared to take a sip of her wine, breathing in the fresh, floral aroma with a hint of melon. She'd been so pleased by its distinctive and appealing bouquet. Assessing it once again, she decided the taste was rich in cherry, strawberry, and wild herbs, with a tang of citrus providing a pleasantly dry finish.

"How do you make a rosé?" Jean-Pierre asked. "Do you mix red and white wine together?"

Nadia rolled her eyes at him affectionately.

"That is frowned upon or even disallowed. Rosé wine is traditionally made from red grapes. The striking color is achieved by leaving the skins on the grapes for a very short time during the process—one or two days only."

Olivia nodded. She'd left the skins in contact with the wine for twenty-four hours.

"With red wine, the skins are left on for much longer," Nadia continued, gesticulating expressively to emphasize the importance of her words. "The shorter contact with the red grape skins allows for the magnifico pink shade of rosé, and gives an exquisite flavor, without the heaviness of a traditional red, which some do not enjoy. While white wines are more specific in their menu pairing, a rosé is a far more versatile wine, which can be enjoyed with any food. So there is your wine education for the day."

She raised her glass in a toast to Olivia, who was still too stunned with amazement to speak a word.

"I was going to tackle Project Rosé next year as I believed we would need to manufacture our rosé primarily from sangiovese grapes, and this year we had a shortage of these. But Olivia used a creative blend of red grapes. She was so clever!" Nadia stared at her admiringly. "She mixed and matched the final harvests of the season, including a little of the dark-skinned Colorino grapes, which have imparted a brilliant color I have never seen before."

Finally, Olivia found her voice.

"I'm so relieved that you're not angry with me. I didn't realize that you meant me to use only what was in the winemaking room, and not the new harvests. When Antonio said that you had already reserved the new grapes for specific wines, I was worried I was in trouble."

Nadia shrugged.

"Independently, those small final harvests would not have produced meaningful amounts, and were simply add-ons. Combined, they have produced quantities high enough for us to take this rosé to market."

Jean-Pierre sipped appreciatively.

"It's excellent. I am so proud my boss made this wine."

Glancing toward the restaurant again, she saw Gabriella glowering. As she turned her head, the other woman slunk out of her view, clearly disappointed that Olivia wasn't getting reprimanded or even fired.

Finally, Olivia allowed herself to admire the bright, gleaming color of her first-ever wine creation without feeling guilty about it.

"The timing is perfect," Nadia explained. "The most prestigious wine critic in Tuscany, Raffaele di Maggio, is visiting our winery this week to taste and grade our new launches, so we can introduce him to this rosé. A favorable review on his Tuscan Wine Tourism website would give this wine an incredible boost. He is very influential and his site has become extremely popular."

"I remember his name," Olivia said. She'd heard it mentioned by visitors, and knew that a lot of tourists followed his site, which seemed to have gained an enormous audience in recent times.

She felt a thrill of nerves and realized she was more intimidated than flattered by this news. Having her rosé reviewed by such a high-profile critic was scary. It was enough of a miracle that Nadia had loved her new creation, but she wasn't ready for her first ever wine to be tested by a renowned expert. What if he felt differently and didn't like it at all?

A few hard-working hours later, Olivia locked up the tasting room and stepped outside. A chilly breeze was gusting and she knew that she would enjoy the brisk, warming walk home.

Then she saw Marcello's car heading up the winding driveway and forgot about the cold completely.

The SUV parked under the spreading olive tree and Marcello scrambled out, clearly in a hurry. Olivia's heart sank as she saw this. It seemed that ever since the end of summer, when they'd indulged in some glorious moments of flirtation and even a day exploring Pisa, Marcello's life had become busier and busier. She'd guessed heading into winter would be a quieter time for him, but it didn't seem that way.

She'd had hopes of lingering evening chats by the fire that burned in the tasting room's entrance foyer on cold days. She'd had dreams of more than that!

Of course, she'd also been far busier than she expected. In addition to her foray into winemaking, her work on the winery's marketing had meant spending hours in the office at the back of the storage room, out of sight and with only her laptop for company.

Now, as he saw her, Marcello smiled, white teeth flashing in his tanned face and his blue eyes warming.

Olivia thought he looked pleased but also self-conscious, as if he, too, was aware that there were matters between them that had been neglected.

"Olivia, it is good to see you," he said. "Nadia called me. She said you have created a rosé that will be a unique and award-winning addition. I am so proud of you."

To think that yesterday she'd been composing an apology letter to him, believing herself to be in serious trouble. Olivia felt stunned by how her situation had changed.

"Thank you," she said. "I'm so glad it turned out well, even if it was due to beginner's luck."

She added a smidgeon of flirtatiousness to the words. After all, if she could succeed beyond her wildest dreams in one aspect of her life, perhaps she could do it in another!

"Not at all. Due to skill," Marcello emphasized. "Don't underestimate your talents. I am proud we will have such a new and delightful wine to offer this leading critic when he arrives."

Olivia felt her stomach clench at the thought. Deciding to change the topic to a less scary one, she spoke hurriedly.

"Have you finished work for the day? Got any plans for the evening?"

As the words left her mouth, Olivia wished she could take them back, because she'd ended up sounding far too forward. She was practically asking Marcello if he was free tonight. That was a no-go. Olivia had resolved months ago that if any romance was going to happen, the first step had to be made by her gorgeous boss. She couldn't push the issue from her side, as there was too much at stake. She might jeopardize her job, and her future at the winery, if things went wrong.

"I have a conference call later tonight with a supplier in the States." Marcello quirked an eyebrow. "The new rosé will be exciting news for that discussion."

Disappointed, Olivia forced a polite smile. This was not what she'd hoped he would say.

But then he spoke again, this time in a flirtatious tone.

"Apart from that, I will be enjoying a glass of red wine and making pasta. The dish I have planned for this evening is Ragu al Cinghiale. It is a traditional, delicious Tuscan dish made using wild boar, which is currently in stock at the village butchery."

"Wild boar?" Olivia asked.

Marcello nodded. "Wild boar breed prolifically, so every year, registered hunters cull a limited number in this region. That way, the populations in the forests remain healthy and sustainable, and the boar are not forced to raid the vineyards or farms in search of food, which of course could be dangerous."

"Really?" Olivia asked, fascinated. Wild boar living in the woods? She'd never known!

"I make this tasty dish during the colder months, when the meat is seasonally available. I feel I am close to perfecting the recipe. Next time, perhaps I can invite you to try it."

Olivia's head spun. This was an invitation. Well, not a direct one, but at least it was progress.

"I'd love to," she said. "My cooking is rather basic, but I think my biggest success so far has been the Pappa al Pomodoro stew, made with leftover bread, beans, and tomatoes. When I get that dish right, I'd love your opinion on it."

"I will take you up on that," Marcello promised. He drew a deep breath. "And in the meantime—"

Olivia's heart leaped. There was potential in the way he said those words. She felt herself twitch all over in anticipation of what might follow.

Then his phone rang.

With an apologetic frown, he checked the caller ID, before answering and heading briskly toward his office.

Olivia gasped in disappointment.

They had been a moment away from making an arrangement. She was certain of it. Now he'd been sidetracked again, who knew for how long? This was exquisitely frustrating, and she was starting to wonder if their budding romance might have stalled forever.

With a frustrated sigh, she turned away and headed up the driveway, hearing the familiar patter of hooves as Erba joined her on the walk.

Marcello wasn't seeing anyone else, Olivia decided. She'd fretted about that many times over the past weeks but had decided against it. He was preoccupied with his business, which was stretched thin financially due to recent expansion. Also, Olivia guessed he was scared of getting involved again, especially with an employee.

After Gabriella, she couldn't blame him, Olivia thought resentfully.

To her surprise, when they reached home, Erba did not head straight into the barn as she usually did, to wait for her post-walk alfalfa snack. She trotted up to the enormous doorway, peered inside, but then shied away from the darkened space as if she'd been spooked, and came prancing back to Olivia.

"What's up?" she asked the goat, puzzled.

Then Olivia's eyes widened as she heard a distant scraping, thudding noise coming from inside the barn.

She swallowed hard.

Someone—or something—was in there, and Erba had sensed it.

Olivia approached cautiously, remembering what Marcello had said about the wild boar. What if one of those aggressive creatures had ventured out of the woods and moved into her future winemaking building?

Olivia started to doubt the wisdom of her decision to go and look. It could be dangerous.

She should at least have a weapon, she decided. Thankfully, the shovel she'd used to plant some bulbs a few days ago was still propped against the wall. Her untidy habits were proving a blessing, for once.

Olivia picked up the shovel and held it in a two-handed grip, like a baseball bat.

As she swung it experimentally, a clod of earth that had been stuck to the shovel's blade thudded down onto her head.

"Damn," Olivia muttered, as loose soil cascaded over her face. A large amount of it was lodged in her hair. She'd hoped to have a peaceful evening. By now, she should have fed Erba and be making a start on dinner. Instead, here she was, getting showered with earth while attempting to defend herself against an unknown peril.

Olivia shook the soil away, feeling it scatter over her shoulders as she sneaked toward the barn.

She paused at the doorway. The scraping, grinding noise had stopped. Was that good or bad? She didn't know.

Suddenly, Olivia couldn't take the suspense any longer. She sprang around the doorway, waving the shovel above her head and yelling, "Get out!"

Then she screamed in alarm as she came face to face with a dark-clad figure wearing a purple spiky hat, and holding a spade himself.

Chapter Four

"Aaargh!" the figure yelled in terror, dropping the tool and waving his arms as Olivia jumped back. The shovel felt slippery in her cold, damp hands and her heart was racing.

But, as her eyes adjusted to the dark, she realized this was no intruder.

It was her friend Danilo, who lived on a farm on the other side of the village.

Danilo stared at her in consternation.

"Olivia. What are you doing? It's rather late in the day and I was coming to find you."

Olivia lowered the shovel, embarrassed by having suspected the worst.

She remembered that the last time they had spoken, Danilo had said he would come by to help her clear the massive pile of rubble in the barn whenever he had time.

Here he was. He'd driven his pickup into the barn, which was why she hadn't seen it outside the farmhouse.

"I—I didn't know what the noise was," she muttered.

Danilo nodded approvingly.

"It is good to be careful. Next time I will message you first."

Olivia suspected he was trying to conceal a smile. She sensed that he thought this entire encounter was hilariously funny, but that he was doing his utmost not to let her see his amusement.

Looking more closely, she could see his dark eyes were bulging with the effort of holding his laughter in.

When they'd first met, they'd gotten off on the wrong foot. Olivia had taken offense to Danilo's directness in telling her she was planting her vines wrong. She had indeed been planting them wrong, but thought he could have said so in a politer way.

Now, she guessed that Danilo was trying his best not to damage the easy friendship they had developed, and not to let Olivia know how much he wanted to laugh.

She'd better not laugh either, she decided, sucking in her cheeks to avoid a sudden guffaw from breaking free. This embarrassing misunderstanding was best treated with the seriousness neither of them thought it deserved.

"I see your hair is purple," Olivia said, changing the subject to a safer topic. Danilo had explained to her that his niece, who was studying hairdressing, used him as her model, although "victim" was the word Danilo mentioned more often when explaining his uber-trendy, constantly changing colors and cuts.

Olivia liked the purple accents. They were bright, but suited his olive skin tone, and the cut was very sharp.

"Yes." Danilo grimaced. "Better than pink, I suppose." He looked at her with a puzzled frown. "I see you have some sand in your hair tonight."

They both fell quiet, recognizing that this might mean a return to the subject they'd managed to steer away from.

"If you bend forward, I will brush it out for you," Danilo offered, and Olivia leaned gratefully forward so he could tease the sand from her hair.

"Did you find anything interesting here?" she asked.

"I brought my car in to provide light," Danilo explained. "The barn is very dark, and I did not want to miss anything important."

Olivia sighed. "I'm beginning to think that one rare bottle of wine I found at the end of summer was the only artifact in the pile, and all we're doing by sifting through the rest is ensuring it takes a year, when a bucket loader could do it in a day."

The barn was frustrating her. She was not a patient person, although she knew that wine farming would teach her patience, forcibly if needed. But this rubble was weighing on her mind. It seemed unnecessary. A bright, clean barn would be a step closer to her dream. Was it possible this dusty heap could house any priceless artifacts, or was it all a huge waste of time?

"I am certain there is more to be found," Danilo insisted.

Olivia could see he was passionate about the search. Perhaps the dubious promise of this dusty pile had awakened his inner treasure hunter.

Personally, Olivia held more hope that the locked storeroom, hidden in the trees at the top of the hill in a remote part of the twenty-acre farm, would be a treasure trove.

And yet, she hadn't called a locksmith or tried to force the door open, but had decided to wait and see if she could find the original key. Whatever was in the solid stone room wasn't going anywhere and had been locked away for decades. A few more weeks wouldn't make a difference.

Also, Olivia realized she thought of that secret place as Schrodinger's Storeroom. Unopened, it was potentially full of treasures. Opened, it might contain nothing but emptiness and disappointment.

For now, it was better to address the rubbish pile, which was large and visible, cluttering her winemaking room and needing removal. Once the pile was cleared, Olivia resolved she would make a decision about the storeroom. At least, if the key was in the pile, it would have turned up by then.

"Let's work a while longer," she said, knowing that Danilo would probably continue anyway. "It's my day off tomorrow so I don't mind how dusty and dirty I get. Plus, I need to keep myself busy, because there's a famous local critic visiting the winery the following day. He runs a big website, and is going to review my new rosé. I'm feeling nervous about it already!"

"Is Raffaele di Maggio visiting you?" To her surprise, Danilo frowned, as if he didn't think this was good news. "I am sure he will love your rosé," he added emphatically, but Olivia suspected he was trying to convince himself, as well as her.

Now she was frowning, too, perturbed by Danilo's odd reaction as she rolled up her sleeves and began sifting through the rubble. It was painstaking and dusty work, but Olivia had to admit that the glow of the headlights made it easier.

"Aha!" she cried, as she spied a bright gleam of glass.

"You have found something?" Danilo rushed over to look.

Carefully, Olivia drew a large shard out of the mound.

"It's only a broken piece," she said, disappointed. "For a moment, I thought it looked like a whole bottle. You can see it was, once. Look at the odd shape. The entire neck is there, and part of the side."

She held it up to the light. It had come from an unusually shaped bottle, with a wide, flared curve to it, and it was colored a dark, mottled green.

"There may be more of it buried here," Danilo said. "Perhaps it will be like fitting puzzle pieces together." He frowned thoughtfully. "I have a friend in Florence who is a wine dealer, and an expert on the area's history. He might be able to provide more information from this piece alone. I am going to Florence tomorrow to pick up some bronze drawer handles, so I could consult him."

"Really? That's so kind of you," Olivia said.

As they stared down at the bottle together, Olivia realized their heads were almost touching. Her blond hair must be tickling Danilo's face. He didn't seem to mind or even notice, and she was glad that they'd reached this level of ease in each other's company.

Even though their relationship had gotten off on the wrong foot, Olivia was thrilled to count him as a good friend now. He was such a fun person. And how rare was it to have a relaxed, platonic friendship with someone of the opposite sex? She felt very fortunate, and hoped that Danilo felt the same way.

She hadn't yet asked him if he had anyone special in his life. Olivia made a note to do so when the time was right.

Danilo paused, dusting off his hands.

"If tomorrow is your day off, would you like to come with me? I am sure you could learn something from the wine history expert, and we could see the sights also. It is supposed to be a fine day. We could make the most of it!"

Olivia's heart soared. Her ambitious plans for exploring the area had taken a back seat in recent weeks. Managing the winery's marketing as well as working in the tasting room had kept her very busy, and at the farm, her list of chores seemed to grow constantly longer. Every time she walked up to the front door, she noticed a new detail that required her urgent attention. Just yesterday, it had been the window box outside the family room window. The wood had rotted, causing the entire box, with its flowerpots, to list sideward. If Olivia hadn't shored it up with some planks, it could have collapsed.

A day out in the company of a friend would be something to look forward to. Not only would it be a wonderful treat, but it would also help to pass the long, anxious hours until the critic's visit. She was sure that in Danilo's company, the day would fly by and there wouldn't be a moment for her to worry.

"I'd love to!" she agreed, and Danilo's face lit up at her words.

CHAPTER FIVE

A t nine a.m. next morning, Danilo pulled up outside Olivia's front gate. She'd been eagerly looking out for his pickup, and as soon as she saw it, she sprinted downstairs, calling goodbye to Erba, who was perched on the family room window box, enjoying the morning sun.

It occurred to Olivia, as she ran down the sand driveway, that the goat's preference for this perch might have something to do with the fact it had almost collapsed a while ago. She needed to goat-proof her sills and balconies. Perhaps Danilo, who was a carpenter and woodworker by trade, could take on the project when he had time.

"Good morning," she called, as Danilo pushed open the door.

Olivia scrambled inside.

She'd wrapped the shard in thick layers of newspaper before putting it in a carrier bag. She placed the bag on the pickup's back seat.

The leather-upholstered interior was sparkling clean and remarkably luxurious. Since Danilo used the vehicle for delivering his finely made cabinets and other hand-crafted creations, Olivia had assumed it would be filled with sawdust and loose nails. Quite the opposite. She was riding in style today.

Danilo passed her a coffee.

"I picked these up at the bakery," he said. "What would a road trip be without to-go coffee?"

"It's an essential," Olivia agreed, sipping from the steaming cup.

Great coffee, and an adventure in Tuscany's capital city to look forward to. This was already turning out to be a wonderful day, she decided, relaxing in her seat and admiring the passing countryside, which sped by as Danilo accelerated onto the main road.

"My aunt lives just outside Florence," Danilo explained. "When my sister and I were younger, we would spend weekends at her house and go into the city center and see the sights. Each time we would walk a different route. That is the good thing about this city. It is much smaller than you would think."

"You can walk the whole of it?" Olivia asked, surprised.

"It takes less than an hour to walk from one side of central Florence to the other. Of course, you end up spending longer than that, as there is a lot to see along the way. Too much for one day, so I will try to remember what we enjoyed the most. What do you want to see, Olivia?"

"Ponte Vecchio has always been on my bucket list," Olivia said. "And although it's not in the city center, I've been longing to visit Castello del Trebbio. If we can see both of those today, I'm going to announce it on social media and post photos as we go."

Danilo grinned.

"We can. My sister used to work in a jewelry store in Ponte Vecchio. I will show you the shop where she had a summer job."

Olivia couldn't help sighing in envy. Did the Italians even know how lucky they were, to live their lives in and around such history? Imagine landing a summer job at a neighborhood store that happened to be located on the most famous bridge in the world.

"I am glad we have missed the worst of the traffic," Danilo said, accelerating onto the Autostrada. "Before nine a.m. this highway is usually chaos."

Danilo weaved the pickup expertly between a few slower-moving cars before claiming his place in the fast lane. In a few minutes, the city came into sight. Olivia saw turrets and towers, gleaming gold in the morning sun, against a majestic backdrop of hills.

"North of the city are Fiesole and Settignano, two very scenic towns," Danilo said, noticing Olivia's fascination with the landscape ahead. "As they are high-lying, you have a panoramic view of Florence from both of them. Perhaps we can visit them another day."

"I think a trip to both just got added to my bucket list," Olivia said. She suspected that the list might grow much longer as the day progressed.

Leaving the highway, Danilo wove through a maze of increasingly narrower streets.

"We stop here," he announced a few minutes later, swerving into a parking space just after a tour bus vacated it. "If we go any farther into the city, we reach the *zona a traffico limitato*, where you may only drive if you have a special permit."

With the car parked, they climbed out. Danilo reached into the back and took out a stylish brown leather jacket. As he pulled it over his white T-shirt, Olivia couldn't help admiring how toned and muscular his arms were. Her friend was seriously fit!

Of course, there was no reason for her to linger over watching him, given their platonic friendship. It was simply a casual observation, Olivia reminded herself, averting her gaze with some difficulty, taking her own jacket from the car and putting on her sunglasses.

There was no shortage of other scenery to admire. Olivia caught her breath as she took in the beauty of the stone buildings surrounding her, remembering that Florence was considered to be the birthplace of the Renaissance. And that wasn't just because of the magnificence of its architecture, with its ornate masonry and dramatic turrets and spires, but also because of the cultural treasures housed within them.

"Down here is an excellent place to have a breakfast panini. We need some food for strength before our tour, no?" Danilo said, heading down the narrow, cobbled street.

"Absolutely," Olivia concurred. She hadn't realized Danilo would prove to be such a like-minded traveling companion. Olivia wasn't a big eater first thing in the morning, so she'd been starving by the time he stopped the car.

He led the way to a tiny restaurant, little more than a cubicle, with four stools crammed next to its counter.

"*Salve, salve*," he greeted the owner. "What do you want to eat?" he asked Olivia.

Olivia scanned the menu, pleased that her Italian language skills were improving. At a glance, she recognized the words for artichokes, chicken, roasted peppers, and sun-dried tomatoes.

"How brave are you feeling today?" Danilo asked, with a sideward grin. "Because I see *panini di lampredotto* is on the menu. It is one of the most traditional dishes in Florence but I should warn you, it is made from the stomach of the cow."

"The stomach of the—say what?" Olivia asked in alarm.

"It tastes delicious. Trust me. The meat is chewy, but packed with flavor."

"All right," Olivia agreed dubiously.

She was starting to doubt her life choices. What would she do if it was inedible? Would Danilo be offended?

When the food was served, she had to admit, the meat packed into the crusty roll didn't look appetizing. The pale, triangular chunks did nothing to lure her in.

"Um," she said, wondering how she could decline without offending him.

"It is a Tuscan comfort food," Danilo explained, giving her an encouraging smile. "In our history, with so many in this city being poor, every part of the animal was used. Some foods became a traditional delicacy and endured through the centuries. Smell it. Go on."

She sniffed nervously, and to her surprise, found that the aroma emanating from this odd-looking panini was mouthwatering.

Olivia took a deep breath and bravely bit into the roll, hoping she wouldn't projectile vomit all over the floor when she tasted it. That would be an inauspicious start to their exciting day.

To her relief and surprise, the meat was chewy, but it was delicious. The flavors exploded onto her tongue, rich and meaty and unlike anything she'd eaten before.

Imagine being a Tuscan peasant living hundreds of years ago, and coming home from a long day's labor to smell this slow-cooking in the pot? Olivia could imagine how the dish must have been appreciated for its taste, as well as its rich nutritional content.

At any rate, she was glad she'd tried it, and didn't find it in the least difficult to finish every bite. She could see that Danilo was delighted with her adventurousness.

"Now, follow me. Down the road here is the Accademia Gallery."

Scrambling off her chair, Olivia headed out of the tiny eatery and walked alongside Danilo. She could see a short line of people waiting at a door ahead, but had no idea what was inside. The street was narrow—something Olivia was already growing used to in this city—and there was a flag flying outside the doorway.

"This is where many of the most famous sculptures in Florence are housed, including Michelangelo's *David*," Danilo said.

Olivia caught her breath. Never had she dreamed she would be seeing this statue in the flesh. She had forgotten it was housed in Florence.

"Let me buy the tickets," she volunteered, eager to contribute to the sightseeing that they were enjoying.

She caught her breath again as they entered.

Ahead of her was a form which she recognized as the *Rape of the Sabine Women*.

"This is the Hall of the Colossus," Danilo told her. "And that is the plaster model for the original marble statue crafted by Giambologna. As you would also know by heart if your aunt had told you twenty times until you wanted to run away forever, this was done as an exercise in sculpture. The challenge was to form a group of three closely positioned figures from one large block of marble. This was the first example in history, and required a huge amount of skill."

Olivia could have admired the intertwined figures for hours, mesmerized by the poetry of their movement, but there was so much more to see in the hall. Renaissance paintings and altar pieces lined the walls, and she moved from one to the next, entranced by the stories that these artworks told, and the glimpse into bygone centuries that was contained inside their extravagant frames.

"The *Cassone Adimari* is another must-see in this hall," Danilo said, pointing to a richly illustrated artwork. "This is a wedding scene, set in downtown Florence, as you can see because the Baptistry of St John the Baptist is visible in the background. It's such a detailed snapshot of early Renaissance life, which is why it is so famous."

"The outfits are amazing. The embroidery. The hats!" Olivia exclaimed, looking closely at the finery of the noblemen and women depicted in the scene.

"Before we reach the Tribune, where Michelangelo's *David* can be viewed, we will walk through the Hall of the Prisoners. Here are the famous *Slaves* that Michelangelo sculpted," Danilo said.

Heading eagerly into the long hall, Olivia stared in awe at the unfinished sculptures. She guessed this was why the hall had received its name, as the figures did look imprisoned in their marble beds. Admiring the stonework, Olivia was awestruck by the artist's perfect sense of proportion and the beauty he imparted to his work—even when it was incomplete.

Of course, the highlight of the tour was viewing the famous statue of *David*, which she learned had originally been displayed outdoors, but had been moved indoors in 1873 to protect it from damage and weathering. Even though she'd seen it numerous times in photos, admiring this pristine, seventeen-foot-high statue in real life, and being able to walk around it and view it from different angles, completed Olivia's bucket list experience to the full.

She could have taken an entire day to explore this spellbinding location, but Danilo warned her that if she wanted to reach her other must-see destinations, it was time to leave the Accademia Gallery.

"We have to make an additional stop before we reach Ponte Vecchio, as there is another museum I think you will enjoy," Danilo said.

Exiting the gallery, Olivia set off energetically. Danilo was right—this city was made for adventuring on foot. And feet turned out to be the theme of their next destination.

She burst into amazed laughter as she reached the entrance of Museo Salvatore Ferragamo—dedicated to shoe and fashion history.

"Only in Italy," she smiled.

She was fascinated to learn that the legendary Salvatore Ferragamo, who was born into a large, poverty-stricken family, had made his first pair of shoes for his sister when he was only nine years old, and had opened his own shoe store at the age of thirteen. After moving to the United States where he stayed for more than a decade and became known as "Shoemaker to the Stars," he returned to Florence and began creating shoes for the wealthiest and most powerful women in the world.

The interior was even more engaging than she'd expected. With a focus on environmentalism and sustainability, the historic footwear on display was fascinating, and included models of shoes that were created and owned by Ferragamo from 1920 to 1960, as well as shoes from the 1960s to the present day.

What intrigued Olivia the most was that despite his fame, Ferragamo had been dissatisfied with making shoes that were beautiful to look at but agonizing to wear. As a result, he'd studied a university course in anatomy during his stay in the United States. Looking at the exquisite shoes on display that had been custom-made for Marilyn Monroe, Greta Garbo, and Audrey Hepburn, Olivia wondered if they'd fallen into the "painful" or "comfortable" category. As she knew all too well, you couldn't tell just by looking.

Leaving the museum, all Olivia could think of was shoe shopping, but fortunately for her budget, there was no time, because Danilo led her down another winding alleyway and pointed ahead.

"Ponte Vecchio," he said.

Olivia gazed in amazement. The quaint, scenic bridge looked as if it had a train crossing it—but it wasn't a train, it was rows of closely packed shops. On top of a bridge!

"This was the only bridge that remained intact during World War Two," Danilo explained.

Treading on the stone-tiled walkway, Olivia felt as if she was walking through history. The ranks of stores on either side of the bridge didn't allow in much sunlight, but the shop windows were brightly lit and glittering with treasures, and glancing up, she saw rows of lights strung across the narrow strip of open space. At night, they must transform the bridge into a fairytale destination, she thought.

"The prices don't seem so bad," she said, gazing at a delicate gold chain that had caught her eye. "Lower than in the States. I guess you can get these items cheaper elsewhere."

She frowned at the price tag. Was her math correct when translating Euros to dollars? Would this be a great deal or was it a rip-off? It was a lot of money to spend, which she couldn't really afford, but she'd coveted a gold chain for years.

"You can get the same goods for cheaper elsewhere," Danilo agreed, "but then you will not have bought them in Ponte Vecchio. At any rate, that is what my sister always used to tell the tourists. She worked in that store opposite, and made a lot of sales."

"I'm sure she did," Olivia agreed. The logic was inarguable. If she bought this bracelet, she would always remember this special day, and the extraordinary experience of shopping on this stone bridge, with the bustle of tourists all around her and the sparkle of jewelry in those bright, enticing windows.

"It has to be done," Olivia resolved, stepping into the store. After all, she'd saved a lot by not buying any shoes.

"Good decision," Danilo agreed, admiring the chain in its elegant velvet box as Olivia took it to the counter. "It is eighteen carat, as most gold sold here is. Top quality."

Olivia's heart was in her mouth as she paid for it. This was a big investment to make, but how could she say no to something she'd dreamed about for years?

"Congratulations!" Danilo wrapped his arm around her and squeezed her shoulder as they left the store.

Olivia felt as if she was walking on air. What a day. Sightseeing that she would remember all her life, and the purchase of a piece of jewelry that she would treasure for the rest of her days. And they hadn't even gotten to the real reason for their trip yet. The light weight of the shopping bag over her arm reminded her why they were here.

"My friend's store is south of here, a few blocks away from the Arno River," Danilo explained. "The specialist store that makes the brass handles is on the same street so we can visit it straight afterward. Do you want to walk there? Once we have picked up the drawer handles, we can take a cab back to where we parked."

"I'm fine to walk," Olivia said.

Eagerly she followed Danilo through the maze of walkways, noticing that as they left the city's epicenter, they were also leaving the tourist mecca. Suddenly, the streets were quieter again and they were skirting a grassy park, heading for a building beyond.

"Begni, my friend, has his office in the basement. You will love this place," Danilo said, pushing the entrance door open and heading down a flight of stone stairs.

Olivia followed him into the cool, dim interior feeling nervous.

She wondered if this expert would be able to identify the glass fragment, and whether it would give her further insight into her farm's mysterious past.

CHAPTER SIX

Danilo knocked on the wooden door at the bottom of the stairs. Two knocks in quick succession, a pause, and then another two. The person on the other side of the door must have known who to expect, because Olivia heard a delighted shout.

"Danilo!"

A sturdy man with short, gray hair threw open the door and enfolded Danilo in an embrace before clasping Olivia's hand in his warm grip.

"Begni, this is my friend Olivia, who bought the old, neglected farm on the hill."

"And you are uncovering some wonderful finds?" Begni asked her.

"I'm hoping so," Olivia agreed.

Following Begni into the brightly lit room, Olivia realized they had entered a treasure trove.

Glass-fronted cupboards lined the opposite wall, each one filled with shelves of bottles whose glass gleamed in the tiny spotlights. The other walls were lined with framed posters and pictures, old newspaper reports, and catalogs.

"Begni owned a wine shop in the city," Danilo explained. "He sold it a few years ago, and started following his passion, which is the wine history of the region. He is the go-to person for all the antique and wine dealers—a consultant and historian with excellent wine knowledge."

Olivia could imagine how valuable that information could be. But would Begni be able to make any sense of the shapely, but narrow, fragment of glass she had unearthed?

She took the paper-wrapped bundle out of her shopping bag, realizing how light it was. There was hardly any glass in it at all. Most likely this would be a fruitless quest, but perhaps this guru would share some of his local knowledge with her. That would make the trip more than worthwhile.

"Place it here, and let us see what you have found," Begni said, indicating a white mat on his desk with a light positioned above it.

Olivia placed the shard on the mat.

Using a soft wipe saturated in astringent-smelling liquid, Begni cleaned the shard. Olivia was amazed by the depth of color it revealed. In the glow of the light, the mottled glass cast bright and dark patches of green on the pristine mat.

Whistling to himself, Begni reached under his desk and produced a massive lever-arch file. He flipped through, scanning the cardboard dividers until he found the one he wanted.

When he reached the page, his whistle changed from a tuneful melody to something that sounded—well, it sounded like a hoot of amazement.

Olivia bit her lip. She stood next to Danilo, their shoulders brushing as they bent forward to watch. She felt like grabbing his hand. This was nerve-racking.

"I have never seen this before," Begni announced in a solemn tone.

"Is that good or bad?" Olivia asked. Her voice sounded squeaky.

"It is interesting," the gray-haired man stated, before flipping through his file again.

Then he returned to the original page and gave a decisive nod.

"Have a seat," he said. "Can I offer you some coffee?"

Danilo fetched two wooden chairs while Begni made espresso in a stainless steel Moka pot.

He poured it, and passed around the sugar bowl. Olivia stirred and sipped, enjoying the sweet, strong flavor. She was growing used to drinking straight espresso with no cream, and sugar only—most Italians topped up this concentrated brew with plenty of sugar.

"You have purchased a very interesting piece of land," Begni confirmed. "Danilo mentioned you have already uncovered an undamaged wine bottle at least a century old."

Olivia nodded. That historic bottle had been her first find. She'd sent it to an antiques dealer to get the label restored. After that, she wasn't sure what she would do with it. She could sell it, but was tempted to keep it. After all, it was a part of her farm's heritage.

"This shard is far more ancient," Begni explained. "So I will start by giving you some history of wine storage, for my friend Danilo, who needs all the education he can get!"

Danilo grinned, clearly enjoying the teasing.

"The Romans loved wine, of course. And they used and sold it in such quantities that big wooden barrels became the preferred method of storage and transportation. Over the centuries, they discovered by chance that oak barrel storage improved the wine, and this is why so many vintages today are aged in oak."

Olivia nodded, impressed by the historical facts she was learning. Danilo had been right. This was turning out to be an educational meeting.

"For smaller quantities, earthen jugs or clay flasks—amphorae— were the only alternatives, but they were difficult to transport and unsuitable for long-term use, so wine was seldom kept for long periods of time."

Olivia could imagine.

"But the Romans invented glass, too, no?" Danilo asked, and Begni nodded, smiling at his friend.

"Exactly so. I am glad you asked. Why not glass, when the Romans had just invented it, and when it was perfect for wine storage? Do you know, Danilo?"

Danilo shook his head.

"And you, Olivia?"

Although she racked her brains, she could think of no reason why not. She shook her head in puzzlement.

"To understand why glass was a problem, we have to look into the minds of the ancient Romans. They were sticklers for order and accuracy. Look at their maps. Look at their roads and their armies and their rules. Everything had to be uniform, uniform, uniform!" Begni wagged his finger playfully as he spoke. "In the early stages of glassblowing, nothing was uniform. The handmade bottles all came out different shapes and sizes. So as you can imagine, that drove the Romans mad. There was no way to tell how much wine was in each one! Instead of order, you had complete chaos. Nobody could trade fairly when every bottle looked unique and held different quantities. They couldn't handle it at all, it made them crazy, crazy!" He tapped his head. "So they banned the sale of wine in glass. And for the Roman era, that was that."

Begni dusted his hands off, looking amused.

"Let us move forward to the 1600s. Now, glass was produced that was stronger, thicker, darker. The dark glass, of course, helped protect the wine from sunlight."

Begni poured them all another round of espressos, stirring sugar into his with enjoyment while he continued.

"Champagne became possible thanks to this stronger glass. It takes strength to contain the bubbles, and in particular, the curve at the base of the bottle—the 'punt'—has to be deep and thick to protect against the pressure produced by a sparkling wine. Otherwise—poof! You have an explosion, and no more champagne."

Olivia nodded. Now that she thought about it, all sparkling wine bottles did have that pronounced dent in their thick and solid base. So this was part of the bottle's structure, to protect it from bursting apart under the pressure of the contents within!

Begni put down his cup and opened the folder, pointing to some line drawings.

"The bottles we know today began to be made in the seventeenth century. As you can see, they were thick and squat at first. Really old-fashioned, no?"

Olivia grinned. No doubt the bottle makers had thought their creations the height of stylishness.

"What made them become more streamlined?" she asked.

"Well, by then, corks were being used as stoppers, and liquid contact with the cork was essential to prevent it from drying out. So the manufacturers changed the bottle shape to allow them to be stored on their sides for cork contact. Each area produced their own distinctive shape to differentiate their wine. Burgundy—which today is the sloping shape of most white wine bottles, Bordeaux—your typical red wine bottle, with higher, broader shoulders. Port, Riesling, if I name the wine, you can probably think of the bottle it is packaged in."

Olivia nodded. She could.

She peered at the drawings again. Begni's illustration showed how the bottles evolved and the shapes that their specialized areas of production had taken on.

"So, what about the piece of bottle Olivia found?" Danilo asked.

Immersed in the history and evolution of the glass bottles, Olivia had all but forgotten the reasons for their visit. She stared down at the gleaming fragment again, and this time, her eye could see some of what Begni had been explaining.

"Your fragment," Begni explained, "is part of a 'shaft and globe' wine bottle that was manufactured in the late 1600s."

Olivia caught her breath, hearing Danilo give an identical gasp. This shard was ancient. She wished she knew how it had ended up in her old barn.

"It is extremely rare. An intact bottle from this era would be a collector's item worth thousands of dollars," Begni told her. "Should such a bottle be found unopened, it would be worth many times more."

Hearing that, Olivia felt motivated to drive straight back to the farmhouse and search that pile some more, unearthing all the buried treasures that might be waiting there.

"But this shard is different," Begni continued.

Olivia's hopes settled. Presumably, her find was not as valuable.

Then she nearly fell off her chair as Begni explained.

"The color of this fragment is what sets it apart. This unique, marbled color is from an exclusive batch of glass, custom-made for one of the area's leading vineyards. We have only pictures, descriptions, and records—and now, this one piece. Not a single bottle is known to exist anymore. If you were to find one, it would be a priceless discovery."

Danilo and Olivia exchanged amazed glances and Olivia saw her own incredulity reflected in his eyes.

"Who knows what you will unearth next?" Begni asked. "Keep me in the loop, as you say!"

"We will, and thank you so much for this background," Olivia said, standing up reluctantly. "Would you like to keep the shard?"

"I would." The expert nodded. "It will provide important historical evidence, helping us understand the winemaking industry in that area.

And perhaps, one day, we can piece together an entire bottle, if your search progresses."

"I hope so," Olivia said.

An hour after leaving Bengi's basement headquarters, Olivia headed into another subterranean site. Her skin prickled in the cooler air as she walked downstairs, her arm brushing against the smooth stone wall, ready to explore the old wine cellars of the imposing Castello del Trebbio.

As she headed into the gloom, her phone buzzed and she saw it was a message from Charlotte.

She was about to read it, when the tour guide began explaining the castle's history. Eager to hear every word, Olivia slipped her phone back into her purse. She'd read the message later, she decided.

"In the twelfth century, this castle belonged to the Pazzi family. This family opposed the powerful de Medicis, who dominated the region at the time. In fact, the Pazzis planned a conspiracy to kill the de Medicis in this very castle," the guide explained, smiling as she shook back her dark ponytail. "It is said that even the Archbishop of Pisa was part of the plot, as the de Medicis were hated by many, and there were also many who stood to benefit if they died."

Olivia felt a shiver run down her spine that had nothing to do with the cold temperatures of this subterranean area. It seemed that nefarious motives, and murder, were an integral part of this area's history. Putting herself in the conspirators' shoes, she wondered if they might have discussed their plans down here, in this cold underground space. It was certainly giving her the chills.

She was grateful that as the tour group crowded close to admire the display of ancient olive jars, Danilo removed his jacket and slung it over her shoulders.

How considerate of him, Olivia thought, worried that he was now cold, but glad for the extra layer of warmth which still radiated his body heat.

"Initially, the plan was to poison the two de Medici brothers at a banquet, but when one of the brothers fell ill, the conspirators decided to attack the following day, during the celebration of Mass at Florence Cathedral. Despite a scene of mayhem playing out in the cathedral as the conspirators attacked with daggers and swords, the murder plan failed. Although one of the de Medici brothers was killed, the other survived," the tour guide concluded.

After learning about the castle's colorful history, Olivia was glad to head upstairs and find a seat in the warm and attractive tasting room. She paged through a brochure, learning that in the twentieth century, the estate had been abandoned and fallen into ruin.

Abandoning such a magnificent place? How could that be possible? Olivia felt shocked. But then, she supposed, her farm had been deserted, too. There had been nobody living there for decades.

In the 1960s, she learned, the new owners had set about the mammoth task of restoring the dilapidated buildings and grounds, bringing it to fresh life as a productive wine farm and tourist destination. The tasting menu included the winery's glorious Chianti as well as the famous Tuscan Special blend and, to Olivia's delight, one of the amphora-matured red wines.

"This wine has a lovely, deep texture," Olivia observed. "I'm definitely going to order a few bottles."

"I guess the clay is a middle ground between steel and oak. It allows for maturation and the exchange of air, but without any oaken flavor. It makes it very unusual for a red wine," Danilo agreed.

From the next-door table, Olivia overheard a familiar name as the group of visitors discussed the wine. She tuned into the conversation and listened in increasing alarm.

"It's no wonder Raffaele di Maggio gave this Chianti such a positive rating," the closest woman said. "It's an extremely well made wine."

Her friend leaned closer, nodding enthusiastically. "He seems to be very discerning and there certainly aren't many wines he's enjoyed recently. At any rate, he's not shy to say when he hates a wine, but I agree with him about the quality of this gorgeous red. If there are no other estates he recommends in this area then perhaps we can spend the afternoon shopping instead."

In a rush, Olivia's fears returned and her stomach twisted. A moment ago, she'd been hungrily dreaming about what food this wine would pair best with, and lunch had been uppermost on her mind. Now, she didn't think she could force down as much as a bread stick.

Danilo was looking at her in concern.

"Is everything all right?" he asked.

"Yes, I'm having a wonderful time," Olivia said, hearing the quiver in her own voice. This critic sounded impossible to please! She felt like running away! Since that was impossible, perhaps a walk would distract her from her worries.

"Should we take a stroll around the vineyards before lunch?" she asked.

"Good idea," Danilo agreed.

Outside, she and Danilo stood for a moment in the warm sunshine. This side of the castle was sheltered from the breeze, and had a glorious view over the rows of vines.

Looking at the verdant plantations stretching into the distance, she felt encouraged to think that what she saw today had been salvaged from an abandoned ruin. It gave her hope—something that she felt in dire need of at this point.

"Oh, you forgot your jacket in the tasting room," she told Danilo.

"Glad you remembered," he said gratefully. "I will run and fetch it. You stay in the sun."

As Olivia waited in the pleasantly warm spot, she heard the sound of voices, and a couple approached along the walkway. Olivia glanced at the woman, picking up on her American accent as she pointed to the vista of fields that she and Danilo had been admiring.

She was a petite, auburn-haired woman with an impossibly slim figure. Olivia had always longed for narrow shoulders and a wasp-waist like that. Her problem was, she wasn't built that way. Even at her thinnest, people called her "fit" and "athletic" and worst of all, "healthy," Nobody had ever complimented her on her tiny waist and nobody ever would.

The man with his arm around that delicate waist had his back turned and was staring out over the vineyards. Something about the set of his shoulders made Olivia take another look. Why did he seem familiar? Did she know him?

He turned around, planting a kiss on the petite woman's perfectly styled auburn waves, and Olivia nearly fell down the stairs in shock.

It was Matt, her ex-boyfriend.

CHAPTER SEVEN

As Olivia gaped at the couple in disbelief, Matt saw her.

"Oh, hey!" he called.

He sounded surprised—but yet, he didn't.

A dark suspicion began forming in Olivia's mind as she remembered how she'd announced on social media that she would be visiting this historic site in the afternoon.

Perhaps this wasn't such a random coincidence as she'd first supposed.

"What are you doing here?" Olivia asked as he headed purposefully up the stairs toward her. Her voice sounded shrill. That wasn't good. She needed to keep control of this unprecedented situation.

"Fancy bumping into you! You know, I'd totally forgotten you'd moved to Italy," Matt announced. "I mean, totally. That fact had slipped my mind completely. Now that I'm seeing you here, of course, I remember and it's all coming back to me. What a surprise. By the way, this is Xanthe, my new girlfriend. Xanthe, this is Olivia. Did I ever mention her to you?"

Xanthe's pretty mouth curved in a smile.

"Nice to meet you," she said, taking out her phone and checking her lipstick before snapping some selfies with the vines and hills in the background.

"What a romantic trip this has been," Matt said to Xanthe, slipping his arm tenderly around her minuscule waist.

His dark hair, streaked gray at the temples, was longer and he was wearing a navy blue top that she hadn't seen before. He sported a trace of designer stubble which was new to her, too. For his work as an invest-ment fund manager he had kept rigorously clean-shaven, so perhaps he was letting his hair—or beard—down while on vacation. Maybe he didn't even work for the same place anymore. What did she know?

The unpleasantness of their last encounter, Olivia's realization that he'd cheated on her—all of it was coming back to her in lurid technicolor, as if it had been buried in her mind, but waiting to surface. This must be why Charlotte had been messaging nonstop. She'd clearly gotten the news he was traveling to Tuscany, and had been trying to warn Olivia. She wished she'd read those messages earlier.

"You're here on your own, I guess?" Matt said in a satisfied tone. "Or are you with a tour group?"

Olivia hesitated, not knowing what to say, her face burning at his correct assumption that she was single.

And then she felt a strong hand rest on her shoulders, before sliding down to cup her arm.

"She is with me," Danilo said in a deep, caressing voice, moving to stand beside her and staring into her eyes as if she was—well, as if she was a bottle of the amphora-fermented wine they'd both fallen in love with.

Olivia couldn't help noticing, in her shock, that Danilo's Italian accent seemed stronger than she remembered. And he hadn't yet put his jacket on. She could feel the bulge of his bicep against her arm.

Danilo gave her a quick, conspiratorial wink that told Olivia he understood the situation and was doing his best to support her.

He'd done so very cleverly, Olivia thought in amazement. He hadn't said anything untrue, but had merely hinted that Olivia might not be quite as single as Matt was assuming she was.

They both turned to look at Matt, who was blinking fast. He seemed disoriented by the speedy turn events had taken.

"This is Danilo," Olivia said, hoping Matt hadn't picked up on her surprise at Danilo's emergency action.

Olivia saw him take in Danilo's sharply styled, purple-highlighted hair. Suddenly, Matt's locks looked unkempt and shaggy in comparison.

She felt a surge of glee as she saw him run a thoughtful hand through his hair, but she thought his worried gaze was more focused on Danilo's toned muscles.

Matt had always complained he'd never had enough time for the gym, she recalled. He'd bemoaned the fact he'd never reached the athletic promise waiting to be fulfilled in his slim, though poorly toned, body.

Olivia had often thought that there would have been enough time if he hadn't been addicted to watching Netflix sci-fi series on his massive flat-screen TV.

Luckily a well-cut suit hid a multitude of sins. No wonder Matt was wedded to his sharp Armani outfits, Olivia realized.

"Er," Matt said.

Olivia saw him pull in his stomach as he drew Xanthe closer. Xanthe gazed at him, angling her phone so that they were both in the frame.

"Smile, honey," she told Matt.

Regaining his composure, Matt stretched his handsome lips in a grin.

"What a wonderful vacation we've had so far, my love. Our five-star accommodations are worth every penny I spent on it. Not to mention the business-class flight. I always feel that if you travel, you should do it in style. I can't imagine a better use of my massive bonus than making you happy."

"It's been unforgettable. And we're only on our second day!" Xanthe agreed, putting her phone away and planting a kiss on Matt's bestubbled chin.

"Remember, we still have lots of shopping to do," Matt reminded her in a loving tone. "I promised to buy you a gold bracelet, and we'll have to spend time in the shoe stores."

"Ooh, I can't wait," Xanthe squealed.

"However, I feel we need to linger in this amazing location. Perhaps a late lunch in the restaurant?"

Olivia stopped herself from squeaking in alarm. That was where they were planning to go.

"I'm on a water-and-lettuce day, remember?" Xanthe reminded him with a toss of her auburn head. "Although I did see they have a magnificent mixed-leaf salad on the menu. If they left out the cucumber, artichokes, olives, and parmesan, it could be the perfect lunch for me!"

Olivia had heard enough.

"Well, enjoy yourselves. We'll be heading on."

Her dark suspicion had solidified. She was sure Matt planned to lurk around the place for as long as she was there, doing his best to ruin her experience. She couldn't have forced down a mouthful of food, knowing they were staring at her while wasp-waisted Xanthe picked at her stupid lettuce leaves.

"Perhaps we should make a move, too," Matt said, cementing Olivia's fears.

Unable to stomach another moment of Matt's presence, she turned away, speed-walking toward the parking lot and the safety of Danilo's pickup.

After four years of dating, for most of which they'd lived together, Matt knew exactly how to push her buttons. Clearly, he was in button-pushing mode, and when he got that way, he didn't let up.

"Lunch is on me," she murmured to Danilo. "But we need to have it somewhere else. Can you drive fast, and lose them if that horrendous error of judgment, otherwise known as my ex-boyfriend, tries to tail us?"

"I am onto it," Danilo said. "There is a good place in a village close to here. They serve delicious homemade pasta and have a great wine list. We will go there, and whatever it takes, they will not follow!"

He sounded energized by the challenge.

Olivia wished she shared his optimism. Matt and Xanthe were two days into their vacation. They still had plenty of time left, and from what Matt said, they were spending all of it in Tuscany.

For the next couple of weeks, she would need to look over her shoulder, and be careful about giving away her whereabouts.

Matt would be stalking her. She was certain of it.

CHAPTER EIGHT

The next morning Olivia woke an hour before her alarm, feeling breathless with excitement and dread about what the day would hold.

The famous wine critic was visiting La Leggenda today and would review her rosé. She bit her lip, nerves surging inside her as she thought about how powerful his opinion was, and how popular his website had become.

Positive comments on her first-ever wine blend would be a massive coup for the winery, and for her. It would be a tourist draw card that would bring his followers flocking to their tasting room.

A negative review, on the other hand—would that have the opposite effect?

Unable to consider the damage that might do, Olivia scrambled out of bed. She dressed extra smartly for this important day, deciding that since rain was expected again in the afternoon, she would take her pickup to work.

She headed over to Pirate, who was perched on the windowsill watching the sun rise.

"Sweet kitty," she said, tentatively clasping her hands around the cat.

He allowed her to pick him up and hold him for a few moments before starting to struggle.

"Good, good cat," Olivia praised him, setting him on the bed and rubbing him at the base of his tail. Progress was being made! She was sure in a week or two, the cat would have gotten used to being handled. Then she could put him into a carrier and take him to the vet for neutering, and his shots, and a health checkup.

Purring loudly, Pirate settled down, and Olivia regarded him with affection as he turned in circles before choosing the perfect spot on the peach-colored duvet to resume his rest.

Olivia hoped this small success boded well for the day ahead. Encouraged, she headed downstairs. While she made coffee, she decided to take a quick peek at the famous website to see if she could find a photograph of Raffaele di Maggio. That way, she would recognize the expert as soon as he arrived. Someone famous would expect to be recognized.

As the site materialized in her browser, she started to feel seriously intimidated.

Even though it was a relatively new site, the hit counter was already in the millions!

The flashing header banner read, "Italy's Most Popular Wine Site!"

Alongside it was a Photoshopped head shot of the expert himself. His skin and hair looked immaculately smooth and he gazed at her from under dark, perfectly shaped brows.

She saw a number of social photos dotted around, where Raffaele stood in posed shots with groups of people at various wineries. Everyone looked as if they were dressed for a wedding, and Olivia noted that the expert seemed very tall, well over six feet in height. His commanding presence dominated each picture.

He towered out of the frames, seeming to stare directly into her astonished eyes.

She felt a cold sweat break out on her forehead.

This was all feeling like far too much pressure.

She wished her brand new wine had been able to have a soft release, being assessed by less high profile critics. Maybe a focus group of wine enthusiasts, or a book club, or reviewed in the area's community newsletter. That seemed less frightening to her. As it was, the opinion of this expert was terrifying.

Feeling lightheaded with nerves, she downed her coffee, and a few minutes later, she and Erba were ready to leave for work.

As soon as she arrived at the winery, Olivia picked up the tension in the air.

Paolo had been uprooted from his restaurant work, and was scrubbing and polishing the brass doorknob and hinges of the imposing front door.

Nadia had removed the old doormat and was taking a fresh new one out of a plastic wrapper.

"Quick, clean around it," she told Paolo, pointing to the dusty square where the old mat had rested.

Olivia waited for the new mat to be put into place, and then hesitated. Should she step on it or over it? If she stepped over it, she'd tread dirt inside. If she stepped on it, it wouldn't be new anymore.

As she dithered over this difficult choice, Paolo came to her rescue.

"Here, lift up your shoe, I will brush it," he offered.

"Thank you," Olivia said gratefully.

She balanced, stork-like, on one leg while Paolo brushed her shoe. She then took a giant step over the mat and onto the stone hallway floor, sticking her other leg out behind her like a ballerina while Paolo brushed that shoe, too.

"You are good to go," he told her.

Olivia went in, confused to see that the winery's entrance hall was filled with white flowers. There must have been eight different vases placed on the hall table, and in the corners, and on the oak sideboard on the far wall.

Nadia was putting the finishing touches to the arrangements.

"Olivia," she called. "Does this one look better here?" She moved the vase a foot to the left. "Or here?"

"Um," Olivia said. "The first one."

"Good," Nadia said, sounding relieved. "I thought so, too. Signor Raffaele di Maggio has an eye for symmetry."

"This is for him?" Olivia asked, surprised. "I thought maybe there was a wedding here today, or something."

Nadia shook her head. Her chin jutted determinedly.

"White flowers are his favorite. It is well known."

Feeling as if she might have woken in an alternate universe, Olivia headed through to the tasting room.

It, too, was festooned with more arrangements of white blossoms, which were set out on the starched white cloths that now covered the tables.

Marcello was straightening a cloth on the far side of the room.

When he saw her, he hurried over. He was smiling, but the expression looked strained.

"We have been up since six a.m. preparing. This is the chance of a lifetime and our winery must look its best," he said.

He clasped her arm and caressed her shoulder with his other hand while he kissed her hello. As his warm lips brushed her cheeks, Olivia felt her heart beat faster. Perhaps their talk the day before yesterday had cleared the air, and now their relationship would move forward.

"Can I make you a coffee?" she asked.

It was the right question. Marcello looked at her in gratitude.

"That would be so kind," he said.

Pleased to be playing an active role in the day's preparations, Olivia hurried into the restaurant and headed to the massive coffee machine that was set up next to the bar.

She loved Italian coffee machines. They were one of her favorite items in Italy. From the most humble manual Moka pot, to the most complicated, chrome-finished machine such as this, every single device spoke of the love and passion Italians shared for their strong, intensely flavored brews.

"Be careful," she heard hissed words behind her. "I just spent an hour cleaning that machine. Wrap tissue paper round your hand when you use it!"

Glancing behind her, Olivia saw Gabriella glaring at her from the far side of the restaurant, where she was polishing glasses to a blinding shine.

With the coffee delivered, Olivia headed back into the tasting room, where Jean-Pierre was attacking the wooden counter with a cloth, buffing nonexistent stains to oblivion as he worked.

"Good morning," he greeted her. "Is it not an exciting day today?"

Olivia swallowed. "To be honest, I'm petrified," she confessed.

Jean-Pierre nodded. "So am I. This man seems very exacting! I am afraid of him before I have even met him."

"I know, I feel the same," Olivia said. "You won't do anything wrong, though. How could you? You're so friendly and professional."

Jean-Pierre smiled in relief at her praise, and resumed his cleaning duties with even more vigor.

Remembering that the maestro loved white, Olivia placed a white cloth over the center of the counter, and arranged glasses on it. Handling the tasting glasses was one of the favorite parts of her job. They were elegant in shape, finely made, and had the winery's logo emblazoned in gold. She loved to think of the tourists keeping them and using them back home, the glass bringing back all the memories of their visit to the notable estate.

As she put the finishing touches to her display, there was an officious click of heels from outside.

Olivia jumped, nearly dropping a glass. Surely he wasn't arriving yet? He was due in an hour, and she still had to assemble the bottles. What if he was early, and found her unprepared?

However, the person who strutted in on her silver-white Sergio Rossi stilettos was alone.

She was a petite, attractive woman who looked in her mid-twenties, but had the authority and confidence of somebody older. She wore platinum-framed eyeglasses, a white business suit with navy trim, and her dark hair was tied up in a neat bun.

"*Buon giorno*," she said to Olivia.

Marcello hurried out of his office.

"*Buon giorno*," he greeted her. "You are Brigitta, the maestro's assistant, no? I am Marcello Vescovi. What a pleasure it is to meet you."

The woman's arrogant expression softened as she accepted Marcello's charming greeting.

"We have some rules to go through before the Maestro arrives. Shall we do the briefing in here?" the woman asked.

Olivia bit her lip. Rules? This wasn't what she had expected. What rules could there be?

"Of course!" Marcello spread his hands in welcome. "I will call Nadia, and Gabriella from our restaurant. This is our sommelier, Olivia, and her assistant, Jean-Pierre."

Brigitta gave them a tight smile. Clearly, her warmth was reserved for the handsome Marcello alone.

The others hurried in and they clustered around Brigitta in a small, anxious group. Glancing at the doorway, Olivia noticed Paolo doing his best to eavesdrop on their discussion as he wielded a feather duster to remove nonexistent specks of dirt from the lintel.

"When Maestro Raffaele di Maggio tastes, he requests a glass of filtered water at room temperature, as well as a few slices of Tuscan bread—unsalted, and a plate of crackers—also unsalted. Kindly ensure both are fresh; the Maestro has a delicate palate and any hint of staleness sickens him."

Sickens him? Olivia's mind boggled. A cracker a few days old had that effect? She couldn't help visualizing the awful consequences of staleness. What would he do? Yell in rage? Projectile vomit over the tasting room floor? Storm out, never to return?

Thinking what could play out over the crackers helped her avoid the terrifying thought of what might occur when he tasted her wine.

This person didn't seem like a normal human being. She'd dealt with prima donnas in her previous life in the ad agency, and none of them had come close to this level of fussiness. She remembered one client who owned a chain of bars, and who had insisted that hard rock music be played at deafening levels during every meeting. That had made life complicated—but it had been fun, in a way. It had gotten them into the spirit of his business. The campaign they'd put together for him had been great, and people had flocked to his bars. This, though, was another level.

Olivia was jolted back to the present moment as the instructions continued.

"Maestro Raffaele will not be spoken to while he tastes. He finds it distracting. You will provide a printed sheet—on white paper—giving any pertinent information on the wine. Good quality paper, not photocopy paper, please."

Did that also make the maestro nauseous? Olivia wondered, feeling confused.

Marcello was nodding solemnly. His face gave nothing away. She couldn't tell if he was struggling to hide his incredulity like she was. Marcello, she thought, would make an excellent poker player.

Nadia caught her eye and Olivia was relieved to see the winemaker pull a quick, disbelieving face. Olivia grinned in response, and then both of them hastily resumed a grave expression as Brigitta spoke again.

"Ensure no background noise, no distractions, no music, and the maestro prefers an ambient temperature of around sixteen degrees Centigrade or sixty degrees Fahrenheit. Your tasting room seems to be at that temperature now." Brigitta nodded her approval.

"Finally, as a gesture of respect to the Maestro since it is his signature color, and per our instructions yesterday so that the photographs are visually pleasing, it will be fitting if everybody who interacts with him today is wearing white, or mostly white."

She surveyed the group. "I see that everyone is complying." Then her gaze fell on Olivia. "Almost everyone," she amended, with a disapproving frown.

Olivia's jaw dropped. She thought she might have heard it hitting the ground.

As she scrutinized the others, her panic rising, she saw that they were all, in fact, wearing white.

Marcello's long-sleeved, stylish knit top in pale cream was paired with light gray chinos. Nadia was wearing a vanilla jacket over a dove-gray blouse, with cream pants. Gabriella looked stunning in a scoop-necked, figure-hugging woolen dress in stripes of eggshell and beige. And even Jean-Pierre was sporting an ivory colored leather waistcoat over the long-sleeved white dress shirt he always wore.

That was why every shot on the website had looked as if it was taken at a wedding, Olivia realized, too late.

She had been off yesterday. She hadn't known about any of this. That morning, she'd decided to power-dress in a way that would pay homage to the beauty of her wine. She'd chosen a smart black pant suit, together with a vivid pink blouse.

She couldn't have gotten the dress code more wrong! How had this catastrophe happened?

She felt her face turning the same color as her top under Brigitta's critical scrutiny.

Gabriella cleared her throat.

"Oh, *mio Dio*, Olivia, did you not receive my email? Since you normally wear white, I did not think it was necessary to call you. What a pity."

The restaurateur smiled slyly at Olivia, who was staring at her in outrage.

Always wearing white? What a lie. Her wardrobe was vibrantly multicolored. As any blond woman well knew, white could leach all color from skin, especially after a summer tan faded. She thought she might have gained a reputation for the bright, cheerful colors she chose each day.

Clearly, she had, Olivia realized. And Gabriella hadn't sent an email. That was another, even bigger lie! Olivia had checked her mails after looking at Raffaele's website, and a communication from Gabriella would have stood out like a sore thumb! Olivia would have opened it immediately to see why on earth her foe was getting in touch.

Brigitta turned away. Olivia thought her body language had become cold.

"Maestro will be arriving in forty-nine minutes. Be prepared," she emphasized, and clattered out on her ridiculous heels.

CHAPTER NINE

I n the blink of an eye, Gabriella disappeared into the depths of the restaurant, and Marcello rushed off to answer his ringing phone.

Olivia stared at Nadia in consternation.

"*Puttana!*" Nadia spat, glancing in the direction Gabriella had gone.

The Italian insult summarized Olivia's feelings in one perfectly chosen word.

"What should I do?" she asked, staring down at her ill-chosen outfit and plucking nervously at her bright pink top as if her touch could somehow transform it to pale cream.

Nadia made a face.

"I have other jackets, but they may not fit you. Perhaps we should try, though."

There was no other option in these desperate times.

After gabbling instructions to Jean-Pierre, Olivia dashed out of the winery and powered her way up the steep, winding road that led to Nadia's house.

She'd only ever been as far as the porch before, and had never seen what the inside looked like. All three Vescovis lived on the estate, but Nadia had gotten the old family home as her residence, and lived in the large, warm, welcoming two-story house.

"Come upstairs," she invited Olivia, who was goggling at the beauty of the interior, with its wood paneling and raw stone walls and fabric hangings, all juxtaposed in a way that created glowing charm out of what could have been mismatched chaos.

She traipsed up the stairs and was met on the landing by Nadia, who already had an armful of jackets in her hand.

"Try this, quick," she advised.

Olivia threaded her arms through the sleeves, feeling pessimistic. The sleeves alone felt tight and restrictive. Nadia had a personality ten times her actual size, and it made people forget how small she was.

Shoulder size was a barrier that could not easily be overcome.

"Um," Olivia gasped.

She felt as if she was trapped in a straitjacket. She could just force this stylish garment onto her shoulders, but there was no way she could bring her arms forward. That would result in a terrifying ripping sound, as the seams of this well-cut garment gave under the inexorable stress.

"Okay, it's a no-go," Nadia agreed, with an impatient sigh. "Try this?"

The next two had the same result. No jacket in this wardrobe was going to fit Olivia.

"Damn, damn," Nadia spat, completing her statement with a few choice Italian curses. "Let us rethink."

She disappeared into her bedroom again, and returned holding a white silk scarf in triumph.

"Here. You can wear it round your neck. At least it is something, no?"

The blue-white scarf did not marry with the rest of Olivia's color scheme at all. She didn't even think a stylish Italian could have carried it off. But it was this or nothing, no matter how absurdly mismatched it looked.

"Thank you," she said with a grateful smile, wrapping the scarf around her neck.

Sporting her white accessory, she hurried back to the vineyard, returning through the side passage that led past Marcello's office so as not to tread any dirt into the doormat.

Marcello hurried out of his office behind her, carrying a sign that read: This Entrance Closed: Please Use Alternative Restaurant Entrance. Inside the restaurant, a temporary wine tasting table had been set up to accommodate visitors while the maestro occupied the tasting room.

Olivia started to feel nauseous. Where had the time gone? There were twelve minutes left till his arrival, if he was as punctual as his assistant had hinted. And Olivia was sure he would be.

She slunk into the back room to rearrange her scarf and check her make-up. Then it was back to the tasting counter for a final tidy up, ensuring that the wines were perfectly arranged before she and the others formed a group, ready to welcome him.

With a click of heels, Brigitta led the way into the tasting room once again, followed by a dark-haired man whose stern features Olivia recognized from the photo on the site. He stalked inside as if he'd just taken ownership of the place after paying rock-bottom price for it.

He was wearing an exquisitely cut, bright white suit and his coiffure was sprayed and styled into an immovable helmet. He cast a brief, disparaging glance at the La Leggenda team, clustered together in the corner of the tasting room.

To Olivia's astonishment, he wasn't nearly as tall as she'd expected him to be from the photos. In fact, he was a fairly short man.

As she struggled to take in this weird reality, she saw his dark, piercing eyes rest for a disapproving moment on her bright pink top.

She shuffled to the left, trying to hide behind Jean-Pierre, but it wasn't any use because he was shuffling left too, trying to get behind Gabriella. Nobody wanted to be caught in the laser-beam of this man's unfriendly gaze.

"Maestro Raffaele, we welcome you to La Leggenda. What an honor to have you here!"

Marcello rushed forward with his hand outstretched.

For an awful moment, Olivia thought that the wine expert was not going to shake it. He stared at Marcello, expressionless, for long enough that Olivia felt the air start swimming around her and realized she'd forgotten to breathe.

Then he extended a perfectly manicured hand and gave Marcello the briefest handshake Olivia had ever seen.

She didn't know whether to gasp with relief or burst into tears. The room felt as if it was about to crack open with tension.

"Thank you," the maestro said in a reserved voice. "From my impression so far, you have an attractive winery."

Praise? Olivia felt as if she might be able to swallow her heart down again.

"Perhaps if there is time, after the tasting, you would care for a vineyard tour?" Marcello persisted. Olivia could see he was employing every iota of charm he possessed to break through Raffaele di Maggio's icy facade. She felt overwhelmed by admiration for her boss, summoning up this level of genuine warmth, and showing such strength of character in difficult circumstances. His devotion to his beloved winery was visible for all to see.

"My day is very busy." Raffaele paused. "Perhaps there will be time."

"Our team members are excited to welcome you, all except my brother, Antonio, who is on vacation." Marcello waved the group forward with an expansive gesture.

Olivia was reminded of a Roman soldiers' formation, sticking close together, with shields guarding their perimeter. That was how she felt as everyone shuffled forward, all trying to keep behind each other, especially her.

Nadia was the first one to break out of their protective huddle. She stepped forward, beaming.

"What a privilege and joy to have you here in our humble winery, Maestro! It is no exaggeration to say I have been counting down the days on my calendar, and indeed the hours, to your arrival."

Olivia wondered if this might be construed as being too over-the-top. She'd never heard Nadia so gushy before. Might this expert think it was fake?

To her surprise, Raffaele's harsh expression softened slightly, as if Nadia's unadulterated praise had been what he expected.

"A true privilege," Gabriella murmured, dropping almost to her knees in an exaggerated curtsy.

Taking his lead from her, Jean-Pierre bowed deeply. "An honor," he stated.

Then Olivia was the only one left in his steely gaze, with nobody to hide behind, conscious that the white scarf emphasized the flamingo-like contrast of her pink-and-black outfit.

She'd just have to do her best with praise, she decided.

"Maestro, as a relative newcomer to the wine industry, I am left breathless by the privilege of your visit," she whispered.

Hopefully, this would explain why she did, in fact, sound out of breath.

Ice formed inside Olivia's stomach as she saw his tanned forehead furrow at her words. Had she said something wrong? Or was it her outfit? It must be her outfit, she decided, sidling behind the counter as speedily as she could.

Marcello invited the maestro to take a seat at the table, where all the accoutrements he'd requested were waiting.

From his jacket pocket, he took out a long, gleaming, and—Olivia thought—cruel-looking fountain pen. It had a sharp, curved, steely nib and a solid-looking white shaft that looked like ivory.

Was ivory even allowed these days? Was it politically correct? Olivia couldn't remember at that moment. Her brain felt addled by panic. Perhaps it wasn't ivory in any case, but something else white and shiny and expensive-looking.

"Maestro, we have three new launches for you to taste," Marcello announced, as Nadia carried a silver tray to the table.

"The first is our new-season vermentino white blend. This time round, we have increased the percentage of vermentino, aiming for a more distinctive flavor and finish."

Marcello stepped back.

You could have cut the silence with a knife, Olivia thought. The chink of crystal as Raffaele picked up the glass was as loud as a shout.

Nobody dared to breathe.

Jean-Pierre clapped a hand over his stomach as it rumbled. The thunderous sound seemed to fill the room.

She watched wide-eyed as the critic swirled and smelled the wine. He took a long time over it. Then he sipped. This, too, was done in a deliberate way and he seemed to hold the wine in his mouth for eons.

Then he leaned forward to the white porcelain spittoon on the table and spat the mouthful out.

Even though she knew that was what professional tasters did, and had seen people do it occasionally at La Leggenda, the vast majority of visitors drank their wine down. Watching someone spit it out was a surprisingly novel sight.

For Jean-Pierre, standing beside her, Olivia realized it was a totally new experience.

A *gurrmph* noise escaped the young sommelier's mouth, as if he'd had a sudden surge of nausea and was struggling to suppress it. Olivia glanced at him anxiously, noticing he'd turned as pale as his crisp white shirt.

Now there was a new sound—the deliberate scratching of that ivory fountain pen in the expert's white, leather-covered notebook.

Raffaele set the glass down, and everyone watched while he ate one of the fresh, crunchy, salt-free crackers and took a sip of water.

"You may present the next wine."

"Our Spirito—a new red blend incorporating sangiovese, merlot, and cabernet sauvignon." Marcello poured it with a flourish.

Again, the silence felt oppressive as the maestro carefully swirled, smelled, and then tasted the wine.

He gave a small nod and his face creased into an almost invisible smile. Olivia felt as if her insides were tying themselves in knots. What did a nod mean? Average? Good? Excellent?

The critic leaned forward to the spittoon again and spat his mouthful out, and yet again, Olivia heard a hasty *gurrmph* from Jean-Pierre and glanced at him again, noting his lips were pressed tightly together and a cold sweat was breaking out on his forehead.

She was glad there was only one more wine to go, because she wasn't sure how many *gurrmphs* her young assistant still had within him before something more drastic occurred.

This time, Raffaele chose a cube of Tuscan bread to clear his palate before making more notes. The process seemed to take forever.

"The last wine, please."

There it was—her wine. In its brand new bottle, with the modern label which she had designed herself. Olivia felt a surge of pride. It looked beautiful, modern, appealing. If the visuals of the bottle were anything to go by, she was sure it was off to a good start.

"This is a new addition to our vineyard's offering—a modern, dry, blended rosé formulated by our own sommelier."

Marcello indicated Olivia, who smiled nervously. She wasn't sure if she wanted to be in this particular spotlight.

The expert smelled the rosé. Olivia had never seen anyone so expressionless. What did he think? Surely he had to reveal some emotion, some of the time? It couldn't be healthy to keep it all bottled up.

Bottled up.

She had to suppress a nervous giggle at the pun.

He tasted the wine, and seemed to take time savoring it before he looked in the direction of the spittoon.

"*Gurrmph.*" Jean-Pierre's shoulders convulsed in anticipation, and Olivia bit her lip in nervousness. This might be his third and last attempt at keeping down his gorge, and the critic hadn't yet spat.

She waited, feeling the seconds draw out, each one seeming to take a year to pass.

Then the critic did something totally unexpected. He swallowed the mouthful and reached for a cube of bread.

Jean-Pierre let out a huge, relieved sigh and discreetly wiped his temples with a trembling fingertip.

Olivia felt her heart accelerate.

Did that mean this icon liked her wine? Or was it traditional for him not to spit the last mouthful out?

She had no idea.

Then he frowned and shook his head ever so slightly, and Olivia thought that the crash as her heart hit the floor might be audible from outside.

CHAPTER TEN

Maestro Raffaele placed the empty rosé glass on the table and scribbled notes in the leather-bound book. Although Olivia couldn't see what he wrote, she noticed that he underlined the final sentence very firmly and a number of times.

Then he snapped his fingers.

As if from nowhere, Brigitta materialized, her heels tapping a loud percussion as she hurried to the desk.

"I have made my decision on these wines."

"Thank you, Maestro. We shall do a group photograph now, in front of the tasting table."

Brigitta turned to the group.

"Come over here, please. If we could have the two Vescovis on either side of Maestro Raffaele. Then on either side of them, you two." She pointed to Gabriella and Jean-Pierre.

Then she stared at Olivia as if wondering what on earth to do with her.

"I don't need to be in the photo," Olivia said hurriedly.

"No, no, you must!" Marcello insisted.

Brigitta gave her a cold stare. Clearly her presence would ruin both the color scheme and the symmetry of this group photo.

"You can stand next to the assistant sommelier," she relented.

Olivia sidled into the picture and they all stood in a row.

Brigitta stepped back.

"Perhaps we can make the picture look more balanced," she suggested in a tone filled with meaning.

Suddenly, Olivia realized why Raffaele looked the tallest in all his photos.

Marcello was the first to understand what had to be done. He bent his knees so that his six-foot frame appeared just a little shorter than Raffaele di Maggio's compact physique.

Olivia winced as she heard one of his knee joints click audibly.

On the far side, she heard the scrape of heels on tiles as Gabriella went into a deep knee bend. Olivia was sure she regretted wearing those platforms now. Beside her, the tall Jean-Pierre folded his legs down until he was well below the Maestro's height.

Petite Nadia was the only one who stood comfortably without needing to make any muscle-burning adjustments.

Olivia sank into a semi-crouch, glancing at the others to make sure she was in line with them.

The tasting room was filled with tiny exhalations and whimpers as all of them strove to maintain this uncomfortable posture, while Brigitta took her time with a leisurely change of lenses.

Olivia's legs were on fire. Her pasted-on smile had become a painful rictus. Wouldn't it be easier to ask Raffaele to stand on a box? she wondered. She guessed the mere insinuation that he was short would cause him to fly into a temper. It wasn't that he was short. It was that everyone else was too tall, and they were being forced to pay for it. What a ridiculous display of ego this was. Her quadriceps were trembling. She was sure they'd be in agony tomorrow.

"Look natural, everyone, please," Brigitta encouraged, and Olivia was sure she could hear a sadistic note in the assistant's voice. "Some of you are looking tight and nervous."

Olivia wanted to yell out that they were looking tortured.

She didn't, of course. She just tried to control her quaking muscles, and her agonized facial expression, until what felt like a year later, when Brigitta finally decided she'd gotten the perfect shot.

"All done," she said in a satisfied tone, putting the camera away.

Olivia straightened up and staggered forward. Her quivering legs nearly gave way under her. Beside her, Jean-Pierre cried out in agony and doubled over, massaging his calf, which had cramped. They limped to the safety of the counter, while Gabriella tottered back to the restaurant.

Then Raffaele turned to Marcello.

"I will accompany you on a vineyard tour. I have an hour to spare before we must leave."

Marcello looked as if the sun had come out. He must think this was a good sign, Olivia guessed. Perhaps she'd been wrong about that frown. Maybe it had been a pleased frown, if such a thing was possible.

"Olivia, come with us," Marcello invited her. "You saw many of these fields being planted. It will be good for you to observe how they have grown."

Still feeling self-conscious about her attire, Olivia hurried out and scrambled into the back of the SUV.

Raffaele climbed into the front seat, and Marcello turned toward the sand road that led to the vineyards. Olivia stared out the window at the sleek, white Lamborghini on the opposite side of the parking lot.

"Is that your car?" she asked Raffaele.

He nodded coolly in reply.

"I've always wanted to drive one of those," Olivia enthused. Then, worried that the maestro might think she was hinting he should give her a ride in it, she continued hastily. "In theory, of course. In practice, I'm happy just looking at them."

As they passed the car she noticed a gold-framed sign at the back.

"Courtesy Car for Maestro Raffaele di Maggio from Sporting Passion, Florence, Proudly Supporting Tuscan Wine Tourism!"

So it wasn't his car. It was loaned to him by a sports car manufacturer, whether permanently or just for this trip, she didn't know.

Silence fell. The car discussion had stalled. Desperately, Olivia searched for a topic that might spark some easy conversation.

"Do you live nearby?" she asked. "Or are you staying in a hotel while you're here?"

"My villa is located south of Montepulciano," he told her. "While in this part of Tuscany, I am staying at the Gardens of Florence."

Olivia caught her breath. That was the area's most expensive five-star hotel, set in acres of landscaped surrounds a few miles from the city, and with a Michelin-starred restaurant on site.

"Oh, how wonderful. Are you enjoying it?" she asked. She'd visited the hotel's website after a tourist had mentioned it, and had thought it looked like the last word in luxury.

He shrugged. "I was expecting my suite to be roomier. I find the accommodation poky and old-fashioned. It is not a quality establishment. In fact, I have told them I refuse to pay the full room price and will only pay what I feel their hospitality is worth."

"Er, oh. I see," Olivia said.

That comment had killed the line of conversation stone dead and she was struggling to find another. Luckily, at that moment, Marcello took over.

"We are approaching the first vineyard. On our right is a brand new plantation of Sangiovese grapes. We are finding this wine so popular, and the grapes so hardy and easy to grow, that planting small, arid, sloping areas such as this is worthwhile. It produces low, but top quality, yields."

Olivia felt herself relax. Finally, the need for small talk was over, and Marcello could pick up the reins. As they drove along the winding tracks between the vine plantations, she felt herself relax. In such a picturesque setting, accompanied by knowledgeable commentary, how could the maestro find fault with this excursion?

After a journey around the entire estate, Olivia returned feeling more positive. She felt proud to have seen the checkerboard of well-tended vineyards, each given the love and care they needed to produce the best possible wines.

"Thank you again, Maestro Raffaele. Have a good day," she said.

He didn't respond and gave no sign he'd even heard her words.

Deflated, Olivia climbed out of the car and walked into the winery, almost colliding with Brigitta on the way out.

"Do you know when the information will appear on the site?" she asked the assistant anxiously.

Brigitta gave her a cool nod.

"Maestro Raffaele prides himself on the swift publication of his critiques. Your new wines will be reviewed by midnight tonight, and the content will go live on the site at four a.m. tomorrow morning. Have a pleasant day."

So early? Olivia didn't know how she would sleep a wink. It was terrifying to think that in such a short time, his opinions would be published. Good or bad, they would appear on his famous site for Tuscany and the world to see.

By the day's end, Olivia felt shattered. The stress of the visit had taken its toll, and drizzle had set in. It wasn't thunderstorm-grade, but was threatening to turn that way at any moment.

She was glad to hurry from the warm tasting room to the shelter of her pickup. Heading up the service road, she stopped at the point nearest the goat dairy.

Erba recognized the sound of her car. In a moment, the goat trotted up and waited for Olivia to open the back door.

As she headed home, Olivia thought gratefully of her lasagna portions in the freezer. She'd bought four premade portions from the bakery and they had been life-savers for those evenings where her cookery mojo was nowhere to be found.

While dinner heated, Olivia did her chores and put the goat to bed. Then she changed into warm, dry, shabby sweatpants and a fleece top. She poured herself a large glass of wine and sat by the fire.

Finally, she allowed herself to decompress after the extraordinary day.

She cast her mind back to that surreal tasting experience. It felt as if every expression and nuance was etched in her mind. The problem was, the more she remembered, the surer she was that the famous maestro had not enjoyed her rosé.

He might have swallowed the sip he took, but the way he'd frowned afterwards was how he felt. She was certain of it.

She took her lasagna out of the oven. At least it was perfect. Bubbly, cheesy, and blackened around the edges. Just the way she loved it.

As she dug her fork into the sumptuous dish, her phone rang. It was Danilo.

"How did it go today?" he asked. "Did that expert like your wine?"

Olivia felt touched that he'd remembered.

"I don't know," she confessed. "I don't think he did."

"Surely he must have," Danilo countered. Then, after a pause, he added, "Do you want some company? I could bring wine and takeout pizza."

Olivia sighed.

"If you'd called a half hour ago I would have said yes. But as it is, I'm about to eat a portion of lasagna, I've almost finished a huge glass of wine, and I'm not sure I'll be able to keep my eyes open once the food is gone. That's how stressful the day was. Shall we make it another time?"

Danilo laughed.

"Enjoy your dinner. I will check out the website tomorrow and see what the verdict is."

Olivia disconnected, smiling.

Almost immediately, her phone rang again.

This time, it was Charlotte.

After messaging back and forth the previous evening following her urgent warning about Matt, they had a chance to chat.

Plus, her friend wouldn't mind if she spoke with her mouth full.

"Hey," Olivia answered. "Thank you for the heads-up on Matt!"

She could visualize Charlotte, sitting in her small, neat apartment, with her russet-streaked hair tied back in a ponytail. Probably, her friend would have been to the gym across the road from her place, and would be working from home, which she did a couple of days a week. Olivia always looked forward to a possible phone call on those days.

"I cannot believe he stalked your Instagram and arrived at that *castello* at the same time as you did. Olivia, I was frantic when I heard he'd gone over to Tuscany with his new girlfriend. I was so worried he'd find you and there'd be a scene. I knew his intentions were dishonorable."

"It was a shock to see him," Olivia said.

"On vacation with someone else, after cheating on you with his assistant and then busting up with you? How does one keep up with his romantic life? I saw the photos of the new one. She looks like she weighs about ninety pounds and would blow away in a strong wind. What's her name? Pixie, or something?"

"Xanthe," Olivia said, giggling. "And she was on a lettuce day."

Charlotte snorted. "A lettuce day on a Tuscan vacation? That tells you everything you need to know. I hope it wasn't hurtful for you to see her."

"It would have been worse if I was on my own. Luckily I was with Danilo."

She remembered again what a hero her purple-haired friend had been.

"Talking of cute Italian men, is there any progress with Marcello?" Charlotte asked.

Olivia sighed. How wonderful it would be to be able to give good news on that front. But there was none.

"We have an intense, unspoken romance that is completely stalled," she said, describing her frustrating situation as best she could.

Charlotte gave an impatient growl. "I was feeling so positive about that. Perhaps it was me being there that helped your relationship progress. I'd better come back!"

"As soon as possible and for as long as you like," Olivia entreated her. "Every time I step into my kitchen, I remember what fun we had cooking together. Cooking for one is not nearly so entertaining. And I miss your jokes."

"And I miss yours," Charlotte agreed. "Oops. My boss is on the line. I'll call you again soon and we can chat for longer. Byeee!"

After finishing her tasty meal, Olivia headed straight up to bed. Even though she was shattered with tiredness, she felt a thrill of nerves every time she thought about the website reviews, what the influential critic would write, and what it would mean for her career and for the winery.

She hoped that tomorrow would bring positive feedback from this egotistical and unlikable man.

CHAPTER ELEVEN

Olivia had set her alarm for seven-thirty a.m. Even though it was forecast to be a drizzly, cold morning, she was surprised when the shrill sound interrupted her slumber, and she opened her eyes to pitch darkness.

Was it storming? she wondered, reaching blearily for her phone on the bedside table and managing to knock it onto the rug below.

"Damn it," she muttered, turning on the light.

As her sleep dissolved, she realized two things.

Firstly, it was still pitch dark outside, and very early morning.

Secondly, it wasn't her alarm at all. It was her phone ringing.

Olivia looked at the screen, and her heart jumped into her mouth as she saw it was Nadia—calling at six-thirty a.m.

Suddenly, she felt wide awake. More wakeful and more nervous than she'd ever been in her life. What was the reason for this unexpected call? Would it signal success or failure for her precious new wine?

"Hello?" she said.

"Olivia!"

Nadia shrieked her name at full volume. Her voice filled the room, causing Pirate to give Olivia a reproachful look and leap off the bed.

"What—what is it?" Olivia asked. Her voice was quivering.

"*Mio Dio!*" Nadia yelled. Olivia blinked at the string of vociferous oaths that followed—some in Italian, some in English, and she even recognized a couple in French.

"Please, Olivia. Come to the winery at eight a.m. this morning! We need to have an urgent meeting."

"Is the review up?" Olivia swallowed hard. Her throat felt dry.

"It is up. And it is disastrous! This could destroy us," Nadia cried.

Olivia was horrified to hear that the winemaker sounded on the point of tears.

She was hyperventilating as she scrambled out of bed and threw on some clothes, grabbing whatever warm items were closest to hand. Yesterday's careful wardrobe choice seemed like a dim, faraway memory as she sprinted to the bathroom, yanked a brush through her tousled hair, and tried her best to apply make-up as fast as she could with a shaking hand.

The review had been bad? How bad was bad?

After stabbing buttons on the coffee machine, Olivia shivered her way across the cold kitchen and opened her laptop.

What had Maestro Raffaele said? Why had he hated her wine so much?

She'd feared that he might think it ordinary and unremarkable. But terrible? How was it even possible?

As the page refreshed, Olivia scrambled up from her seat and made herself a double-size, double-strength Americano. She took a large gulp—nearly burning the roof of her mouth off—and then returned to her chair to stare anxiously at the site.

A horrified gurgle escaped from her mouth. She let out a soft whimper. It felt as if night had fallen again, and the farmhouse had collapsed, and everything that was right with the world had gone wrong.

This could not be worse.

She, and La Leggenda, had just hit rock bottom.

Maestro Raffaele di Maggio had a simple grading system on his site.

A top quality, brilliant wine received a platinum bunch of grapes— this award was, unsurprisingly, silver-white.

An excellent wine received a gold bunch of grapes, and a good wine received a copper grading.

A wine that was average received a humble green bunch of grapes. A wine that was disappointing received a gray grading.

Then a wine that was unpalatable, trash, a wine so badly formulated it would probably poison you and which you should on no account ever touch—a wine of the Valley Wines standard—those wines received a black bunch of grapes.

The two La Leggenda wines that the maestro had tasted before her blend had received humiliating gray gradings.

And hers—Olivia stared, aghast, at the condemning bunch of black grapes positioned alongside the clear visual of her beautiful bottle.

His words assaulted her eyes.

"Unpalatable, poorly made, a ridiculous color. The taste was nauseating. You would do better buying cheap grape juice in a supermarket. Or even cough mixture. A wine to avoid at all costs!"

Olivia let out a sob.

He had hated it. He'd thought it was absolute rubbish. There had not been one single redeeming feature about her wine in his eyes. In addition to those excruciating words of criticism, the wine itself was graded as abysmal, a must-avoid.

As a result of these scathing ratings, La Leggenda itself had dropped off the list of "Wineries You Must Visit in Tuscany."

The winery had become invisible.

The maestro had not only killed her precious wine's prospects, he had also obliterated La Leggenda from the map. Tourists searching for a venue to visit wouldn't know the winery existed.

Olivia downed the rest of her coffee. It scorched its way along her throat but she barely felt the pain. It was nothing compared to the raw agony of having to stare at the trash, ruinous review.

No wonder Nadia had freaked out, Olivia thought. She felt as if she'd woken into a terrible nightmare.

But this was no nightmare. Erba's nose pushing up against the kitchen window reminded Olivia of the harsh reality of her predicament.

She climbed to her feet, feeling as if all strength had drained from her legs—which were aching after the deep knee bends she'd done during that ridiculous photo shoot. All that pain for nothing. She might as well have told Maestro Raffaele to stand on a box. The outcome couldn't have been any worse.

With her thoughts in hopeless turmoil, she took a handful of carrots from the bag in the fridge and dropped them into Erba's bowl.

"There you go," she told the goat in a dull, toneless voice. "The carrots don't matter. Nothing matters anymore."

She felt the rain spattering onto her jacket's hood. Its cold grayness suited her mood.

This was it, there was nothing left to do but to succumb to despair. Perhaps Nadia would fire her after all. That was fine. Olivia deserved it. She'd used up precious grapes to produce a wine that was so terrible, it was lucky the maestro had survived that sip!

Erba looked up at her, and Olivia sensed a clear message. The goat thought she was being a drama queen.

Erba tilted her head and then did something she'd never, ever done before. She leaped forward and butted Olivia in her thighs.

With a startled squawk, Olivia tumbled backward into a thick, spiky rosemary bush.

"Erba!" Now the rain was spattering into her eyes! Olivia blinked it away, to see a solemn white face, with an orange spot on the forehead, staring down at her.

"Geez! What was that all about?"

With some difficulty, Olivia extricated herself from the bush's fragrant clutches.

"Erba! Why did you do that? It was so naughty! My pants are soaked now! And I have rosemary inside my collar!"

Running a finger inside her jacket's neckline, Olivia removed the scratchy fronds.

She glared down at the goat, but Erba ignored her, returning to her carrots as if nothing had happened at all.

With a dramatic shrug, Olivia retreated inside.

At least her backward plunge had distracted her from her predicament. She didn't feel anguished any longer. Instead, she felt annoyed with the damned goat!

And, as she stamped leaves and soil off her feet, her emotions changed again.

Now she was angry.

She was furious!

What right did he have to judge a wine as undrinkable that experts— and she considered Nadia an expert—had praised?

Raffaele was insufferable and egotistical and opinionated. Either he'd made a massive misjudgment, or else this wasn't about the wine at all, but that he'd been in a bad mood when he tasted it.

In that moment, Olivia realized that the goat had acted deliberately. Sensing that her adopted owner was suffering from a personal crisis, Erba had intervened to jolt Olivia out of it. Landing on her backside had been the shock she needed to overcome her self-pity.

Was she going to take this career-ending obliteration of her wine without a fight?

Erba didn't think she should.

Olivia clenched her jaw, plucking at the rear of her damp jeans.

Nor did she! She was not going to give up without fighting back. After all, what did she have to lose?

Thanks to the conversation they'd had yesterday, she knew where Raffaele stayed. The Gardens of Florence was a half-hour drive away. She was going to head straight to his hotel and confront him, and demand that he remove the review if he couldn't give her a good reason why he'd hated her wine. She was going to face down this unpleasant, opinionated little man who seemed to live in a bubble far removed from reality. And she was going to see justice served.

Adrenaline surging inside her, she grabbed her purse from the hall table, her jacket from the hook on the door, and headed out at a run.

Chapter Twelve

Olivia leaped into the Fiat, turning the heater to max as she accelerated down the driveway.

The local radio station was playing Italian rock. Olivia didn't understand all the words, so she made up her own, singing along at the top of her voice as she headed onto the main road. The music kept her motivated and by the time she arrived at the wide, treed avenue that led to the Gardens of Florence, she hadn't lost a shred of her resolve.

In fact, she was even more hell bent on having it out with him.

The rain had eased up, and Olivia breathed in the cold, fresh air as she climbed out of her pickup in the paved parking lot.

There was Raffaele's loaned Lamborghini, parked across two bays. She guessed he behaved like a selfish pig so that nobody would park too close and dent the supercar with their doors.

"Humph," Olivia snorted. She was all out of patience with him and his pretentious ways.

Warm air caressed her face as she stepped through the hotel's glass-paneled front doors. She breathed in the scent of jasmine and rose wafting through the air while her feet sank into the midnight-blue, thick-pile carpet.

The butler at the door bowed to her as she passed, and ahead, the receptionist gave a welcoming smile.

Olivia realized she'd gotten ahead of herself.

This was a five-star establishment that hosted many international celebrities. Raffaele di Maggio himself had achieved worldwide fame. They weren't going to let her storm in and bang on his bedroom door. Their guests paid top dollar for privacy. Well, most of the guests. Raffaele, of course, had said he'd pay what he "thought it was worth."

Smiling nervously at the receptionist, Olivia bought some time by pretending to take a phone call. She patted her purse with an expression of surprise, pulled her cell phone out, and made as if she was answering.

"Hello?" she said, pacing in circles on the plush carpet. "Yes. No. Yes."

Meanwhile, she was thinking furiously about how to find out which room the critic was staying in.

Then Olivia had a stroke of luck.

She glimpsed a familiar high-heeled figure clip-clopping past the reception desk and into the dining room, where the clink of cutlery and the aroma of freshly brewed coffee signaled breakfast was underway.

Brigitta was en route to her table, and that meant Olivia could seize the moment.

"Oh, hello!" she cried, abandoning her fake call and rushing to the dining room in pursuit.

"Hello there!" she shouted again.

This time, Brigitta heard her.

The petite woman turned and stared at Olivia, a surprised frown crinkling her otherwise flawless forehead.

"You?" she asked, looking thoughtful. "You were at the winery yesterday, no?"

Early though it was, Brigitta was flawlessly made up and her hair was swept into a perfect chignon. She was wearing another power suit today; this one in pale cream, with a silver blouse.

"I need to speak to your boss," Olivia demanded. "Where is he?"

Brigitta glared officiously at her. "He is still in his rooms. He does not accept visits from members of the public. If you wish to meet with him, you must make an appointment."

Olivia hadn't driven all this way in the rain to be given the brush-off from an assistant who also had an inflated opinion of herself, thanks to their website's surge in popularity.

"Well, it's urgent," she said.

She watched Brigitta closely. Perhaps her body language would give something away, or offer a hint as to the direction of the maestro's room.

"I do not care." Brigitta smiled smugly.

"He trashed my wine on the site this morning. And I want to speak to him about it."

Brigitta shrugged.

"Many people are disappointed when they receive a reality check on the quality of their products. You are not the only one to have been brought down to earth. Maestro Raffaele is very discerning."

"Discerning? He's deranged!" Olivia retorted. "He acts like a spoiled movie star. Requiring total silence while he tastes wines? I ask you. Does he taste with his ears? And wanting to be the tallest person in the room? It's ridiculous to think that a grown man can be so childish and egotistical."

Brigitta drew herself up to her full height, which even in her platform stilettos only took her as far as Olivia's nose. Looking down at her, Olivia was beginning to understand how she'd landed this role, and what the primary job requirement might have been.

"He is a world-renowned expert who has made a fortune from his skill!" Brigitta snapped.

"He probably got his money from a family trust fund," Olivia shot back.

"Oh. So you think he built his site from a trust fund?" Clearly, Olivia had hit a nerve and now Brigitta was on the attack. "Do you think he grew his following from a trust fund? Do you think he is invited to travel all over Italy and the world, staying in the very best accommodations, insisting on the presidential suite in every hotel he visits, because of a trust fund?"

Olivia beamed at her.

"The presidential suite? Thank you."

There was a signboard on the wall pointing in its direction. The suite wasn't part of the main hotel at all. If she'd known where it was, she could have walked straight there from the parking lot.

She could see it through the glass side door. It was a palatial building, set high on the hill above the hotel.

"No! You can't go there!" Brigitta pleaded. She leaped forward, trying to grab Olivia's arm, but she was too slow and Olivia jumped away.

She had lightning reactions this morning. It must have been the plus-sized coffee she'd had. Her reflexes were as fast as Erba's!

Slipping through the side door, she jogged up the paved path, hearing breathless cries from behind her. Glancing around, she saw Brigitta was struggling to keep up. Her platform stiletto heels were not made for running, or even power walking.

The presidential suite had a tall, arched front door with a brass knocker.

Olivia raised the knocker and rapped hard on the door.

The noise was loud and commanding.

She waited, hoping to hear the sound of footsteps from inside, but the only sound she picked up was the hurried clip-clop of Brigitta approaching from behind.

"Maestro Raffaele is going to be angry," she said breathlessly.

"Not as angry as I am." Olivia hammered on the door again. "Why isn't he answering? Is he still asleep? In the shower?"

Brigitta looked doubtful.

"By now, he should be having breakfast," she said. "He usually calls reception and orders it direct with them."

Thinking of another solution, Olivia tried the door.

To her surprise, it was open.

Ignoring Brigitta's warning yelp, she stepped inside.

The suite opened into a luxurious dining room on the right, and a lounge with cream leather couches on the left.

Olivia saw the maestro instantly, even as Brigitta drew in a horrified gasp.

He was lying face-down on the fluffy rug behind the coffee table, with his arms outstretched.

Looking at the rigid stillness of his body and the ice-white paleness of his outflung hand, she was certain he was dead.

CHAPTER THIRTEEN

"We should leave the room," Olivia advised Brigitta in a quivering voice, as the assistant knelt down on the fluffy rug next to the body.

"He has no pulse. He is icy cold," she whispered.

"We must call the police. And let's go outside while we do it, in case we contaminate the scene."

Olivia was shaking all over, but she was grateful for this fragment of coherent thought that allowed her to act sensibly.

"Contaminate? What do you mean?"

"I mean the detectives will need to investigate if the death is suspicious."

Olivia hauled the hyperventilating assistant to her feet and hustled her out of the suite. Her mind was spinning with shock. They mustn't touch anything. Even touching the front door handle had been a big mistake, which could land her in trouble.

"You think this was not natural causes, Olivia?" Brigitta asked, as Olivia herded her outside into the cold morning.

"We need to wait for the police," Olivia said, not wanting to spook the assistant further. The unlocked front door was troubling her. Had someone visited the maestro and left in a hurry after a fight?

There was an ornate wooden bench outside the suite.

"Let's sit down," she suggested.

Her legs felt weak, and not only because of the torture Brigitta had put them through during yesterday's photo shoot. Plus, it was freezing out here in the chilly wind. Rummaging in her jacket pocket, Olivia was pleased to find a pair of woolen gloves. She put them on, hoping they would help stop her shivering.

She thumped down onto the bench. As she dialed the police, her mind kept returning to the unsettling sight of the maestro, lying prone on that fluffy carpet.

Brigitta bent over and buried her face in her hands.

"I do not believe this," she muttered.

He hadn't merely died. Olivia was certain.

Somebody as unlikable as him must have many enemies, and she strongly suspected one of them had killed him.

Fifteen minutes later, a retinue of people made their way up the hill toward the presidential suite. In front was the hotel receptionist. She was followed by the butler, and another well-dressed and anxious-looking man who Olivia guessed was the hotel manager.

Behind them were three police detectives and two dark-clad men wheeling a stretcher.

As the group neared the suite, Olivia's heart sank even further into her shoes.

Detective Caputi was among them. Olivia recognized her shiny gray-bobbed hair and her aggressive walk before she even saw her face.

She'd had two run-ins with the scary detective before. It seemed to be Detective Caputi's life goal to arrest Olivia for murder. Thanks to Olivia's unwitting arrival at this scene, she might have a third chance at doing so.

She had been hoping that the detective might have been on vacation. Did she never rest?

Olivia saw the flash of suspicion in the detective's eyes as she recognized her.

"Well!" Detective Caputi said, sounding satisfied, as if the process of getting Olivia behind bars would now be as simple as filling in the paperwork.

"We thought we'd call you, in case there was foul play," Olivia explained, annoyed that she could already hear the defensiveness in her own voice. It was something to do with the other woman's dark, piercing gaze. The way she looked at you, Olivia thought, it was as if she knew you'd done it and that even if you thought you were innocent, it was probably due to an unfortunate memory lapse.

"Signora Detective!" The manager was wringing his hands. "Please, as soon as you can, reassure me what has occurred? A suspicious death at our prestigious hotel will be most catastrophic for our ratings!"

Olivia couldn't help the swift, uncharitable thought that Raffaele wasn't being good for anyone's ratings at the moment. The man was sinking businesses with every action he took—including his own demise.

The manager joined them on the bench, sitting to Olivia's right. He was a one-man hive of activity, messaging on his phone, plucking at a stray thread on his smart jacket, and lighting a silver e-cigarette which he puffed on energetically.

It didn't take long for Detective Caputi to reappear.

"Signor di Maggio's death is, indeed, suspicious," she confirmed, and the manager dropped his Twisp.

As he scrabbled to pick it up, the detective continued, gazing implacably at Olivia.

"Did Signor di Maggio use an ivory fountain pen, to your knowledge?"

So it was ivory, Olivia thought. It was Brigitta who replied in an anxious voice.

"Yes, he did, Detective. He has owned the pen for years."

"Someone"—and the detective put a particular spin on the word—"stabbed him with it. Clearly a lucky blow. It appears to have pierced his heart, and he died at once."

The manager dropped his Twisp again. This time, Olivia thought she heard the casing crack.

"Unbelievable!" he muttered. "We cannot keep guests safe from being attacked by their own personal stationery. The one-star reviews are going to annihilate us."

Olivia's mind was racing.

"Can't you fingerprint the pen?" she asked.

Detective Caputi's eyes narrowed.

"Forensics will do their work, of course," she said in a grim tone. "However, there is a strong likelihood that given the weather conditions, the killer would have worn gloves."

She stared meaningfully down at Olivia's blue woolen mitts.

Hastily, Olivia sat on her hands. "How—how long has he been dead for?" she asked.

The policewoman gazed at her with a cynical expression, as if she thought Olivia might know only too well.

"I will ask the questions here," she announced. "Olivia Glass, I will interview you first."

With a glance in their direction, she scattered the other two occupants off the bench.

The manager stumbled down the pathway. As he went, he dropped his Twisp yet again and this time, stood on it. Olivia heard the sad crunching sound that signified the second fatality on the premises that morning. It was followed by a hollow cry of grief.

Brigitta moved to the groomed lawn, where she paced up and down with some difficulty, as her needle-like heels kept sinking into the soft, damp ground.

With a sense of doom, Olivia saw the detective was taking out her tape recorder.

"Why did you arrive here this morning?" Detective Caputi asked.

Olivia stared at her, struggling to remain calm. She knew how the detective's unsettling questions could trick people into appearing guilty of a crime they hadn't even committed. She would have to tread carefully, especially since she had arrived with angry intentions.

"Yesterday, Raffaele di Maggio visited our winery and tasted three new wines. He published the reviews this morning and they were very bad. I didn't think that his opinion was fair, so I decided to speak to him in person, and ask him to remove the negative reviews."

"Is that so?" Detective Caputi looked thoughtful. Olivia had a sudden suspicion that she was remembering how the death had occurred, and that the critic had been stabbed with his trademark pen. "How did you know where he was staying?"

"He mentioned it while he was at La Leggenda."

"What time did you arrive here?"

"About half an hour ago. Nadia from the winery phoned me at around six-thirty a.m. She said the review was terrible, and I must come into work at eight for an emergency meeting. I decided that maybe I could solve the problem by asking Raffaele to remove the review. I drove straight here and saw Brigitta, his assistant, going into breakfast. She mentioned he was in the presidential suite. I came straight here, with Brigitta following."

Olivia felt relieved. She'd managed to negotiate the questioning without feeling as if handcuffs were imminent. From experience, though, she knew she wasn't out of danger. Her honesty had bought her, at the most, a temporary reprieve.

For some weird reason, the detective seemed to think she was a serial liar. Or maybe she thought that way about everyone. Olivia guessed it went with the job, particularly if you were a scary and ferocious detective with no people skills. Innocent people would do anything—yes, even blurt out an untruth—when trapped in the glare of Caputi's dark eyes.

Olivia knew that if she had somehow managed to escape the first pass of Caputi's handcuff run, it would only make the policewoman more focused on everyone else at La Leggenda. After all, just a few hours ago, the winery's products and reputation had been annihilated.

"That is all you have to say?" Detective Caputi asked in a tone of finality.

Olivia stared at her in disbelief. She was being let go? She hesitated, ready to give the detective a second chance to arrest her, in case it had slipped her mind.

It didn't seem to have.

But at that moment, a terrible thought occurred to her.

Now that Raffaele di Maggio was dead, there was no way to erase his review. It would remain in perpetuity unless there was a way it could be removed.

"May I ask you a question?" she dared to say.

"What?" Caputi snapped.

Olivia knew she was already breaching the limits of the detective's patience.

"Now that Signor di Maggio is deceased, could somebody—the website host, for instance—take the site down or at least remove recent content? I mean, it would be sad for his grieving relatives to have to read the very last reviews he wrote," Olivia said, although she wasn't sure that any of those relatives existed.

Detective Caputi shook her head firmly.

"We will contact the domain host and ensure that the site is sealed and no content is tampered with. The information may comprise valuable evidence. Only when this crime is solved will we allow any changes to be made."

She gave Olivia a meaningful glance.

The message was clear.

Detective Caputi was hinting that if anyone at the winery was involved, they should confess sooner, rather than later, in order to save the business.

The more time that went by without an arrest being made, the faster La Leggenda's reputation and presence would be destroyed.

Olivia scrambled to her feet. The interview, though short, had been unsettling, and she felt worried about the winery's future.

Then the detective cleared her throat.

"In case we need it, do you have an alibi for earlier this morning?" she asked casually.

Olivia stared at her in concern. How could she have thought she was out of trouble?

Detective Caputi had saved the biggest bombshell for last. Olivia knew she would not consider a cat's or a goat's testimony to be reliable, but that was all she could offer.

The detective was implying that Raffaele might have been killed after the publication of that dreadful review. If that was the case, it put Olivia and the others at La Leggenda squarely in her crosshairs.

CHAPTER FOURTEEN

Marcello and Nadia were waiting anxiously by the entrance when Olivia arrived at the winery, still quivering with tension after the police interview. As soon as Nadia saw her car, she rushed over.

Before Olivia had even climbed out, she was assaulted by the mini-whirlwind that was Nadia in an excitable mood.

"Olivia! What is this I hear? Detective Caputi called and said that awful little man is dead? And you were there this morning, at the hotel? What has happened? Explain to us!" Nadia added in a lower voice, "Leave out any details you would prefer to keep to yourself."

Olivia goggled at her.

"I didn't kill him!" she protested.

Did Nadia think she was capable of such a terrible act? Olivia wasn't sure, but she knew it was important to explain the circumstances carefully. She didn't want there to be any confusion about this.

"I decided to confront him after you called. I thought I could pressure him to take the review down if I explained how unfair and mean it was," she said. "When I arrived there, I found him dead. Someone had stabbed him with that pen he used."

Nadia nodded loyally, pacing alongside Olivia as she headed to the winery's entrance.

Marcello's expression looked etched in stone.

Olivia hadn't expected him to draw her into a tight embrace.

Her heart started thudding even harder than it had during her police interview, as she felt Marcello's strong arms around her and smelled the faint sandalwood aroma of his aftershave.

"Olivia, I am thankful that you are all right. When the detective called and told us that you had arrived at his hotel and there had been a murder, I thought for one terrible moment…" He embraced her harder, clearly reluctant to voice what he'd feared.

"Come, now, we need to talk inside." Nadia tugged at his arm. As Marcello released her, Olivia could see the concern in his deep blue eyes.

"You are all right. That is the best news I could have received. But now, we are all under suspicion. And, of course, those words he wrote cannot be erased."

"The police are sealing the site until the murder's solved. That could take ages," Olivia said, frowning. "What are we going to do about it? Did you decide anything in the meeting? I'm sorry I wasn't in time. My morning didn't go as planned."

Nadia shrugged.

"In the end, we did not hold the meeting. You did not arrive, and Jean-Pierre did not answer his phone—he only got here half an hour ago. Instead of having a meeting, I went and tasted your rosé again. Olivia, it is world class. There is nothing wrong with that wine and it is high quality. It did not deserve that review. Not at all!"

Nadia stamped her foot.

"If we could rewind time, I would not have given that nasty critic any wines to taste at all and would have told him we had nothing new to offer. Idiot! Imbecile!"

Muttering angrily to herself, she stomped off in the direction of the winemaking building.

Olivia hurried through to the tasting room. She was late for work, and worried that Jean-Pierre would have been overwhelmed with the morning rush.

As she entered the large room, where a crackling fire was banishing the coolness of the morning, she realized there had been no need for concern, because there wasn't a morning rush.

She stared in bewilderment at the lone tourist seated at the counter preparing to sample the wines, with Jean-Pierre in anxious attendance.

The dreadful reviews had erased La Leggenda's presence from the local map. This was more than serious; it was a crisis.

Jean-Pierre hurried over to her and spoke in a low voice.

"Olivia, this is craziness. Your wine is incredible and that man was wrong. He calls himself an expert? He knows nothing, nothing! Now he is dead and we cannot take the review away?"

Jean-Pierre punched the air in frustration.

Olivia smiled sympathetically.

"It's a very serious situation. We must try to do our best today. It's all we can do," she encouraged her young trainee sommelier.

Pressing his lips together and jutting his chin, Jean-Pierre nodded in agreement.

Putting on her game face, Olivia headed to the single tourist. In these difficult times, every guest at La Leggenda needed to be treated like gold. She couldn't allow the customers, or Jean-Pierre, to see how upset or distracted she was.

She greeted the middle-aged man warmly and invited him to start his wine tasting.

"First on the menu today is La Leggenda's famous vermentino-based white blend," she said.

Well, it had been famous until Raffaele had trashed it.

"It's a classic and excellent example of its type," she continued, knowing Jean-Pierre was watching her and taking in what she said. "You may have enjoyed vermentino wine before, as it's a grape native to Tuscany?"

The man shook his head. "It's new to me. It'll be novel to try something so different. In our local village, it seems that apart from sauvignon blanc and chardonnay, there are no other white wines at all!"

Olivia smiled in sympathy.

"I loved the vermentino as soon as I tasted it," she explained. "It's a light type of wine, but a good vermentino can be deliciously complex, and we've managed to convert quite a few sauvignon blanc drinkers to this as their new favorite." She smiled. "As you taste, you may pick up pear, lime, and pink grapefruit, and the wine has a distinctive aftertaste—it's subtly bitter and many people compare it to green almonds. This latest vintage has a small percentage of sémillon and chenin blanc added to it for balance, but the local grapes are the star of the show."

Olivia felt better as she picked up on his enthusiasm at experiencing this brand new varietal of white wine. Interacting with customers was the activity she loved above all else. What a joy it was to introduce them to the incredible wines La Leggenda offered.

She poured the tasting portion with a flourish, and then stepped back to allow the gray-haired gentleman to savor its characteristic citrus taste.

As soon as she turned away from the counter, her brain started buzzing again.

Somebody had committed murder—but who?

Staring at the almost-empty tasting room, Olivia realized how drastic this crisis was.

The police were investigating, but that could take weeks, and how much damage would the winery suffer in the meantime? Tourism was the lifeblood of the winery, not only in terms of direct sales, but also word-of-mouth referrals, reorders, and even restaurant wine sales. Visitors who'd loved their experience at La Leggenda would be far more likely to order the same wine from a restaurant menu.

This situation had to be resolved as fast as possible. It was a time for emergency action!

Drawing in a deep breath, Olivia decided that she would have to start her own investigation. She desperately needed to clear her own name, but more importantly, she had to solve the case so that the website could be changed and the horrific reviews removed.

After all, as long as she stayed out of Detective Caputi's shiny, steel-gray hair, there was no reason why she shouldn't pursue her own research. If she uncovered anything helpful, she could tell the police immediately.

She knew that the detective would suspect Nadia and Marcello as well as herself, but it couldn't have been either of the Vescovis, because as soon as they had read the review, they'd leaped into action, organizing an urgent meeting.

The other suspect who came to mind was Brigitta, the maestro's assistant.

Olivia mulled over this possibility for a while as she watched her lone customer sip and smile, appreciating the lively, fresh white wine.

Brigitta had been the closest to the maestro, without a doubt. And based on how badly he treated others, why should he treat his staff any different? In Olivia's experience, nasty people acted the same to everyone across the board. Perhaps Brigitta had snapped.

Olivia also remembered that the maestro had refused to pay the Gardens of Florence the full rate because he'd been dissatisfied with the palatial presidential suite.

That meant she would have to widen her net to include the hotel manager. No doubt, Raffaele was the guest from hell who'd complained about everything. He could have called the manager to his room in the early hours of the morning over some minor problem. Possibly, the annoyed manager had reacted with violence.

The manager had dropped his Twisp several times, Olivia remembered. Had it been through genuine shock, or the fear of being found out?

Olivia's musings were interrupted by raised voices from the restaurant. Looking toward the entrance, she saw Jean-Pierre and Gabriella were clashing yet again.

"You must let red wine breathe. Customers should be offered a decanter," Jean-Pierre implored.

"We have protocols in our restaurant! And they have been devised in consultation with Marcello! Customers like wine from the bottle. Only young wines need to breathe, and we have very few of them on our menu. You are a little squeak, with no knowledge and a huuuge ego!"

As she hurried to the restaurant to break up this fight, Olivia saw Gabriella emphasizing the size of Jean-Pierre's ego by spreading her arms apart, as wide as they would go.

"Stupid spotty teenager!" Gabriella spat.

Jean-Pierre really was getting under the restaurateur's skin, but as Olivia approached, she realized that Jean-Pierre himself was even more upset.

He danced from foot to foot to express his extreme annoyance.

"I have had no pimples since I was seventeen! My skin is clear as I rinse with lemon water every morning. Why will you not use a decanter, just for those wines?" he asked. "Why are you so set in your ways? My father—"

"Worked in a Michelin restaurant," Gabriella taunted. "What did he do? Wash dishes?"

"He was the manager!" Jean-Pierre shouted, sounding agonized. "Horrible, rude woman. How dare you insult my family!"

To Olivia's horror, Jean-Pierre picked up the nearest implement, which happened to be the ballpoint pen that Gabriella had been using to take down a booking.

Her eyes widened as Jean-Pierre brandished it as if it were a knife.

Then, with an exasperated shout, he stabbed it into the appointment book so hard that the nib snapped off and ink splattered over the pristine white page.

CHAPTER FIFTEEN

By the end of the long, quiet day, Olivia couldn't bear the suspense any longer. She had to start by clearing Jean-Pierre. She couldn't stop thinking about the shocking episode she'd witnessed in the restaurant, or forget the moment when her assistant sommelier had plunged the pen furiously into the page.

Had this been an inadvertent confession? Had Jean-Pierre committed the crime?

She knew he had a terrible temper and acted impulsively. He was an emotional person who didn't stop to think first.

Olivia also remembered, with a frisson of unease, that Nadia had said Jean-Pierre hadn't answered when she'd called to summon him to the morning meeting. Had that been because he was already leaving the murder scene and speeding back home?

She hoped that he wasn't guilty. It would be a catastrophe if such a talented newcomer to the world of winemaking landed himself in jail through his own reckless actions.

The opportunity for chitchat came while they were clearing the tasting sheets and glasses from the counter, and buffing its wooden surface to an immaculate shine.

"Jean-Pierre, you didn't attend the meeting this morning, did you?" she asked in a casual tone.

"No. I missed Nadia's phone call. I was jogging at the time."

Jogging? It had been an unpleasantly cold, rainy morning. However, Olivia was the first to acknowledge that running enthusiasts were not normal people. They didn't seem to care whether it was rain, snow, or shine. They and their Fit Bit would be out on the roads, if the roads were not actually underwater.

"And afterward?" Olivia questioned, keeping her voice light and conversational. "Did you notice the missed call when you got back?"

Jean-Pierre nodded. "Yes. I saw the message when I returned, and was preparing to come in early. However, I then discovered that my cat, Absinthe, was nowhere to be found and I concluded he must have escaped from the house when I went for my run. I had to find him. I was worried he would be wet and cold. I searched the garden for nearly an hour."

Olivia stared at Jean-Pierre in concern.

"Did you find him?"

Jean-Pierre smiled happily.

"Yes. Absinthe was asleep in my sock drawer. I had overlooked him. As soon as I was reassured he was safe, I came to work."

"Well, that's a big relief," Olivia said, but she had to force the cheerfulness into her tone. Jean-Pierre's story was as full of holes as—as a well-worn sock. Had he not used footwear for his exercise? How was it possible to reach into a drawer for running socks and not encounter the annoyed, sleeping cat who was occupying that drawer?

If Olivia had reservations about Jean-Pierre's story, she didn't even want to imagine what Detective Caputi would make of it.

She imagined how the detective would tilt her head in that disbelieving way she had, and rudely insinuate that Jean-Pierre was lying.

Then what would happen?

An outburst of temper from Jean-Pierre could be fatal at that point in the interview, and there was no guarantee Jean-Pierre would exercise restraint. He was a young, volatile, passionate Frenchman!

Who might, or might not, have made a habit of stabbing pens into things, Olivia acknowledged with a nervous twist of her stomach.

Although Jean-Pierre was an unfortunate fixture on her suspect list for the time being, Olivia wasn't going to let this setback prevent her from doing a thorough job in widening the net. After all, there must be many others who'd had it in for Raffaele. All she had to do was find them.

As Olivia was tidying the fridges under the counter, her last job for the day, she heard someone arrive in the tasting room.

She scrambled up from her kneeling position. Even though it was past closing time, they needed every visitor that came their way, and she was more than willing to help out with an after-hours tasting.

To her astonishment, she saw the new arrival was Brigitta.

What was she doing here? Olivia had been planning to track her down for further questioning. She hadn't expected the critic's assistant to be leaning her elbows on the counter, looking exhausted and fed up, but with a determined glint in her eyes.

The assistant's well-coiffed hair had come loose from its chignon and flopped around her face in lifeless strands. Olivia noticed a few leaves lodged in her bangs. There were several smears of dirt on her silver blouse, and large grass stains on the elbows of her white power suit.

"Hello," Olivia said. "Why are you here?"

Brigitta drew herself up to her five-feet-nothing and raised her chin.

"I am busy investigating the murder of my boss and would like your help. May I ask you some questions?"

Olivia stared at her in amazement.

Was the assistant telling the truth, or was this an elaborate setup? She could be looking to frame somebody else for the murder, Olivia thought. She would have to be careful that person wasn't herself.

She wasn't ready to trust Brigitta, but even so, she was curious about her disheveled state.

"What happened to you?" Olivia asked.

Brigitta brushed impatiently at her hair. A few leaves fluttered out.

"It was that detective," she said. "She interviewed me twice. Once in the morning and then again in the afternoon. She made me feel so stressed. I started to believe I was the guilty one! After the second interview I was so tired that my heels stuck in the grass while I was walking away, and I fell into a bush. I left the shoes there. I didn't care anymore. I just wanted to get away from her."

Hopping around on one leg, she showed Olivia her stockinged foot.

Olivia felt an unexpected flare of sympathy for the unfortunate assistant.

"You're going to catch cold."

Brigitta shrugged, looking fatalistic.

"So be it."

Annoying as Olivia thought she was, she couldn't let her catch her death traipsing around in stockings on a cold, wet evening.

"What size are you?"

"Thirty-seven."

"I'm going to try and find you some shoes."

Olivia's knowledge of European shoe sizes was sketchy, but she remembered Nadia was that size, which she thought was the equivalent of a six in the States. Quickly, she called the vintner and explained the situation.

There was a stony silence.

"I do not like that woman," Nadia said eventually. "Now I must give her shoes?"

"Any shoes. Just on loan. Perhaps you have a pair you don't want, or don't wear anymore? She might know something useful," Olivia added, lowering her voice so Brigitta couldn't hear.

Nadia hummed, sounding thoughtful.

"Hold on," she said.

Fifteen minutes later, Brigitta followed Olivia out of the winery. She was wearing bright pink, pointy-toed, calf-length boots covered in oversized cerise sequins. Her footsteps were blinding. Even in the mellow light of evening, Olivia had to blink and look away.

"There's a good restaurant close to where I live," Olivia suggested. "We could go and discuss this over pizza and wine. If you drink too much, we can get a cab to take you back to the hotel, and you can fetch your car tomorrow."

She hoped that in the circumstances, Brigitta might drink enough to speak without inhibition. That would help Olivia no end.

"Let us do it!" Brigitta sounded enthusiastic about the outing. "I will follow you there."

She seemed like a nicer person now that she wasn't at the beck and call of Maestro Raffaele, Olivia thought, climbing into her car. She reminded herself not to be too trusting. After all, she could well be heading out to dine with Raffaele's killer. She would have to be on the alert, ready for Brigitta to bluff and double bluff. She mustn't take her words at face value, Olivia warned herself.

Inside the restaurant, a table by the fireside had just been vacated. The waiter showed them to it, and they sat down in the warmth. Brigitta stretched her legs onto the tiles in front of the dancing flames.

"This is a lovely place," she enthused, paging through the menu hungrily. "I have been getting so sick of refined restaurant food. Maestro Raffaele liked Michelin-starred dishes and, apart from breakfast, I had to eat every meal with him."

The waiter arrived, and Olivia saw the round-faced owner hovering behind him. She looked anxious.

"Please can I have a large glass of your cheapest vermentino white wine, and a mushroom and salami pizza?" Brigitta asked.

"Of course, signorina, but we have to ask you a favor."

Brigitta looked up, surprised. "Sure. What is it?"

"The lights are reflecting onto your boots and spreading over the whole room." He gestured apologetically upward. "Customers are complaining that they feel as if they are in a disco."

Olivia looked up. Sure enough, the walls and ceiling were covered with bright pink, dancing pinpricks of reflected light.

Brigitta moved her boots, and the reflections shifted above them. It was dizzying.

"Sorry," she said, sounding embarrassed, and put her feet under the table.

"I'll have the same as her," Olivia said.

With Brigitta at a disadvantage thanks to her flamboyant footwear, Olivia decided to make a start on her questioning.

"Why did you decide to investigate your boss's death?" she asked.

Brigitta gave her a considering stare as their wine arrived.

"I am not sure I should confide in somebody who could have committed the crime themselves," she said in a low voice.

Olivia nearly choked on her first sip.

"Me? You suspect me? Why would I have needed to trick you into telling me where he was staying, if I'd already been there to murder him?" she asked incredulously.

"You tricked me once. What's to stop you doing it twice?" the assistant replied with inarguable logic.

"Well, I've been thinking about who could have done this, and you're a person who comes to mind!" Olivia retorted.

"Me?" Brigitta sounded outraged.

They glared at each other in silence, and drank more wine.

Olivia was doubtful whether she should say anything more to the assistant. She didn't trust her at all! But if she wanted to gain any information, she'd have to open up. What if her words were used against her, though?

She had another sip of the vermentino while continuing with her internal debate.

Across the table, Brigitta raised her glass again, staring at Olivia through narrowed eyes. Olivia guessed she was thinking exactly the same.

Olivia sighed, deciding to capitulate and offer some information. Perhaps the wine was having the unintended consequence of loosening her own tongue, too.

"I was asleep until six-thirty, when Nadia called me to say the review was published," she explained. "There's no way I could have done it, but I don't have an alibi as I live alone."

Brigitta nodded, and now Olivia thought she looked more sympathetic.

"The police detective suspects me, I am sure," she confided. "I am guilty—not of the murder, but that I let it happen. I feel I should have been able to prevent it from occurring. I was not alert enough."

"Why do you say that?" Olivia asked curiously.

Although she didn't think Brigitta trusted her completely, Olivia had the sense she wanted to unburden. She listened intently as the assistant shared her reasons.

"Maestro Raffaele was a night owl, who liked to work late into the evening. He insisted that I be at his beck and call during his waking hours. He would forward all his correspondence to me, for immediate reply, and I had to deal with all the website queries. He would sometimes send me questions about the wineries that I had to look up and answer within a few minutes. So I worked very long days."

"I can imagine," Olivia sympathized.

"Last night being the final night of his Tuscan winery tour, I was exhausted. I dozed off while waiting for him to read one of my messages, and only awoke in the morning. That was an unforgivable sin in his world. I expected to be in serious trouble for neglecting my duties, and even more so for letting you knock on his door. Instead, my laziness had an even worse outcome. If I had stayed awake, I would have known something was wrong."

Olivia nodded. Brigitta's story seemed plausible, and it explained her anxious pursuit of Olivia as she'd stormed up to the presidential suite.

The pizzas arrived. Olivia stared gratefully at her plate. Was there a more welcome sight after a stressful day than this crisp, fragrant combination of crust, cheese, and sumptuous toppings?

She didn't think there was. Life was beginning to seem better.

"The detective asked me a lot of questions about you," Brigitta added, and Olivia froze, with the first delicious wedge on its way to her mouth.

"She did?"

Brigitta nodded. "More wine, please!" she asked the waiter, before turning back to Olivia. "Questions like: had I seen you in the hotel before? Had you appeared familiar with the layout of the premises? Had you previously asked which room Maestro Raffaelo was staying in? She even asked me if you had appeared angry when he visited the winery yesterday."

Olivia lowered the pizza slice, frowning in worry.

"I hope you answered no to all of them," she said.

Brigitta gestured expressively with the black pepper grinder.

"She put me under pressure so my memory is hazy. I said 'I don't know' to most of her questions. I don't think I said yes to any of them." She paused. "At any rate, not more than one or two. Three, at the most. You did seem a little belligerent yesterday, or perhaps it was just the unfortunate effect of your black outfit."

Olivia crammed the pizza into her mouth. She was a stress-eater, no doubt about it, and she was stressed now, because Brigitta had just told her she'd thrown Olivia under the bus. Detective Caputi might already be organizing the arrest warrant, she thought, with a flicker of dread.

Concerning as this was, she couldn't blame Brigitta. In the circumstances, she might have done the same.

Luckily, the rush of carbs and cheese gave her some inspiration, and she thought of an important question.

"Did the detective mention if she knew the time of death?"

Brigitta shook her head.

"During the second interview, the pathologist interrupted us to say that it could have been any time between one and five a.m. They couldn't be more accurate than that."

Olivia munched another slice while considering this information. The timeframe was troubling. If the time could be confirmed as earlier than four-thirty a.m., then she would be off the hook, and so would the others at La Leggenda.

"That's a shame," she said. "If only they could narrow it down."

Brigitta downed her second glass of wine and hiccupped.

"I think I know what time it happened," she said.

"Really?" Olivia's eyes widened. "How do you know?"

With a confident, if slightly unfocused smile, Brigitta took out her phone.

"Remember what I said earlier, that if I'd stayed awake I would have known something was wrong? This is why." She pointed to the screen with a manicured nail. "You see here? I replied to Maestro Raffaele's question at one a.m., before I fell asleep. He always—and I mean, always—reads his messages within a few minutes, and he would have gotten back to me on this one, asking for more information. He never read this message, which should have been a big warning sign to me. I should have gone and checked on him immediately."

"So you think he didn't reply because he had a visitor?"

Brigitta nodded. "Yes. Whoever it was must have distracted him from his messages, and then killed him. Therefore, I think that the time of death was very close to one a.m. and couldn't have been much later."

"Did you tell the detective?"

Brigitta picked a piece of salami off her last slice of pizza.

"No, because I didn't think she would understand. She seemed so angry with me, I thought it might make things worse," she said, and hic-cupped again.

Olivia nodded, feeling relieved.

At least the unread message might provide Olivia with a temporary reprieve if Detective Caputi did arrive at the winery with handcuffs in tow. Most importantly, in Olivia's eyes, the earlier timeframe cleared everyone at La Leggenda. At one a.m. the review had not yet gone live, and that meant nobody from the winery, including Jean-Pierre, would have had a motive for the murder. Olivia was relieved that she could cross Jean-Pierre off her suspect list, in the light of this new evidence.

Olivia stared longingly at her final slice of pizza. She was too full to fit it in, even though she could hardly bear to leave it on the plate.

"We'd better call you a cab," she told Brigitta, who was starting to droop in her chair.

Olivia paid for the meal and helped Brigitta out of her chair. She teetered drowsily on her flashy boots toward the door.

Out in the fresh air, she hiccupped yet again.

"I didn't tell you someshing—shomething—another very intereshting thing," she confided as she lurched up the paved path to the waiting cab.

"What's that?" Olivia asked.

"I washn't going to tell anyone but I think I can tell you. You see, when I went into the presidential suite this afternoon, to pack up some things before the police came back, I saw Maestro Raffaele's notebook was missing."

"His notebook?" Olivia repeated, puzzled.

Brigitta nodded wisely as she half-climbed, half-sprawled into the cab.

"That white leather-bound book he used to write all his notes in. It was gone! Gone! I couldn't find it anywhere." Brigitta squinted at Olivia from the cab's back seat. "I shink—what I think is that the person who killed him must have stolen that book. And if we can find the book, we will know who the murderer was."

CHAPTER SIXTEEN

That night, Olivia found it difficult to sleep. Her mind was racing after learning that Raffaele had probably been murdered close to one a.m. and that this accounted for the unread message on Brigitta's phone.

Everyone from La Leggenda was off the hook if this was the case, but who was on the hook? And who had stolen that white, leather-covered notebook and why? The two crimes surely had to be related.

After tossing and turning for what felt like an eternity, Olivia opened her eyes wide at six a.m. to find Pirate staring into them. The cat's paw was raised, ready to bat Olivia on her nose.

In fact, she thought he might have done that already. The remnants of a weird dream where she'd been trying to fend off an aggressive pot-scourer came back to her. With a shock, Olivia remembered her feline responsibilities.

She'd been so distracted when she arrived home last night that she'd forgotten to top up Pirate's kibble bowl.

"Pirate! I'm sorry!"

She jumped out of bed, pulled on warm clothes, and headed downstairs to refill his bowl with the expensive pellets that the village vet had recommended for optimal health.

Pirate began crunching enthusiastically. After topping up his water, Olivia decided to make the most of her early start and research the theories that had been milling around in her head all night.

Brigitta had mentioned that La Leggenda was the last stop on Maestro Raffaele's Tuscan wine criticism tour. Olivia decided to look back over the past days and see if any other local wineries had suffered similar harsh treatment. That could provide her with important clues.

Opening the website, Olivia saw that the day before La Leggenda's trash review, Raffaele had visited a vineyard a few miles south of La Leggenda.

Quercia Winery was a small but excellent vineyard specializing in red wines, which Olivia had heard tourists enthusing about. *Quercia* was the Italian word for "oak," which Olivia thought was a wonderful name for a winery that produced wooded reds and had a big oak tree outside its tasting room. She had bought several of their wines from the local store, and loved all of them.

Her eyebrows shot up as she saw that Raffaele hadn't shared her views. He'd thought their two new releases—a Sangiovese red and a blend—were disgusting.

Those were his actual words, Olivia read, as she stared at the gray bunches of grapes he'd chosen as his grading.

"Rough, immature, poorly made from substandard produce, harsh on the palate and with a disgusting aftertaste," he'd slated the wine.

Olivia shook her head. This was impossible. Quercia won awards for its wines every single year. The vineyard would never have released anything that was average, never mind substandard.

The poor grading was as illogical as the critic's condemnation of the La Leggenda wines.

Intrigued, Olivia scrolled back further.

Before visiting Quercia Winery, the maestro had been to two other well-known wine farms in Grosseto, the southernmost province of Tuscany.

These, too, had received scathing critiques and he had slated their wines, unable to find any good in them at all.

Olivia wondered how far she'd have to backtrack to discover any praise. Had Raffaele been on a nonstop negativity spree?

No, he hadn't. Returning to the site, she saw he'd described a wine the previous week as "an incredible new release—a rather promising wine."

That winery, unsurprisingly, had shot up in the rankings. Olivia couldn't help a flare of envy as she gazed at the premier position of Boschetto di Querce winery.

So, last week, at Boschetto de Querce, the critic had been in a good mood, and from that point on, he'd left a trail of destruction and negativity behind him, trashing the efforts of hard-working winemakers who had not only made their wines with expertise and passion, but had also invested a lot of money in them.

The unfair reviews would have affected the egos, the emotions, and also the finances of the winemakers who'd suffered them. Had somebody cracked under the pressure and decided to take justice into their own hands?

Olivia started work at lunch time today, so she had the whole morning to investigate. If she set off now, she could reach the farthest of the affected wineries by the time they opened, and make her way back from there.

This wasn't just going to be an investigation, it would be an adventure. It had been a while since she'd been to the coast, and the route to her first destination, which was about an hour-and-a-half drive away, included a scenic stretch along a winding sea-view road. The winery itself, Olivia realized, might actually overlook the Tyrrhenian Sea.

Eagerly, she climbed into her Fiat and set off, hopeful about what her trip might uncover.

Vino Sul Mare winery did indeed overlook the sea. The stately buildings had a clear view of the waters which, that morning, were gray and restless looking. Olivia loved a moody sea. She could have watched the crashing waves all morning, but she had an important mission to fulfill and could waste no time.

Olivia parked outside the tasting room. The doors were closed, but as she watched, a tall, gangly young man who looked about fourteen years old swung them open. He gave her a friendly smile.

"Good morning," she greeted the young assistant. "Are you open for sales yet?"

"We are," he nodded. "My mother is inside, preparing the tasting room. Please come in."

When Olivia walked in, she was surprised to recognize the attractive, dark-haired woman who was setting out glasses behind the counter.

She'd definitely seen her at La Leggenda before. Had she visited Nadia? Olivia thought she might have. And the sommelier clearly recognized her, too. She regarded her with a puzzled yet welcoming frown.

"I'm from La Leggenda," Olivia said.

"Of course!" The woman beamed. "Now I remember you. I am Venetia, and know your winery well. Nadia is one of my best friends. We play briscola together on the first Sunday of every month."

"Oh, really? I've seen it being played. Is it difficult?" Olivia asked, remembering what fun the card game seemed to be.

How fascinating that Nadia was a lover of such games, she thought. For some reason Olivia hadn't pegged her as a patient enough personality to strategize her way through a game. Briscola, she recalled, was similar to bezique.

"It's easy to learn, but difficult to master and become truly skillful. However, it is a lot of fun. We use the traditional forty-card deck. One of the most exciting parts of the game is signaling—in most of the rounds you are allowed to signal to your partner what cards you hold. It can be a challenge to do that and not be caught out."

Olivia thought it sounded the perfect game to play with friends, whether old or new. Perhaps one rainy winter afternoon, she could ask Nadia to teach her and Jean-Pierre the basics of the game.

She dragged her attention back to the problem at hand. Her job, now, was to see if Venetia would answer her questions openly, or appear to be holding back. Olivia hoped Venetia's expertise in briscola wouldn't give her too much of an advantage.

"I came to buy a bottle of your Sangiovese," she said. "I'm going to give a gift to a friend."

As she spoke, Danilo's dark-eyed, smiling face came into her mind. Her story didn't have to be fiction. She could give this wine to Danilo as a thank-you for all his help and support. In fact, she wondered if Danilo would be free that evening. Perhaps she could invite him around for a drink, to discuss the investigation.

Sleuthing, Olivia realized, was lonely work. Detective Caputi had an entire team to support her. Olivia only had Erba who, though multitalented and endlessly entertaining, was not the ideal partner to bounce ideas off.

"You have chosen one of my favorites. Thank you for the support." The woman smiled.

"Have you been busy this week?" Olivia asked, deciding to broach the difficult topic.

The woman shook her head thoughtfully. "We have definitely had fewer walk-in tourists than usual. In fact, hardly any have arrived in the past few days. Perhaps it is due to the rainy weather. That is the problem with being located close to the sea. People do not visit the beach when it rains."

Olivia was interested that the winery had been negatively impacted, but that Venetia had not realized why. Or, if she had realized, she was using her expertise in briscola signaling to mislead Olivia.

"Did you hear that famous wine critic was murdered recently?" Olivia asked.

"Yes, I heard. What a shock. He reviewed one of our new wines a few days ago. I haven't even read it yet, and to be honest, he didn't give the impression that he liked our winery very much. We are unpretentious people here and didn't do any of the preparation his assistant demanded. We just carried on with our lives, and put a table aside where he could try the new release," the vintner confessed.

Olivia felt a pang of envy. She wished now that the La Leggenda team had taken the same independently minded stance, and not been swept up in the drama of Raffaele's rules and regulations. All it had done was spoil their day and create a massive sense of expectation around the review.

"It's funny how you always recall what you were doing when you hear about a shocking incident like that, isn't it?" Olivia asked. She hoped this subtle line of questioning would allow her to confirm whether the winemaker had an alibi for the evening.

"Oh, yes, we will never forget it," Venetia replied enthusiastically, as she processed Olivia's payment. "That was the same night that my younger sister, who lives in Japan, gave birth to her first son. My husband and I stayed awake until three a.m. waiting for the news that her boy was born. When we heard he had arrived, we opened a bottle of Metodo Classico sparkling wine and called the extended family to tell them the news. What a wonderful, if unusual, night it was. When we heard about the critic's murder I thought of the great circle of life. A death and a birth. Poignant."

"Congratulations on the arrival of your nephew," Olivia said, taking the tissue-wrapped bottle.

Venetia and her husband had a confirmed alibi, so Olivia could rule this small, seaside winery off her suspect list. And she had bought a fine bottle of wine, too. Her first stop had proven to be a fruitful destination.

Turning away from the sea view, Olivia headed inland to the next winery on her list, Cantina Carducci. This one was a firm favorite on the tourist route and many visitors to La Leggenda had mentioned it. She herself hadn't yet been there, and was eager to see what it was like, as she'd heard a lot of positive comments about it.

To her surprise, rather than traditional Italian, this winery had opted for the height of modernity in their architecture, with sloping, glass-clad buildings that looked more like a trendy office block than a historic winery.

Lavender plants in silver pots were set at intervals around the gray-paved parking lot, which was empty apart from one other car.

Olivia headed through the gigantic glass door and into the tasting room.

The huge space echoed with emptiness. The rows of glasses set out on the counter, and the expectant faces of the two sommeliers, told her that this lack of visitors was unusual. Just like La Leggenda, this winery had been plunged into immediate obscurity after the condemning reviews.

"*Buon giorno* and welcome! Would you like to taste our wines?" the closest sommelier smiled.

"Er—yes. I'd love to!"

She hadn't planned to, but after such a warm welcome and generous invitation, how could she decline? After all, it seemed rude to march in and start asking questions.

"I look forward to introducing you to our wines, which have won many awards," the sommelier said, passing her the tasting sheet. "We specialize in lighter, modern selections here, although we still use many of the traditional winemaking techniques."

"Oh, I see that you have a blanc de noir and a rosé on the menu," Olivia enthused. She couldn't wait to taste and buy another local rosé, and was interested to hear how it had been made.

She admired the rosé as it was poured. It was a softer, subtler color than hers, a fainter pink. In line with their winery's metallic modernism, she thought this shade suited the brand perfectly.

"Could you tell me more about this wine?" she asked the assistant, who was hovering attentively over her in the empty room as there was nothing else to do.

"I can," he smiled. "This is our second year of production. The rosé is formulated mainly from Merlot grapes, as we decided for this wine, to follow a more traditional winemaking approach. However, it has a small percentage of Sangiovese. The skins are left on the grapes for only twelve hours to give it the most subtle color and flavor."

Olivia swirled and tasted the wine, realizing that the winery had achieved exactly what they had set out to do in formulating it.

"It's a triumph," she complimented him. Then, deciding it was time to get down to the real purpose of her visit, she added, "I'd love to speak to the winery owner. Would he be available for a chat?"

Again, the sommelier nodded. "Mr. Carducci has just walked in."

Olivia turned to see a sturdy and solemn-looking man approaching.

"*Buon giorno*," she greeted him before switching to English, feeling relieved that even though tourism was temporarily at a standstill, the staff and owners at all the wineries could understand and speak English, sometimes at a basic level, but more often fluently. She wasn't yet up to the task of asking probing questions in Italian, or fully understanding the answers.

"I'm Olivia Glass. I work at La Leggenda and I'm treating myself to a tasting on my morning off," she continued.

"La Leggenda?" She saw immediate recognition in Mr. Carducci's eyes. Suddenly, the atmosphere in the tasting room changed.

Mr. Carducci was suspicious of why she was here. This wasn't just picking up on a familiar local name, she thought. It went beyond that.

This was the type of recognition you gave a winery that happened to be listed below yours, at the bottom of the rankings of a very famous website, after the critic had been murdered.

Had he ended up in a violent confrontation with the unlikable Raffaele?

Olivia knew she would have to use all her newfound investigative skills to get truthful answers from him.

Chapter Seventeen

"Are you finding business quieter than usual in recent days?" Olivia asked Mr. Carducci innocently

Mr. Carducci shrugged, eyeing her uneasily. "Winter is very unpredictable," he said. "One cannot tell what the day, or the week, will bring. A tour bus comes by and—bam!—suddenly you are running off your feet to keep up. Then a rainy spell hits, and the trade slows down. My vintner and I were discussing this just yesterday, in fact."

He gestured toward a tall, lean man who was walking into the tasting room. He was on a phone call, speaking in an imploring tone as he strode in the direction of the offices beyond.

"No, no, please do not cancel your order. The wines are top quality, I promise you, and we have already organized the delivery service to send them to you. You will not regret it. Yes, I know the patrons of your restaurant search online when choosing their wines but there are other sites!"

He headed out of the tasting room, still talking at the top of his voice.

Olivia turned back to Mr. Carducci and they both smiled uneasily.

"Restaurants are so whimsical," Olivia sympathized. "Nadia, our vintner, always says that their wine lists change like the tides."

"Exactly." Mr. Carducci nodded.

"Did you hear that famous critic was murdered recently?" Olivia asked, deciding to move on to the main purpose of her visit.

"Ah, yes. What was his name again? Raffaele, that's the man. I remember reading about that." Mr. Carducci's gaze slid away.

"Did he visit your winery?" Olivia asked.

Mr. Carducci stared thoughtfully at the ceiling.

"He may have. We have had a number of different events and tastings in the past week or two. It's difficult to recall any one in particular, but yes, I think he may have sampled our new wines. I'm not sure if the review is published yet or not. We've been so busy, we haven't had a chance to think!"

He spread his hands as if to encompass the whole enormous, empty tasting room.

From the back office, the younger man's voice came clearly, shouting in an agonized tone.

"Please! Just because that one famous critic didn't like the wines, doesn't mean your restaurant customers will feel the same. We have only had glowing reviews otherwise."

"I think your rosé and blanc de noir are very fine and well-made wines," Olivia said bravely, trying to pretend she didn't hear the impassioned pleas from the office. "I'll have the two, please."

"Two bottles?" He looked at her anxiously.

Olivia thought about the empty winery and what impact a sudden slow-down in sales had on any business that relied on tourism.

She couldn't singlehandedly save the Tuscan wine industry after the decimation it had received—but she surely could try to do her part.

"Two cases. One case of each is what I meant to say," she said.

As Mr. Carducci packed the cases of rosé and blanc de noir, Olivia wondered why he had downplayed the critic's visit to her when it had clearly been a pivotal event. Perhaps he was simply reluctant to think about an encounter which had plummeted their ratings and caused restaurants to cancel orders. Especially since she was a visitor, this might be a sore point that he was purposely avoiding.

But Olivia knew there might be another reason why Mr. Carducci was pretending he didn't remember who the critic was, or when he had been here. And that was because, in a moment of passion, he might have decided to stab the critic with the very pen he'd used.

"Don't you always find you remember what you were doing at the time something shocking happened?" Olivia asked him, striving for a conversational tone. "Do you recall anything about the night of the murder?"

Mr. Carducci shook his head. "On this farm, in winter, we all follow the same routine. We close up at six p.m., lock up by six-thirty, and then

spend a quiet evening. If it is not raining I will take my dogs for a walk—
I have two lovely Italian pointers. Then I will drink wine and make pasta
or stew for dinner, and catch up on any business correspondence I need
to address."

He gazed at her and she couldn't read his expression.

"My vintner usually eats his evening meal at the nearby trattoria, as
he is engaged to one of the waitresses. She stays with him in his cottage
on this vineyard. Our two sommeliers live off-site with their families in
the village nearby."

"It sounds like an enjoyable, but simple life," Olivia enthused, aware
that Mr. Carducci appeared to live alone and therefore had no alibi for
the evening.

Olivia admired this winery and she liked Mr. Carducci and she loved
their modern wines. It pained her to realize how badly their business had
been affected after their online annihilation, and it tore her up to think
that this seemingly good person, who was a well-respected and highly
talented winemaker, had to remain on her suspect list.

"You didn't call anyone when you heard about the murder?" she asked,
in a final effort to obtain information that might clear him. "Perhaps you
went out to visit someone to talk about it?"

Mr. Carducci shrugged.

"That would have been impossible. My car went in for a service on
Monday, and the garage was unable to obtain the right part to fix an elec-
tronic issue I was having. They were out of stock and had to wait for new
parts to be delivered from Florence. I only got it back yesterday. So, the
entire week, I have been confined to the winery, and to our local village
which is walking distance away."

"What an annoyance," Olivia sympathized, feeling as if she could
hug him with relief. His alibi was ninety percent solid. Of course, there
was a slim chance that someone intending to commit murder, or even to
arrive for an angry meeting in the small hours of the morning, would be
foolish enough to use a taxicab. But she didn't think that Mr. Carducci
was such a misguided individual.

"I thank you for your business," the winery owner said. "May I carry
these boxes to your car?"

"Yes, please. I am looking forward to enjoying them, and promise I'll be back again soon," Olivia said.

She climbed into her pickup feeling heavy-hearted. She was finding this angle of investigation surprisingly difficult. It felt as if she was snooping on her neighbors. In these hard times, the wineries should be supporting each other.

But, on the other hand, the damage would continue to worsen until the murder was solved. Unpleasant as this process was, it was necessary—and at least she was buying wine along the way. There was one more winery on her investigation-and-shopping list. She was going to finish her morning's work at Quercia Winery.

Heading back in the direction of La Leggenda, Olivia listened to the eleven o'clock news. It was in Italian—she was working on her language skills, so she tuned in to local radio whenever she was driving. Although she couldn't pick up all the details, she realized that Raffaelo di Maggio's murder was still the top story. Even the newspaper headlines, displayed on a street pole as she left the small town, shouted *"Omicido!"*

Detective Caputi must be under pressure to solve this case fast, Olivia thought. That was good in a way, but risky in another way.

It made it more likely that she might arrest the wrong person, or wrong people, to show that progress was being made. And Olivia could imagine who would be top of her list in that case. She had a nonexistent alibi for the night of the killing, and a strong personal motive since her wine had received the worst ever review on his site.

Speed, Olivia decided, was of the essence. She accelerated onto the main road, determined that she would have made some headway in her investigation by the time she had to go to work.

She arrived at Quercia Winery at the same time as a minibus carrying eight British tourists.

"So is this the right place?" the violet-haired woman in the front passenger seat said, disembarking from the van.

"Yes, I think so, dear." The man who Olivia guessed was her husband climbed out of the driver's side.

"Are you sure, Barry?" one of the others asked as she emerged from the sliding door at the side. "You routed us wrong earlier on. If you'd taken the right road we could have had breakfast in that nearby village before we started on our drunken wine tasting road trip!"

The others laughed as they alighted from the van and stood on the gravel drive, staring at Quercia Winery's façade. Olivia thought it was gorgeous. It was designed in the shape of a mini castle. The owner had even constructed battlements across the front of the tasting room, and had used enormous stones as cladding on the building's front. It reminded her of Castello del Trebbio, only a smaller and more exclusive version. What vision and creativity, and expense, it must have taken to construct this.

To her concern, the tourists didn't share her enthusiasm. One woman, wearing pink-framed spectacles and holding a half finished cornetto roll, took out her phone.

"Wait a minute. Let Miss Navigation set things to right here, because this doesn't look like the picture on that wonderful wine tourism website. This seems to be some sort of fake castle. The place we wanted had a pond in front, and a cluster of trees."

"It was a lake, I think, with an oak grove nearby," her white-haired partner advised, rummaging in his backpack for a well-thumbed map.

"Siri, where is the winery with the lake in front?" a woman at the back of the group addressed her phone in a ringing tone.

"Er," Olivia began faintly, sidling up to the group. "Nice to meet you. I couldn't help overhearing your discussion. This is a very well-known winery. If you enjoy red wines, you will love it."

Only the nearest woman, wearing a red fluffy jacket, took any notice of her. The others were all absorbed in their maps and phones.

"It does look pretty, but we've set ourselves a limit," the red jacket woman confided to Olivia. "Three wineries only this morning, before we head off to a late lunch in Pisa. So we have to choose the best ones. Luckily, there's a great site that we've found so helpful."

Barry nodded knowledgeably.

"What makes it even more of a bucket-list experience is that the critic who owned the site was recently murdered." He peered at Olivia over his eyeglasses. "You might not have heard about that catastrophe, but we were shocked. The site was invaluable when we planned our holiday and thanks to it, we consider ourselves very well informed."

His wife nodded. "On our local We Love Tuscany WhatsApp group, they're saying that because of his death, these ratings will remain as they are forever and a winery at the top of his list will be like one of the seven wonders of the world."

"I only want to go to wineries he recommends—or recommended. This isn't one of them," the woman with the pink-framed spectacles explained. "Barry, I've looked it up and you've misled us again. Although it may not have been your fault. This time it wasn't being directionally challenged, it was the wrong winery name."

"Verbally challenged?" the red jacketed lady suggested.

"Exactly. Who planned our route last night?"

"That was me," Barry admitted.

"I think you must have had too much prosecco! This is Quercia Winery, which in Italian means Oak Tree Winery. The winery we want is Boschetto di Querce, or Oak Grove. Big difference, Barry!"

She waggled her finger at him in playful reprimand.

"We nearly had to settle for one oak when we could have had a whole forest," one of the other men chortled.

"Well, it's an attractive place. Why don't we do a group photo in front of this fascinating building and then be on our way? We don't have time to waste on substandard wines, and there seem to be a surprising number of them in this area. Funny how I always thought this part of Tuscany was one of the top winemaking destinations of the world," the spectacle-wearing lady emphasized.

"But—but—" Olivia gasped. This was like watching a terrible accident play out in front of her. "Don't you think that the winery at least deserves to sell one bottle to you, in exchange for the beautiful photo backdrop? I mean, nobody wants to be perceived as a rude tourist. That would be terrible. There's always one's national reputation to consider."

She gazed appealingly at the spectacle lady, who seemed to be the group's main influencer.

The woman gazed at Olivia over her bifocals. She didn't seem convinced.

"You could always use the wine to cook with." Olivia smiled in a conspiratorial way, hating herself for having to stoop so low in order to make a sale on their behalf. She hoped nobody at Quercia Winery would ever find out she'd said such a thing about their gold-medal-winning vintages.

"True enough," the spectacled lady agreed.

"Would you mind taking our photo?" Barry asked her.

"Sure," Olivia said.

The tourists clustered together in front of the battlements and Olivia snapped a few shots on Barry's phone.

"Smile!" she said.

Then they changed their grouping and she took more photos on the red jacketed lady's phone, and then the lady with the pink spectacles handed her a phone, too. Olivia was starting to wonder if she was going to end up being late for work.

"Will you look at the time!" Barry said, when Olivia had done the last round of photos. "We're going to have to head on now."

Olivia's smile disappeared.

"You mean you're not going to buy any wine from here?"

"Not now. But we have the lovely photos to remember it by."

"Siri, find me Oak Grove Winery," the lady at the back of the group commanded her phone, as she scrambled back into the bus.

With a scrunch of wheels, they were gone, leaving Olivia alone in the parking lot.

"Well," she said.

She felt like saying a lot more. What a frustrating encounter. Short of dragging the group inside, she hadn't been able to persuade them to give this wonderful winery any business. They'd refused to set foot in it as a result of the awful ratings it had received by one man.

She headed into the otherwise empty tasting room.

"Good morning," she greeted the gray-haired, mustached sommelier. "I don't have time to do a tasting, but I'd love to buy—" She hesitated. Her credit card would only stretch so far, and she'd already purchased far more wine than she'd intended to, as well as splashed out on her bucket-list gold chain. That trip to Florence suddenly seemed like a long time ago. How carefree life had been then, Olivia thought with a sigh. She hadn't expected her circumstances to change so dramatically in a couple of short days.

She looked around the empty tasting room, where the castle theme had been carried through with metal grilles and dramatic lanterns and candlesticks. There were even faux-old-style portraits on the walls of Italian noblemen and women with their greyhounds. What a wonderful place.

"I'd love to buy a mixed case of your red wines," she said bravely. "My name's Olivia Glass."

She had to make up for the lack of business, even if it maxed out her card.

The sommelier gave a relieved smile.

"Thank you, Olivia," he said. "I am Gianfranco, the owner of this winery. It is our sommelier's day off today, and I am always glad to have the chance to interact with visitors. However, I apologize for how empty our establishment is. Business has been slow the past week, ever since we got a bad review from a well-known critic."

Olivia felt encouraged that this would be an easy interview if her potential suspect was already volunteering information.

"I know about it," she said. "I work for La Leggenda. He did the same to us."

Gianfranco shook his head. "It is wrong. There should be some checks and balances in place. For one man to have so much power over the local wine industry—I think he ended up misusing it."

He wrapped each bottle carefully in tissue paper before placing them in the case.

"I said to my wife after our review appeared that I would email him and ask if it could be removed altogether as it was unfair. Of course, when it came to it, I could not think what to write. I put it off, but then decided I needed to confront him if I was to have any success."

"When were you planning to do that?" she asked.

"As soon as possible," Gianfranco said. "In fact, I tried to contact him three times before his death. Each time, I was unable to speak to him and his assistant was very obstructive. She wouldn't let me make an appointment after she realized what the purpose of my visit was."

Abruptly, he cut himself short, as if realizing he was sharing too much.

"Did you know where he was staying?" Olivia asked. Her suspicions of this gray-haired winery owner were growing stronger.

"I never met him again." Gianfranco hadn't answered her question directly, and Olivia thought he looked uneasy. His fingers tapped a nervous rhythm on the counter.

"Did you plan to go to the hotel?" Olivia probed, feeling anxious.

"One plans many things in life," Gianfranco replied cryptically, but he looked away and wouldn't meet her eyes. Olivia could sense he'd clammed up and was not going to give her any further information.

She felt conflicted as he carried the heavy box to her car. Gianfranco was holding back, she was sure of it.

Was he the murderer? And if not, why hadn't he opened up and told her everything he knew?

CHAPTER EIGHTEEN

Throughout the long, frustratingly quiet afternoon at the winery, Olivia couldn't shake the uneasy certainty that she'd been lied to. As soon as work was over, she messaged Danilo and asked if he'd like to come around for a drink and snacks, to talk about the case.

She hoped he would say yes. She was desperate to get some perspective on this complex and confusing situation, and to be able to share her thoughts with someone she could trust.

Her heart leaped as he replied immediately.

"I would love to come around! What can I bring?"

"Just some wine!" Olivia texted back, smiling.

She couldn't wait to discuss what she'd learned so far, and find out what he thought the next step should be.

She made a quick stop at the shops on the way home, and as soon as she got inside, began frantically preparing the plates of food.

After the difficult interviews earlier in the day, it was a relief to focus on her snack creations, and take her mind off the troubling case for a while.

She had a lot to do. The only part of the mini feast she'd cheated on was buying the Erbazzone from the bakery. These small, savory pies were filled with spinach, chard, leeks, ham, and Parmesan. They were one of Olivia's favorite Italian snacks. And because they contained spinach and chard, she reckoned they qualified as a health food, too.

Everything else, she decided she would make from scratch.

Olivia's first job was to slice the rustic loaf of bread into thin slices, and then halve them into neat, easy to eat pieces. She brushed them with olive oil and put them under the grill to toast.

At that moment, her phone rang.

Olivia grabbed it, wondering if it would be Danilo. She hoped he wouldn't be calling to cancel, but she also prayed he wouldn't be asking if he could arrive any earlier. She had a lot to do in the next hour.

It was her mother.

"Hello, angel. I thought I'd call at this time when you were likely to be home," Mrs. Glass said. "Although, as you know, I still don't think of Italy as being your home. I feel as if you're simply enjoying an extended vacation there! Home is Chicago, isn't it? Or any other town within a reasonable driving distance of our house."

Olivia stared at the spread of waiting ingredients. There wasn't a moment to lose in her food prep, but equally, she didn't want to offend her mother by saying she couldn't talk right now.

With a sigh, she switched the phone to speaker. She'd have to chat with her mother while simultaneously preparing several different snacks. Even a good multi-tasker would find themselves stretched to the limit trying to juggle all these activities, and Olivia knew from thirty-four years of personal life experience that she wasn't a good multi-tasker.

"Hello, Mom," she said. Yup, the cheerful-yet-strained tone was audible in her own voice, just as she'd expected.

One of these days, she was going to have to take a stand and tell her mother firmly that she was capable of making her own reasoned decisions, had no intention of moving back to the States, and that this was a permanent life choice.

However, Olivia acknowledged that there wasn't going to be time for that difficult conversation right now.

"I have exciting news for you!" her mother announced.

"Really? What is it?" Olivia asked cautiously, taking the fresh asparagus spears out of the paper grocery bag. She had absolutely no idea what the news could be. Had her parents adopted a dog? Were they renovating their kitchen?

A chill ran down her spine as she wondered if the news might be that her mother had booked flights to Italy to visit Olivia. It would be typical of her to reserve the tickets first and only then share the bombshell with her daughter.

Her mother had a knack for inappropriate timing. Arriving while Olivia was embroiled in a murder investigation and trying to avoid being arrested would be typical behavior from Mrs. Glass.

"I'm starting a wine appreciation club," her mother continued. "In fact, I've started it. We've already had our first get-together."

"A wine club?" Olivia was surprised. She'd never have guessed that! She listened carefully, just in case an impulse vacation to Italy proved to be part two of the news.

"You've not known me as a wine lover, and Bailey's Irish Cream has been my tipple of choice in recent years, but let me tell you, I was an avid sherry drinker in my day."

Olivia rinsed the asparagus spears, patted them dry, placed them on a baking tray, and brushed them with olive oil.

"That's very exciting. I'm sure you will enjoy the social aspect," she encouraged her mother.

"As I told Gladys from next door, I can't possibly have a daughter dabbling in the wine trade, even though in a foreign country, without fine-tuning my own already very promising palate. After all, you must have inherited your taste for wine from one of us and your father's never been a drinker at all."

"I'm sure you will make great strides," Olivia said, snatching open the oven door just in time. Another moment and her crostini would have been overdone. Out with the bread, in with the asparagus, and she hoped that she wouldn't forget about them, too.

"I wanted your advice on some good starter wines for the girls and me," her mother continued.

"Er," Olivia said. She guessed semi-sweet might be the best choice, if her mother was used to Bailey's Irish Cream. Perhaps a Gewurztraminer, she thought.

Before she could make the suggestion, her mother continued.

"The peach-flavored sparkling wine we enjoyed in our first session was very nice. Gladys brought it. We weren't sure what it was until we read the label and saw it had sweetened peach juice added. We definitely picked up stone fruit, though, all of us."

"That's excellent," Olivia said cautiously. Peach-flavored sparkling wine? Where had her mother bought it? She didn't think such a thing was readily available in Italy. She could imagine what Nadia would think of mixing sweetened fruit juice with wine.

"Maybe experiment with some different fruit flavors?" she suggested, hoping this would be within the group's comfort zone.

"The other thing I should tell you is that one of the group, a very nice lady who lives opposite the park, brought along a bottle of Valley Red."

Olivia tried to speak, but choked. Quickly, she poured herself a glass of water as her mother continued smoothly.

"We didn't get around to drinking it and I do remember there was some controversy surrounding it after your hugely successful marketing campaign for the wine? Would you recommend we drink it next time? Or should we leave it? I'd like to make a factual decision and not feel that it's sour grapes on my part because you no longer work at the ad agency, even though I'm convinced you'll return to your chosen career after this little break. Oh, did you hear me? I made a pun! Sour grapes!" Her mother laughed merrily.

"I wouldn't advise drinking it," Olivia warned. "If you remember, it was taken off the shelves after the FDA raided the manufacturing premises. Plus, from personal experience, it gives you a terrible headache."

"Oh, of course. It's coming back to me as we speak. Rats in the wine vats, and banned chemicals being used! How could I have forgotten? Perhaps I erased it from my mind?" her mother suggested in a low, horrified voice. "No wonder you decided to take a career sabbatical after being involved in promoting it!"

Olivia rolled her eyes, unable to get in a word of protest as her mother continued.

"I certainly won't drink it in that case, as it doesn't sound healthy. Although, do you think one could use it for cooking, since heat disinfects?"

Cooking! With her memory jogged in the nick of time, Olivia rescued the asparagus spears from the oven.

"I wouldn't recommend that either," she advised.

"Goodness! There doesn't seem to be much use for it, angel."

"No, not really," Olivia admitted.

She scooped a spoonful of ricotta cheese from the tub and spread it onto the first of her crostini. Olivia sighed. It looked instantly messy, as if a preschooler had been playing with food. When Gabriella did the same thing, the ricotta looked perfect, designer-applied.

"I know! I'll start a wine collection!" Mrs. Glass decided. "The Valley Red can be my first bottle. I'll put it down in the rack to mature." She raised her voice. "Andrew, we need to buy a wine rack. A big one—it might need to hold as many as eight or even ten bottles one day in the future if our collection grows. Well, angel, it's been lovely chatting to you. Edna's at the door now so I have to head off on our morning walk."

Abruptly, her mother disconnected, and Olivia shook her head, feeling bemused, as she returned to the urgent job of food prep.

It seemed like only a few minutes later, but was actually more like an hour, when Danilo's truck pulled up outside her front gate.

All the food was ready, and Olivia had refreshed her lipstick and put on a warm but stylish knit top.

Should she light some candles? she wondered, glancing into the dining room as she hurried to the front door.

No, she decided. This was not a romantic occasion, but a working get-together, where they were going to discuss the investigation.

"Hello!" She met Danilo at the front door.

His hair was still purple and the same length—clearly, his niece hadn't had the chance to experiment with any new styles this week—and he was carrying a bottle of wine.

"Thank you for inviting me," he greeted her.

Forgetting her Italian etiquette in the excitement of his arrival, Olivia leaned forward to hug him at the same time that Danilo tried to kiss her cheek.

Their heads collided with an audible thud.

"Oh, dear," Olivia said. She gave an embarrassed laugh. Even though they had such a relaxed, platonic friendship, it seemed prone to these awkward moments. "I was trying to hug you. I forgot my local manners."

"I can learn new customs." Danilo smiled.

Carefully, he leaned toward her and embraced her warmly with his free hand. Her face pressed against his neck, and she felt the smoothness of his leather jacket on her chin.

Then, moving back, Danilo kissed her on each cheek.

Olivia realized her face felt strangely hot. Probably, it was from rushing around making the food look presentable.

"I prepared some snacks for us. And I have some wine for you, as a gift," she said. She had picked out three of the nicest bottles from her morning's shopping; a fine Merlot-Sangiovese blend from Quercia Winery, the rosé from Cantina Carducci, and the Sangiovese she'd bought from the friendly Vino Sul Mare winery.

The dining room table was covered with tasty-looking plates of food.

Olivia had made polpette—Italian meatballs with added parsley, garlic, eggs, and Parmesan. The bite-size, well-browned treats smelled delicious and she'd skewered them with toothpicks and arranged them in a bowl so they'd be easy to eat.

She'd topped her ricotta-spread crostini with a variety of different delights. Some had chopped mixed olives and sundried tomatoes, others were decorated with garlicky fried mushrooms, and others with the roasted asparagus spears.

The only job she'd had with the Erbazzone had been to warm them and transfer them to a plate.

"Wow!" Danilo said, looking at the spread of food. "When you said snacks, I was expecting a packet of Amica potato chips. You are such a good cook. These look delicious."

Olivia realized that in her enthusiasm she'd catered for six people, rather than two. This was a dinner-sized selection. But since it was officially snacks, and not dinner, it didn't count as such.

"I bought the pastries," she admitted, pouring them wine. "Everything else I made, or at least assembled."

Danilo headed over to the fireplace to greet Pirate. The cat meowed a friendly greeting and Danilo got down onto all fours to exchange head bumps with the now-purring animal.

"He is looking good. So tame."

"I'm almost ready to take him to the vet," Olivia said. "He's getting better and better about being picked up."

She handed Danilo his wine and they clinked glasses and sat down.

"*Saluti,*" Danilo toasted her. "Olivia, I have been looking on that site. That critic, he was mad. I have been to a few of those wineries. No way did they deserve those terrible reviews, yours included. And I am appalled he trashed your new rosé. I have not yet tasted it, but if the owners of La Leggenda consider it a fine wine, you can be certain it is. The Vescovis are among the most renowned experts in the area. They are the leaders. Not some guy who got famous through a website."

"You make me feel better by saying that," Olivia said, grateful for his support. "The rosé hasn't launched yet. I was supposed to add it to our tasting menu this week, but after reading the review, we've all been too discouraged to think about it at all."

Danilo transferred a selection of crostini to his plate and munched appreciatively on a meatball.

"So, the pressure's on to fix the problem," Olivia explained. "The police have sealed the website with all its damaging content until the crime is solved, which means that many wineries are suffering with drastically reduced tourist numbers, as I saw today. And Detective Caputi suspects me, among others. She's been interviewing people, looking to gather evidence against me."

"It would have been a big rush for you to have read that website, decided to kill him, and driven there and committed the crime," Danilo observed.

"Even so, the timeframe allows for it," Olivia said. "He was killed sometime between one a.m. and five a.m. Brigitta, his assistant, thinks it was closer to one a.m. as he didn't read a text message she sent. If that's the case it clears everyone at La Leggenda, as our review went live at four a.m."

"Yes, you would have had no motive before reading the review," Danilo agreed.

"The problem is that there were other terrible reviews of wineries published on previous days, and any one of those owners would have had a motive, as well as more time to plan the murder. I interviewed some of them today and I'm sure that one of them, Gianfranco, didn't tell me everything he knew. I could read his body language."

Danilo nodded, looking frustrated.

"There might be many reasons for that. After all, you are a stranger and he had never met you before. Perhaps he did not trust you? Or he was embarrassed about what he did?"

Olivia sighed. What Danilo had suggested was all too possible.

"There's something else that complicates things," she continued. "Brigitta said that the notebook where Raffaele wrote his critiques on the wines was missing from the scene."

"Does she think the killer took it? But why would he, or she, have needed to steal it? How could the notebook change anything?" Danilo asked, confused.

"I don't know! Maybe there were even worse comments in it that the killer didn't want anyone to see?" Olivia hazarded. "Perhaps, if the police found the notebook, they would know instantly who had committed the crime?"

Danilo bit thoughtfully into a roasted asparagus crostini.

"I believe it was a crime of passion, and the perpetrator acted in the heat of the moment," he said, after eating the crostini with evident enjoyment. "Such an action speaks of recklessness. A moment of temper and—bam! The deed is done. And yet, taking the notebook is more logical, as if somebody was thinking ahead. What is the English word I am looking for—computed?"

"Calculated." Olivia nodded. "You're right. It seems as if two different thought processes, or mindsets, were at work. Maybe someone arrived with the intention of stealing the book, and ended up fighting with Raffaele."

"That could be an answer. Are you going to go back to the hotel? Perhaps there is more to be discovered there. What is your next step?" Danilo asked.

"I'm going to speak to Brigitta again," Olivia said. "I need to confirm Gianfranco's story, so if he won't tell me, I have to get the information another way. I want to know if he made an arrangement to see Raffaele. And then I want to find out from the hotel if he arrived there. If the answers to both those are yes …" Olivia stared at Danilo, seeing her excitement reflected in his eyes.

"Then you might have found the murderer," he confirmed.

CHAPTER NINETEEN

Olivia called Brigitta first thing in the morning. To her surprise, she found that the assistant was still in residence at the Gardens of Florence hotel.

"Detective Caputi said I must stay in the area, so the hotel is putting me up for a few more days at no charge," Brigitta said. "They've had a lot of interest in rooms because Maestro Raffaele's death has been all over the news. They said winter bookings are busier than usual as everyone wants to come and see where it happened. They've even had a murder mystery company wanting to partner with them and do a series of events."

"That's incredible," Olivia said, remembering how the manager had bemoaned that this would be bad for ratings. Clearly, it had worked the other way.

She climbed into her car feeling positive. Brigitta had sounded friendlier and more approachable than she had the last time they'd spoken. Perhaps their pizza evening had broken the ice, Olivia hoped. As a bonus, a second visit to the hotel would allow her to interview the manager. After all, he had been on site when this dastardly deed was committed.

Arriving at the hotel a half hour later, Olivia was encouraged to see the manager himself outside. He was puffing on a new, bright white Twisp in the parking lot.

Speaking in a gentle voice, as he was clearly highly strung and prone to dropping things, Olivia greeted him.

"Hello. I remember you from a few days ago."

"Ah, yes, signora. You were the one who found the body, no? Yes, I recall sitting next to you while waiting for the police."

The manager looked suitably sorrowful, and then his lips quirked in an inadvertent smile. Clearly, he was remembering how this event had stimulated bookings.

"I guess he was a difficult guest?" Olivia probed.

"Oh, yes, he was one of our more demanding customers. Nothing was satisfactory. He used to order a Frangelico Dom Pedro every night at two a.m., and if it was not made to his satisfaction, he would shout down the entire hotel. Eventually, I paid our bartender, Celia, extra to stay on and make it for him. She is the only one who can make a perfect Dom Pedro. It's all about the balance between the ice cream, cream, and liqueur, and the blending time is critical, too."

"Did he drink one of those on the night he was murdered?" Olivia asked.

The manager puffed at his Twisp, considering the question.

"No. We expected him to, and in fact, waited in the bar for a while to see if the order came through. We were chatting, we might have shared a glass of wine. We were both officially off duty," the manager added, blushing.

Olivia had the feeling that there was more to the story than a simple desire to help a demanding customer. She felt she was listening to the account of a budding romance!

"So he didn't call?"

"No. He did not ring room service at the usual time. Since I was on duty from eight a.m. and Celia had to be back at noon, we decided to call it a night at two-thirty a.m."

Olivia thought this was interesting information. It provided the manager with an alibi, and also confirmed what Brigitta had said about the murder occurring earlier, rather than later, in the morning.

Another thought occurred to her.

"Do you have a security camera at your hotel entrance?" She hadn't noticed one when she'd driven in, but perhaps it was concealed.

The manager shrugged ruefully.

"We had one, but recently, a departing guest drove into the pole. It fell, and the camera broke. We wrote the incident up in our repair book, so I know the exact date and time it happened. We are only obtaining a replacement tomorrow."

"What a pity," Olivia said.

The manager nodded. "The police said so, also. They said camera footage would have been a very valuable tool, had it been available."

Thanking him, Olivia headed inside.

To her dismay, the first thing—or things—that she saw were two printed signboards directing visitors to upcoming conferences.

The first read: "Murder Mystery Association Planning Meeting: Tuscan Winelands Edition. 11 a.m. in the Oleander Room."

The second was of far bigger concern. It read: "Media Conference and Press Briefing with Detective Caputi. 10 a.m. in the Bougainvillea Room."

The detective was arriving here, and soon. This was where she was updating the local journalists on the progress made in the case.

Olivia swallowed nervously. Already, a waitress was carrying trays of snacks in the direction of the Bougainvillea Room. She didn't want to run into the detective while she was here. That would be extremely awkward. She took her phone from her purse, intending to call Brigitta, but as if summoned by the action, the assistant appeared, heading toward the desk.

"Good morning," she greeted Olivia.

Her hair was held back by sparkling pink and gold clips, and she was wearing a shocking pink jacket over a cotton-candy-colored top, paired with bright blue diamante jeans.

A fiery flash drew Olivia's eye to floor level.

Brigitta was wearing the garish sequined boots that Nadia had loaned her!

She saw the direction of Olivia's gaze.

"I called the winery three times to ask if I could return them. I even spoke to Nadia the third time but she said she was busy and I and the boots must go away."

Olivia was pretty sure Nadia hadn't said go away.

"I am sure she doesn't want them back," she reassured Brigitta.

"Do you think? They are lovely."

Olivia thought the assistant looked much happier. Looking at her changed wardrobe, she could see how stressful, and in fact restrictive, her employment must have been.

"Can we speak somewhere? Over coffee, perhaps? I'm in a bit of a rush. Do you know where we can get served quickly?" Olivia asked.

"How about the bar?" Brigitta suggested.

The bar was in the opposite direction to the Bougainvillea Room. That sounded ideal to her.

They headed into the bar and sat at a table near the window, with a sunlit view of the hotel's gorgeous garden.

"I spoke to a few of the other winery owners who had received appalling reviews," Olivia said. "One of them said that he intended to send an email but had planned to make a personal visit. Only you kept saying Raffaele wasn't available."

Brigitta sighed. "Well, yes. Those were my instructions. Maestro Raffaele said his word was final and he was not willing to enter into correspondence with people who had petty gripes." She scooped up some of the cappuccino's rich cream with her spoon. "It wasn't very nice of him, I know. But what could I do? I was just the assistant."

"Did anyone arrive here looking to see him?" Olivia regarded the other woman closely as she spoke. This information could prove critical.

Brigitta thought back.

"Yes. The day before Maestro visited your winery, an angry man with a graying mustache arrived at reception, demanding to see him. I recognized him from somewhere, probably from one of the wineries Maestro visited during his Tuscan tour. He said that he had sent an email that morning but that he wanted to speak to Maestro in person."

Olivia nodded. This must have been Gianfranco. He'd told her he hadn't sent an email and that he'd only thought about the personal visit. In fact, he'd done both.

Why had he lied to her?

Hopefully, Brigitta could fill in the gaps.

"What did he say when you spoke to him?"

"He became very angry when I said that Maestro Raffaele would not meet with him. He started shouting and would not stop. He stamped his feet and waved his arms, and he kept ringing the bell on the counter, non-stop."

"What happened next?" Olivia asked, eager to know how this drama had played out. It had been an important moment. Emotions had surged. What had the outcome been?

"The hotel manager arrived. He threatened to call the police if the man continued causing a scene. I think that made him realize that he had gone too far. He appeared—embarrassed, almost," Brigitta said, propping her chin on her spoon as she gazed to the ceiling, recalling the encounter.

"And then?" Olivia felt as if she was holding her breath waiting for the answer.

Brigitta gave a small shrug. "Then he turned and marched out. I never saw him at the hotel again."

Olivia let out a long sigh of disappointment. That story had her quivering with expectation. Now, it had ended in anticlimax.

Brigitta giggled. "He was so angry, he drove into a pole as he left the hotel. He knocked it right over! He drives an old Fiat which didn't look to be damaged, but he didn't even stop! Just accelerated away!"

Olivia's eyes widened.

Gianfranco had knocked over the security camera pole!

Had he done so intentionally, not wanting his next visit to be recorded?

Or had it been an accident, a genuine error made in an angry moment of misjudgment?

The evidence, or lack of it, was tantalizing. With the camera gone, there was no way of proving whether he had returned. It frustrated Olivia no end to think that he might have gotten away with murder, and in the process, annihilated the entire local wine industry!

Worst of all, Olivia found that she was having to force herself to be suspicious of the winery owner. Even though he'd lied to her, she instinctively felt he couldn't have committed the crime, and was finding it difficult to align the behavior of the man she had interviewed with that of a brutal, reckless murderer.

"What did his email say?" she asked, hoping it had contained incriminating content that would ramp up her suspicions and get her back on track.

"Oh, I didn't see it," Brigitta explained. There was something in the way she emphasized the word "I" that intrigued Olivia.

"How do you mean? I thought you handled all the communication?"

Brigitta gave her a patient smile.

"I dealt with all the incoming messages and his personal correspondence. Emails sent directly to the website go to the editor. He would answer some of them, or pass them on to Raffaele, or else to me if they were less important."

Olivia clattered her cup back into the saucer.

"Editor?" she said incredulously.

Brigitta nodded, picking up her sugar cookie and nibbling at a corner as if she hadn't realized anything was wrong!

"You never mentioned an editor," Olivia spluttered.

"Well, I wouldn't have mentioned it, because he works from home." Brigitta ate the rest of her cookie.

"What else does he do?" Olivia probed.

"He edits the reviews before they go live. Maestro Raffaele's English is not perfect, and he was aware that the website needed to be. The editor, Silvano, did that job. He corrected the English, did the final design, posted the reviews, and then checked the web emails daily."

Olivia felt as if the whole landscape of this investigation had shifted. This could be a crucially important lead.

"I think it would be very helpful to interview Silvano," she said. "Can you tell me how to get hold of him?"

"Sure," Brigitta said.

She scrabbled in her purse for notepaper and a pen, and wrote an address and phone number down for Olivia.

Letting out a sigh of relief that she hoped was unnoticeable, Olivia took the page and put it into her purse.

She couldn't wait to interview the mysterious editor, but that would have to wait until after her working day at the winery.

Thanking Brigitta, Olivia stood up and checked her watch.

It was just after ten a.m. and Detective Caputi's press briefing would have started.

A thought occurred to her, so sudden and tempting that she couldn't resist.

It might be possible to eavesdrop outside the conference room door. That would provide her with valuable information on the detective's investigation, and on whether she'd made any progress in the case. Perhaps this conference was to announce a breakthrough!

Instead of going outside to the parking lot, Olivia walked past the reception desk and headed purposefully toward the Bougainvillea Room.

CHAPTER TWENTY

Olivia was relieved to see that the Bougainvillea Room's door was closed. Outside, the tea, coffee, and snacks had been well received by the hungry journalists. All that was left on the large trays were two mini cornettos, one small egg and bacon crostini, and several fruit skewers featuring melon and apple, which were clearly the unpopular choice of the spread.

Olivia was tempted to eat the crostini, which looked simply delicious, but reminded herself that it would be very bad manners. She was a stress eater, no doubt about it, drawn to food at moments of tension. But she wasn't here to behave like Goldilocks, greedily guzzling snacks that weren't meant for her, but rather to listen out for the more important tidbits of actual information.

She leaned close to the door.

Faintly, she could hear a voice. It wasn't Caputi speaking, but a male detective, who must be introducing the briefing. Her heart sank as she picked up that he was speaking rapid Italian.

Her Italian was improving every day, but understanding a gabbled, technical address from behind a closed door would be impossible for her at this stage. How frustrating to be able to hear what the detective was saying, but not yet be skilled enough to translate his important words.

Then, to her relief, a woman's clear, bell-like voice rang out.

"Signor Police Detective, I am the editor of the Expats of Britain online community. Could we please have this address in English, if you could be so kind, so that I can convey this important information to my concerned audience?"

"Of course!" The police detective sounded apologetic as he switched languages. "Will all other journalists be able to understand? If not, I can repeat it in both."

From the murmur of asset, Olivia surmised that everyone in the room could understand English. She listened intently as the detective continued.

"Our team has been working around the clock to solve this dastardly crime. The fact that this is a high-profile victim does, of course, place additional pressure on us to provide fast results. However, we are working methodically because by the time we make an arrest, we want the case to be iron-clad. We are confident that if we do the groundwork correctly, our suspect will go straight to jail and will be found guilty, without the possibility of an appeal."

Someone from the audience must have asked a question, which Olivia couldn't hear, and then the police detective spoke again.

"Yes, we are relying on informants as we commonly do in these cases, and are working with several of them at this present time. We have received some important evidence from one person in particular, and this is guiding the direction of our investigation."

Informants? Who were they working with?

The mention that there were several of them sent chills down Olivia's spine, because she'd been roaming around Tuscany, enthusiastically interviewing her list of suspects. For all she knew, one of them could have picked up the phone the minute she'd left and told the police what she'd been asking.

Could she even trust Brigitta? Olivia wondered, with an uneasy twist of her stomach.

It seemed that one of the audience had asked about the informants, because the police detective replied again, sounding as if he was smiling.

"No, no, we cannot disclose their identity, nor any other details. At this stage, the investigation is highly confidential. It is only this way that we will be able to effectively close the net on the perpetrator."

As she stood with her ear pressed to the keyhole, increasingly worried about what she was hearing, Olivia remembered that she must be ready to leap out of the way if it opened. At any time, one of the media might feel the need to hurry outside and snag the last crostini, or possibly force down a fruit skewer.

At that moment, Olivia realized that there was a shadow behind her. The light was not as bright as it had been.

Hurriedly, she straightened up from her ear-to-the-keyhole pose, and turned around to face the corridor behind her.

"Aaargh!" Olivia let out a strangled cry.

She stood face to face with Detective Caputi, dressed in a power suit and wearing gold-framed spectacles, and carrying a folder of documents under her arm.

"Well!" the detective said, in a tone that could have sliced through steel.

This was unprecedented. Why had Caputi been wandering around the hotel picking up papers, instead of safely ensconced inside the conference room where she was advertised as being.

"I—I thought—" Olivia gasped. Her head was spinning with shock.

She was going to blurt out, I thought you were inside, but realized that would be disastrous. The policewoman suspected her already. Now, thanks to Olivia's highly irregular behavior, Caputi would be ten times as motivated to pin the crime on her.

Thinking as fast as her reeling brain would allow, Olivia stammered out an excuse.

"I thought this was the murder mystery conference. I've always been so interested in them. But I see I have the wrong room. I thought I'd listen outside, in case I interrupted anything," she gabbled, stepping hastily aside.

"You do not only have the wrong room," Caputi intonated, in a voice that made it clear she didn't believe one word of Olivia's flimsy and hastily thought up excuse. "You also have the incorrect wing of the hotel, as well as a completely inaccurate starting time."

"Er—what a shame. I'll go and find the right room."

As Olivia hurried away, conscious of Caputi's gaze boring into her back, she realized that this impromptu detour had been a disaster. She'd only learned enough to scare herself, and she now looked guiltier than ever to the suspicious policewoman.

It was time to abandon this line of work for the morning, and head to her real job at the winery.

Although she'd had dreams of seeing tour buses pulling up outside La Leggenda, Olivia's hopes were dashed when she arrived. The parking lot was almost empty, and the few vehicles that were there all seemed to be restaurant patrons. The tasting room was empty and echoing, apart from a worried-looking Jean-Pierre.

Olivia grimaced to herself as she walked inside. The pressure was on! She had to solve this case as fast as she could. If only the hotel's security camera had been working.

She hoped that her visit to the editor later would uncover concrete evidence, because so far there was proving to be a frustrating lack of it.

Putting on a brave face, she smiled at Jean-Pierre.

"This might be a good time to catch up on stocktaking," she suggested. "It's one of those jobs that only ever seem to become important when things are busy. Let's take advantage of this temporary lull."

She emphasized the word "temporary," hoping that if she spoke it, it would prove to be true.

At that moment, Nadia marched through the tasting room, speaking on the phone while heading for Marcello's office.

"What do you mean, you are canceling our order?" the vintner shouted.

With a chill, Olivia realized that this was a repeat of the dialogue that had played out at Cantina Carducci the previous day.

Except, as she listened to the one-sided conversation, Olivia realized that Nadia wasn't going down without a fight.

"We have a year's contract to supply your restaurants." Nadia paused. "I do not care about bad reviews. That is the only bad review this wine has ever had. Have your restaurants had no bad reviews? Maybe I should never visit you again because one critic believed your calamari to be undercooked, or the fish was not well seasoned? I think I will look and see if there are any, and if I find some, we shall warn all our winery visitors not to eat there."

Nadia paused.

"Okay then, I take you a bet. If I go online now and find nothing negative to be said about your restaurants then by all means cancel the wine order. I will start the bet at four thousand euros, since that's the value of your order." She paused before continuing, in a triumphant tone, "All right, I thought so. I am glad common sense has prevailed. Yes, I will send the wines tomorrow. As you have delayed things with this review nonsense, the truck has already departed and I will now have to courier the first batch to you, so there will be a surcharge of fifty euros. I will add it to your invoice."

She disappeared down the corridor.

Olivia breathed a sigh of relief. Nadia had won this battle, but she knew that the war was still raging. The winery was empty. There was no way to remove that damaging review, and its presence was eroding their numbers day by day.

When she returned to the tasting room, she was pleased to hear the growl of an engine from outside. A sports car was speeding up the driveway, its tires screaming over the neat paving. She heard the scrunch of wheels as it pulled to a stop outside. Finally, guests had arrived.

Olivia stood poised by the tasting counter, giving a welcoming smile as the couple entered.

Her smile froze, and then dissolved. This was impossible, it couldn't be happening. She felt plunged into a waking nightmare.

Matt and Xanthe were walking into the winery.

CHAPTER TWENTY ONE

"So, my love, I thought we could do some wine tasting at this excellent vineyard. I looked online and it's rated as one of the best," Matt said in tender tones, staring into Xanthe's eyes as Olivia looked on, appalled.

Matt was lying. In terms of website ratings, La Leggenda had become the black sheep of the Tuscan vineyard family. There was only one way he could have chosen this vineyard out of the hundreds in the area, and that was because he had found out Olivia was working there.

At that moment, Matt looked up and stared straight into Olivia's eyes.

"Well, look who's here!" he announced, his voice ringing with artificial surprise. "What an absolute shock. I don't mind admitting I'm stunned to see you here, Olivia. Are you visiting this place, too?" Matt approached, tilting his head sideways. "No, wait, you're on the wrong side of the counter. That must mean you're working here." Incredulity filled his voice. "My goodness, what a change of pace."

He turned to Xanthe, who'd taken out her phone and was arranging her hair, preparing for a selfie, Olivia guessed. She looked slimmer than ever in skinny jeans that appeared to be painted onto her petite form, and a pair of stylish cream colored, knee-length boots that were clearly brand new and looked expensive. So they had gone shoe shopping, Olivia thought, and to her surprise, felt a sour stab of jealousy.

They really were exquisite boots, damn it. She'd have loved a pair, but after having bought what felt like Tuscany's entire stock of wine, her credit card had reached breaking point and there weren't going to be any shoes in her immediate future. She seethed with resentment toward Matt for trolling her on his carefully planned vacation, with his new girlfriend and her fancy designer footwear.

"You know, when I knew Olivia, she had a real job, back in the States. She worked for one of the top ad agencies in Chicago." Matt announced in piercing tones. "She was quite good at her job, but not everyone can handle the pressure of a normal career."

Beside her, Olivia felt Jean-Pierre tense.

"What does he mean, a real job?" he muttered.

"He's my ex," Olivia whispered. "He's trying to put me down in front of his new girlfriend."

Jean-Pierre glowered at the couple.

"That is terrible of him," he breathed.

Feeling slightly better about the situation thanks to Jean-Pierre's loyal support, Olivia turned back to face her ex. Her prediction had been correct, and Xanthe was, indeed, busy with a selfie.

"So, Olivia, I can't wait to see you on the job, so to speak. We'll definitely do a tasting now. I'm interested to see what you've picked up so far in your new workplace, or I guess it's more of a hobby, really?"

Olivia forced a smile. She wasn't going to allow him to rile her—or at any rate, to show how riled she was.

"Unfortunately, I'm busy stocktaking," she said, indicating her clipboard with a faux-apologetic shrug. "My skilled assistant Jean-Pierre will be more than happy to take you through our tasting journey."

She felt Jean-Pierre tense beside her, clearly unnerved by the bombshell of this responsibility. Sorry as Olivia was to inflict Matt on him when he was in super-annoying mode, she wasn't prepared to spend more time in the company of her dreadful ex. Her feet were itching to leave. Walking out seemed like the best life choice that she could make.

"Oh, no, no, no, I don't think so." Matt shook his head. He had a tone in his voice that Olivia recognized only too well. He used to use it on waiters when he thought they needed putting in their place.

Olivia was sure he would be insufferable during the tasting.

And, as he continued speaking, she realized she was right.

"You see, Olivia, we're not your average tourists. We're wealthy folk, upper-echelon customers, who might possibly buy a few cases of wine to take back home if we're satisfied with the service. And we're discerning individuals. I'm not happy with an assistant who knows nothing. If I have a question, I want it answered by the expert, not the beginner."

Jean-Pierre drew in his breath sharply at this insult. He shifted from foot to foot in a restless way.

"There's no point otherwise," Xanthe added. "I remember at the Ferragamo shoe store in Florence, we had to insist on the manager attending to us, to get any service at all. Otherwise we might not have spent the amount of money there that we did. I agree, we should receive the most expert advice on these wines, or I won't be convinced to buy."

She glanced down at her boots in a satisfied way, and Olivia felt her blood pressure skyrocket. Damn it, she could come to terms with the other woman's wasp waist after an internal battle, but the Ferragamo footwear was really getting to her.

She was groping for the words that would allow her to avoid the torture of an hour in the company of her obnoxious ex, his narcissistic girlfriend, and their new boots, when Jean-Pierre abruptly cracked.

"Actually," he roared, his voice so loud that Matt visibly flinched and Xanthe dropped her phone, "neither of us is available now. You have come at the wrong time, stupid tourists. Can you not see we are holding clipboards? This is the middle of stocktake! There should have been a notice on the door. Perhaps you did not read it or else you blew it away with the passage of your fast car arriving. We do not want you or your idiotic questions or your aggressive speeding into our winery."

Matt and Xanthe were staring at Jean-Pierre in horror. They seemed hypnotized. Olivia guessed they'd never experienced the tornado that was her assistant sommelier when he lost it. Luckily, she had some mileage in that regard and had developed techniques to manage his behavior. However, at this moment, she couldn't bring herself to use them. It was simply too satisfying to watch Matt step back, looking confused and apologetic, and Xanthe stoop to pick up her phone, which Olivia saw now sported a large, star-like crack in the top right corner.

Jean-Pierre rushed around the counter, flapping his clipboard at them as if intending to use it to fan them out the door. His French accent seemed stronger in this moment of high emotion, as he yelled at them.

"Get out! Go away! You cannot stand here and insult us while we are so busy counting up our many excellent wine bottles that we do not want or need to sell to you. It would be an insult to our wine to pass your lips. You are as rude as—as Gino Galletti himself. If you want to return, you make an appointment. Unpleasant guests cannot be accommodated at short notice!"

Olivia couldn't believe her eyes. Somehow, the force of Jean-Pierre's temper had pushed Matt and Xanthe all the way back to the entrance door. As she watched, they turned and hurried out, with her assistant sommelier in hot pursuit.

A moment later, she heard the growl of the car's engine—this time, more subdued, as it departed.

Jean-Pierre returned to the tasting room. His temper had evaporated and now, he appeared repentant.

"I am sorry," he muttered, his head hanging as he slunk up to the tasting room counter. "I could not help myself. Olivia, if you want to dismiss me, I will accept it. I will only say that I was unduly provoked."

Olivia stared at Jean-Pierre admiringly. She'd never have had the guts, or the ability, to shoo her ex out of the winery as if he was a nasty smell that needed to be removed. She was realizing, right there, what an asset her trainee was.

"Who's Gino Galletti?" she asked. The name made her think of ice-cream.

"I do not know him, but my friend, who works at the estate down the road, told me about him. He was the vintner there until a few years ago. He was so arrogant and rude that many other staff resigned from their job rather than work with him. Eventually the owners asked him to leave and he went elsewhere. They still talk about him at that winery. I guess you will ask me to leave, too?" he said humbly.

First things first, Olivia had to consider priorities.

She glanced in the direction of the restaurant. Gabriella was nowhere to be seen.

Jean-Pierre saw where she was looking.

"She has not yet arrived," he confided, in a low voice. "Yesterday I heard her mention she was going to pick up some cases of organic eggs on her way in."

"Well, then," Olivia said, "I think we can safely keep this between us."

Jean-Pierre nodded knowingly. "It did not happen," he ventured.

"We were occupied with counting bottles the whole morning, and noticed no visitors," Olivia confirmed.

"It was exceedingly quiet," Jean-Pierre elaborated, waving his clipboard in the air.

"Now that we've established that without any doubt, let's get back to our stock take, while keeping an eye out for any arrivals who might be the first visitors of the day," Olivia said, smiling in a satisfied way as she took her pen out of the slot and turned back to the storage room.

As soon as the tasting room had closed for the afternoon, Olivia climbed into her car.

The lack of visitors had prompted them to shut the doors a half hour earlier than usual. Clearly, nobody was coming to the winery. That was good, as it gave her more time to get to the editor's house before it grew dark, but it was bad because if this carried on, the winery might not survive. Tourism and direct sales were a huge contributor to profits all year round, and Nadia couldn't bully every restaurant that started canceling orders.

She felt worried as she started the pickup and drove out, heading for the coast.

The editor's address led her to a remote village that was so close to the Tyrrhenian Sea that the local bistro had been named Spruzzo di Mare, or Sea Spray.

Olivia thought that was lovely.

She cruised through the small village, peering curiously from left to right to take in every scenic inch of the pink and cream buildings, the fishmongers, the coffee shops, the stores selling seafaring and hiking gear, and the tiny restaurants.

Then she drove out of town and headed along the seaside lane until she found number thirty a half mile ahead. This was where the editor lived.

She stopped outside, edging the pickup as close to the home's low stone wall as she dared, so that any other passing cars could squeeze by. This really was a tiny road. Olivia guessed it wound up into the hills and ended in a cul-de-sac.

She climbed out, breathing in the tangy, salty scent of the sea. The crash of waves filled her ears, and the wind carried a fine, cold mist from the ocean that made her face and hands tingle.

What a magnificent location and view. Olivia stared out over the sea for a few appreciative moments. If she lived in this simple cottage, she'd also insist on working from home. With the nearby village supplying all one's needs, there might be no reason ever to climb in a car again.

With a sigh, she turned away. She had a murder to solve, if she wanted to work at all.

She opened the low, rusty gate—Olivia was sure that in this brine-filled location, rust must be endemic—and headed to the weathered, green-painted front door.

Her knock was answered in a few moments.

"Ah, you are the lady who called me earlier? Come in, come in. I am Silvano."

The man who answered the door was dressed in a gray tracksuit and comfortable-looking loafers. He was cheery, round-faced, and smiling. A delicious aroma of garlic wafted out of the house.

Olivia followed him through the hallway and into a small living room. There was a compact cabinet in the corner that she guessed might house a television. It seemed seldom used. The main attraction was the huge sheet-glass window overlooking the ocean. Olivia could hardly tear her eyes away from the blue-gray, restless sea to admire the massive wine rack that stretched across the far side of the room. It was filled with bottles. Above it hung three colorful still-life paintings of food, wine, and flowers.

She noticed a state-of-the-art silver laptop on a large wooden desk in the corner of the room. The laptop was the only new item she could see. Everything else was comfortable, weathered, and had seen years of use.

The left side of the two-seater couch was occupied by a small dog with a white, fluffy coat. On seeing Olivia, he gave a welcoming yap and his tail thumped the cushions.

"That is Garibaldi," Silvano said.

"He's cute. Is he a Maltese?" Olivia's knowledge of dog breeds was sketchy. She stretched out a hand and let the little dog sniff it, before patting him and seating herself on the other side of the couch.

"He is part Bolognese, and part who knows what," Silvano explained with a smile. "May I offer you a glass of wine?"

She didn't have a chance to acquiesce. He was already selecting a fine-looking Barbera red from the shelves and reaching for the wine opener.

"You are here regarding Maestro Raffaele's murder?" the editor asked.

"Yes. Have you had anyone else come round and ask questions?"

"Indeed I have." Silvano handed her a glass. "The police came here yesterday and questioned me for an hour. I feel they might have more to ask, although they did not say when they would return."

Again, Olivia felt uneasy. Detective Caputi was a step ahead of her, and had visited the editor before Olivia knew he existed. Was she slipping up, and had she wasted important time heading off in the wrong direction?

"Were you shocked when you heard about Raffaele's murder?" she asked, hoping that this would invite Silvano to open up and share his feelings.

He nodded.

"Shocked, yes, but not surprised. You see, for the past few months, I have felt that he was heading for disaster. I tried to stop him, but he would not listen."

"Why was that?" Olivia asked.

Silvano sat on a leather armchair opposite the couch and sipped his wine.

"His website became so big, so influential. People gave him cars, clothing, jewelry. He was an international celebrity and he was so powerful that he could make or break a winery. And he knew it." The editor sighed. "He stopped caring about what was right or wrong, and only cared about himself. I could see he was making many enemies, but he refused to listen to my warnings. I told him again and again that what he was doing was not ethical. You cannot destroy a winery simply because you felt slighted in some way or you disliked the place for personal reasons. He never thanked me or took my advice. In fact, he started insulting me, and threatened that he would fire me and destroy my reputation if I continued badgering him in that way."

"Is that what he said?" Olivia asked.

The editor nodded sadly. "It became all about his own ego, and not the wineries at all."

Olivia felt stunned by this bombshell. If the Vescovis had known how corrupt and devious the critic was, she was sure that Marcello would never have allowed him to set foot on the property. She wished she could turn back the clock and warn him.

"Did the police ask you not to change the website?" Olivia said. She was sure Detective Caputi would have, but it was surely worth a try.

Silvano nodded. "The site is to remain sealed until the investigation is concluded, or else closed."

Olivia took this disappointment on the chin. It went down easier with another sip of wine. She decided it was time to move on to the original purpose of her visit.

"I was talking to one of the winery owners, who mentioned they had sent an email to Raffaele. Do you recall if any unusual or threatening mails arrived recently, complaining about poor reviews?"

Silvano didn't answer immediately. He frowned, and seemed to be thinking hard.

"I do not recall," he said eventually, shaking his head.

"Could you check?" Olivia asked in her most pleading voice, hoping she wasn't pushing his good nature too far. "It's important. His assistant said that his notebook was stolen from the crime scene. So I can't help thinking that the reviews and the murder are somehow linked."

Silvano's eyebrows shot up. Looking startled, he glanced at his computer but didn't make a move toward it. Olivia was suddenly aware how silent the room was. She could hear Garibaldi's faint snoring, and the crashing rhythm of the nearby waves.

Then, with a loud trill, Silvano's phone rang.

"Excuse me," he said. "My sister in Rome is calling. I will be five minutes. Please, enjoy your wine."

Looking relieved, he headed out the door and she heard him hurry upstairs, talking animatedly in Italian.

Olivia took another sip of her wine and gave the dog a head rub.

She sat on the couch for a full thirty seconds before she realized this was an inexcusable waste of an opportunity. She was alone in Silvano's house, and his computer was on the desk in the corner. If Olivia was lucky, she could manage to access the website herself and remove the appalling review. At any rate, peeking at Silvano's emails would give her a helpful insight, especially since the editor hadn't seemed willing to do so. In fact, she'd been expecting him to refuse.

This was her only chance.

Olivia scrambled hastily to her feet. At any moment Silvano might finish his phone call and return to the lounge. She had to act as fast as possible.

But, as she moved, Garibaldi raised his head and gave a piercing *woof.*

CHAPTER TWENTY TWO

O livia froze, and then sat carefully back down.

"Sssh," she cautioned the dog, her heart accelerating, because a volley of barks would surely bring Silvano rushing back. "It's all okay."

Thankfully, Garibaldi laid his head on his paws again, clearly prioritizing his rest over her untoward activities.

Olivia climbed to her feet—slowly and in a relaxed way, this time. She tiptoed to the desk and jiggled the metallic silver mouse.

The screen shimmered into life.

"Damn," she muttered. It was asking for a password to let her in.

Frustrated, Olivia was starting to regret her life choices. Why had she spent so long in college studying marketing and copywriting? If she'd studied computer programming and learned how to hack, she could already be past this screen and accessing the reviews.

She recalled that her complete inability to do math had ruled out a number of careers, including programming. At any rate, there was no chance she could guess this password, although Olivia did give it one intelligent try, typing in Garibaldi.

Nope, Silvano hadn't used his dog's name. Beyond that, she had no idea. Letting out a frustrated sigh, Olivia dropped her head in defeat.

Her downcast gaze fell on the laptop bag that was propped against the desk.

There was a white object inside the open bag which looked strangely familiar to her. Confused at seeing it out of context, Olivia stared at it for what seemed like a long while before she finally placed it.

Then her mouth fell open.

It was the book!

That distinctive white leather binding, the gold metal reinforcement on the corners. This was the notebook that Raffaele di Maggio had used to scrawl his uncomplimentary thoughts during his tasting.

Olivia drew in a sharp gasp.

She took the book out of the bag, running her fingers over the textured leather in disbelief before opening it at random. A glance was enough to confirm that this was undoubtedly the same book. That deep blue, flamboyant writing was familiar. She could almost hear the scratch of that expensive, deadly pen on the page.

Olivia nearly dropped the book as she realized what this meant.

The editor was the murderer.

He had to be. No wonder he'd looked so shocked when she'd told him she believed the theft of the book and Raffaele's killing were linked.

He hadn't said a word to her about the fact that this book was now in his possession. It was clear evidence of his guilt. And he had even revealed his motive to her. When Silvano tried to speak up against him, Raffaele had insulted him and threatened to fire him and destroy his reputation.

Olivia's heart jumped into her mouth as she realized the phone call might have been a pretext. What if he wasn't talking to his sister at all, but had gone upstairs to find another weapon to use on her, after deciding she had found out too much?

Olivia let out a faint squeak. This situation was dangerous.

Before she could think about the consequences of her actions, she found herself at the front door, still grasping the notebook.

"Goodbye," she whispered to the sleeping dog.

Then she was outside, in the fresh, breezy air, sprinting toward the road and the safety of her car.

By the time she got back to her farmhouse, it was fully dark and starting to drizzle again. She let out a sigh of relief as she parked the car, glad to be safely home. What a stressful afternoon it had been.

Her nerves were still jangling as she set the notebook on the kitchen table.

What would its pages reveal? Her hands were shaking as she poured herself a glass of wine and took a big sip to calm herself down.

She sat at the table and touched the book again with a sense of disbelief, feeling its glossy leather cover, cool and smooth in her hands.

Silvano had said that Raffaele had been getting more and more unreasonable, egotistical, and unfair in his reviews, and had threatened to fire him. Presumably, the editor had reached breaking point. Perhaps he and Raffaele had fought about it.

He had killed Raffaele and stolen the notebook.

Why had he stolen it? Perhaps he'd intended to mislead the police, guessing they would believe, as Olivia had done, that the negative reviews were linked to the murder.

At any rate, the notebook might provide her with more insight, and she hoped she would also learn what Raffaele's honest opinion of her wine had been.

Taking a deep breath, she finally dared to open its plush leather cover.

Here was Cantina Carducci's review. Olivia looked closer, her eyes widening as she read the words.

"Very promising red blend, I enjoyed the addition of Dolcetto grapes. Needs a touch more oak. Excellent new season Sangiovese," the critic had scribbled. And below that—Olivia frowned as she battled to read the angry scrawl.

"Winery owner answered a phone call in front of me while tasting. Rude and inconsiderate! Plus, the tablecloth was not pure white but had ugly tan stripes. Disrespectful again!"

Olivia put her wineglass down.

"Well!" she exclaimed.

An innocent phone call and the winery's choice of table covering had led to Raffaele condemning the wines? Olivia couldn't believe it.

What about Quercia Winery?

Fascinated, Olivia turned the pages, searching for the winery's name. There it was.

"Well made Sangiovese blend, easy drinking, but a little light for a place in a serious collector's cellar. The Merlot-Montepulciano blend was better made, stronger, more character, a very fine wine!"

Clearly, the critic had loved that wine, despite his scathing review. So what had he found fault with at that winery?

She read on: "Hideous pictures of dogs on the walls. Why, oh why? Also, owner has revolting mustache. Made me want to vomit. Like having a dirty scrubbing brush sprouting from under your nose. We have moved on from the disastrous and best forgotten trends of the 1980s! Shave it off, you imbecile!"

Olivia blinked rapidly. Were they even thinking of the same person? She hadn't found Gianfranco's mustache offensive at all. It suited his urbane look just perfectly, and was elegant and well maintained. In fact, she couldn't imagine him without it. And the paintings on the wall were beautiful.

Just after that, Olivia was interested to see, Raffaele had written his notes on Boschetto di Querce. This was the Oak Grove winery that produced the wine he'd described as "incredible" on his site, and where the British tourists had been attempting to go.

"This is the best Sangiovese I have ever tasted! An absolute triumph of winemaking. Egotistical vintner, though."

"Interesting," Olivia said aloud. So Raffaele had toned his review down slightly—while still giving the wine high praise—because he hadn't like the vintner's attitude. But clearly, being egotistical wasn't as big a problem as having a mustache or taking a phone call.

She shook her head, feeling confused, and then she turned the page and nearly choked on her wine, because there it was—the name La Leggenda, scrawled in that confident, dark blue script.

What had he really thought? Olivia was almost too scared to read his words at all.

"Red blend: very well made. Will mature into a certain prizewinner."

"New season Miracolo: upholds all the qualities of previous years, incredibly consistent—how do they do it???"

And then, at the bottom of the list, was hers.

"New rosé: Remarkable. Top quality, perfectly blended, a very fine example of its type, will win awards."

A cry escaped Olivia's lips. He had actually liked—in fact, loved—her creation. There hadn't been anything wrong with the wine at all. She felt giddy with relief.

So what had the problem been, then?

There, in black—or rather, blue—and white, was the scribbled reason for Raffaele's dreadful review.

"American sommelier??? What on earth? Are we short of Europeans to fill this critical job? Unacceptable! What do Americans, the country responsible for Valley Wines, know about the noble heritage of European winemaking! I am disgusted!"

The words "American sommelier" were underlined three times. So was the word "disgusted."

With a shiver, Olivia realized it had been her fault that the expert had condemned La Leggenda. Never mind her dress code faux-pas. Raffaele hadn't even gotten around to mentioning that. As soon as Olivia had opened her mouth, she'd earned the winery those disastrous reviews and that terrible, black bunch of grapes.

As she drained the last of her wine, wishing she'd stayed home that day or at least faked laryngitis, Olivia realized something even worse.

This review blamed her, personally. And that gave her a compelling motive for murdering the critic in anger.

Here she was, alone in the farmhouse, in possession of the critic's notebook. If Detective Caputi arrived now, this would provide damning evidence against her. And Olivia knew only too well what an uncanny knack for bad timing the sharp-eyed policewoman had.

She could say she'd taken it from the editor's bag, and that she was convinced he was the murderer, but there was nobody to corroborate that story, because she'd grabbed it and run away. When she thought of Detective Caputi's merciless, hawk-like stare, her story seemed flimsy and inadequate.

Her reckless actions had been a huge mistake. Worse still, she had no idea how she could fix the damage before she was found out.

CHAPTER TWENTY THREE

Olivia slept badly, and eventually slipped into a weird dream where she was sitting inside a prison cell, waiting for Detective Caputi to interview her. The cell was freezing. Olivia watched as frost formed on the iron bars, and icicles dangled from the ceiling. She was shivering on the hard, steel bench.

When Detective Caputi arrived, she was swathed in a massive white velvet coat, and wearing a fur-lined hat.

"I'm cold," Olivia explained, her teeth chattering.

"So you should be! You deserve to be cold," the detective jeered, reaching through the bars and pulling at the flimsy blanket on the bed. "I'm taking this away! You don't need it! You have a notebook to cover yourself with."

"No!" Olivia cried, and found she'd shouted herself awake.

Her curtains were bright with the first rays of the morning sun, and the room was freezing. She hadn't dreamed the temperature. A cold front had blown in during the night, and the air was so frosty it seemed to burn her goosepimpled skin.

She'd worn summer pajamas last night, and had left the window open. Big mistakes, Olivia realized. The only one adequately prepared for the weather was Pirate, who was curled into the smallest ball she'd ever seen him in, nestled in a warm fold of the summer-weight duvet.

Pirate knew the best way to endure today, that was for sure. Olivia had a more difficult time ahead. She had to work out what to do with the incriminating book, while avoiding being arrested for its possession!

She pulled the curtains back, staring out over the sparkling white, frosty landscape.

Olivia had only a moment to think how perfectly picturesque the scenery looked, before reality descended with a bang.

Her vines! The young plants would not survive a hard, early frost. Danilo had said so. He'd warned her about it.

Olivia pulled on her fluffy slippers and her oldest, warmest pair of sweatpants. Then she wrapped herself in her padded dressing gown and hurried outside, anxiety flaring inside her as she thought about what she would find.

With a patter of feet, Erba emerged from the barn, eager to join Olivia on this morning adventure as she half-walked, half-slid over the icy grass. Olivia was jealous to see how sure-footed the goat was in this terrain, gamboling across the ice-covered tussocks as if her ancestors had lived in the Alps.

Well, for all Olivia knew, they had.

"Come, Erba, we have a serious situation," she advised the goat.

The wind was tugging at her hair, which she hadn't even had time to brush in her haste to examine the vines. The frigid breeze seemed to be blasting straight from the North Pole. Who would have thought Tuscany could get so cold?

As she approached the plantation, Olivia felt her heart sink. The vines didn't look brilliant green, the way they had yesterday. Their baby leaves were brown and withered. Her heart plummeted as she approached.

The plants were well and truly frost-struck.

She plucked at a leaf in horror. It was limp and brown, coated in ice, and it detached from the plant immediately to lie sadly in the palm of her hand.

"Surely this isn't possible?" Olivia whispered, horrified. How could so much be going wrong?

Even Erba, capering high-spiritedly between the rows of sorry-looking vines, could do nothing to lift her spirits.

Olivia didn't know if the plants could survive this. It could well be that this early, hard frost had destroyed them completely. There seemed no hope for the vines. Her lack of experience made her even more despondent.

With a jolt, Olivia thought about the wild vines growing randomly on her farm, laden with grapes that she'd meant to pick and hadn't. With the murder, and her investigation, she'd been distracted and hadn't found the time. Now it was too late, because the grapes would also be frozen. That meant she'd missed out on any chance of making a batch of wine this year, even a small one!

"Oh, Erba," she said mournfully. "Will this farm ever be able to produce wine? Did the previous owners leave because it was too difficult?"

The goat skidded to a stop in front of her and Olivia gave her a friendly head rub.

"At least I'm doing a good job with you," Olivia reminded herself, looking for the bright side in these desperate times. "You seem very well. I would say your energy levels are excellent, for a goat. Perhaps too high."

Olivia tried to picture her farm, the hilly terrain studded with goats of various colors. She was able to visualize it with disturbing clarity. This mountainous land was probably far more suited to goats. If only that was her life goal, but it wasn't. As far as goats went, she was happy with just one.

Frantically, Olivia tried to think of something else positive to cheer herself up.

"There's coffee in the kitchen," she said eventually. It wasn't much, but it provided a small beacon of hope in this suddenly unfriendly world. Coffee made everything better, and she had a package of her favorite beans that were sold at practically every store in the village.

"Coffee for me, carrots for you," she told Erba.

And then her attention was caught by an approaching car, speeding up the sand road toward her farm.

Olivia felt a stab of guilt as she remembered the critic's book was lying in full view on the kitchen counter. She'd considered hiding it away but had decided that would only make her seem guiltier. Now, Olivia was wishing she'd hidden the book.

Perhaps the car was just passing by. Tourists occasionally took this sandy road by mistake.

She narrowed her eyes, fighting the glare of the rising sun. Nope, it was slowing down and turning into her gateway.

Puzzled, Olivia saw that this wasn't the usual gray Fiat she'd come to associate with the detective. Had she upgraded? This was also gray in color, but it was a sleek and sporty model, powerful and low-slung.

She heard exactly how low-slung as a protruding rock scraped the car's undercarriage with an unpleasant grinding noise.

The car skidded to a halt behind her pickup and Olivia watched, breathing rapidly. She raised her chin, summoning up all her inner calmness, readying herself to remain composed during the police search and questioning.

Then Olivia's Zen deserted her and she let out an outraged squawk.

It wasn't the steely-haired policewoman climbing out of this beast of a car.

It was Matt!

Olivia stared, her horror compounding as Xanthe alighted from the passenger seat. She was wrapped in a thick, white duffle coat that accentuated the skinniness of her legs—and she was wearing the gorgeous boots again.

Matt had had his hair cut and it was sharply styled. He'd used a lot of gel, Olivia saw. So much that his hair seemed immovable in the tugging breeze. It reminded her of Raffaele's lacquered helmet-head.

"Well, hello! What an incredible coincidence. I simply cannot believe that you are here. Of all the places in Tuscany, you live in this farmhouse. You? Here? I think I'm getting goose bumps at how eerie this all is. You know, Olivia, I almost feel like you're stalking me," Matt confessed with a deliberately casual laugh.

She was stalking him? Olivia was rendered speechless by outrage.

Luckily, Matt had no shortage of conversational points to keep the morning's dialogue flowing.

"Just got out of bed?" he asked.

With a rush of embarrassment, Olivia remembered that she was still in her nightwear. Well, mostly. The shabby sweatpants were equally hideous whether it was day or night, but the fluffy bunny slippers were most definitely bedtime wear, and so was her well-insulated, but remarkably shapeless, dressing gown.

She hadn't even brushed her hair. Olivia knew she was blushing crimson.

"What—what are you doing here?" she spluttered, wrapping her arms defensively around her body. She'd woken into a new, worse nightmare. She'd rather have been back in that freezing prison cell, facing an Eskimo-like Detective Caputi.

"I found this farm on a for-sale site. We decided we'd go on an early morning adventure, to see what the area has to offer in terms of property investment. I've started a small, but so far brilliantly performing, international portfolio. Haven't I, my love?"

He addressed the question to Xanthe, who didn't seem to hear. She was involved in a complicated exercise, trying to photograph herself with the rising sun behind her.

"This farm is not for sale. I bought it," Olivia said. She had to shout out the words, because she wasn't coming any closer to the happy couple. She was staying right where she was, in the safety of her ruined vine plantation.

Matt quirked an eyebrow. "Is that so? I guess they don't always update the sites regularly. You have to love the Italian chaos that prevails here, don't you?"

Olivia didn't believe a word of it. She was convinced that Matt had networked with his contacts and, through sneaky and cunning means, had found out where she'd bought. The "still for sale" story was a barefaced lie if she'd ever heard one. And, having lived with Matt while he was cheating on her, Olivia thought she had gained some retrospective experience in identifying his bare-faced lies.

"It's very scenic out here. Rustic, though." With his arms folded, Matt turned to stare at her sturdy but humble farmhouse, and then walked confidently toward the front door as if he had bought an entrance ticket that entitled him to a self-guided tour.

Olivia felt her temper rising. She hadn't invited them here. She wanted them to leave, now!

At that moment, Xanthe let out a shriek and Olivia whirled to face her.

Erba had trotted over to see what Xanthe was doing. The goat had stuck her nose inquisitively over Xanthe's shoulder, giving her the fright of her life and ruining her selfie.

Xanthe scrambled to her feet and backed away.

"Does your goat bite?" she called, sounding nervous, as Erba stalked playfully toward her. Clearly, she thought this petite human was trying to start a game.

"She's not my goat," Olivia shouted back. Then, seeing Erba tilt her head into a familiar stance, she added, "She butts, though."

"She what?"

Xanthe shrieked again as Erba charged forward and pushed her fore-head into Xanthe's skinny thighs. Arms windmilling, Xanthe overbalanced and fell backward into Olivia's bulb bed.

Olivia shook her head. She had no idea where the goat had picked up this naughty, and highly antisocial, habit from. Not once had Olivia ever head-butted another person in her goat's presence. She could only think that Erba had learned it from her peers at the winery. Olivia was going to have to school it out of her, and she could see that a lot of loving firmness would be required.

But that was for another day. Now, her more pressing need was to get Matt off her property.

"Where do you think you are going?" she yelled, and he stopped suddenly, turning to face her. She saw a flash of guilt cross his face.

"I was just—I thought I'd have a look around. Check out the interior."

Xanthe clearly wasn't joining him in this exploratory mission. She was busy brushing off her backside and creeping toward the car, using the farmhouse wall as a backstop to prevent herself getting butted a second time.

"No." Olivia folded her arms. "You are not welcome here. This is private property and trespassers will be prosecuted. Did you see the sign at the gate?"

Even though there wasn't a sign at the gate, that line had worked well when Jean-Pierre had used it at the winery. In any case, she was sure Matt would have driven in too fast to notice its presence or absence. He glanced back at the gate, looking unsure.

"I have to get ready for work now," Olivia continued, hoping that she was coming across as calm and firm in spite of her rising internal hysteria. "I do not have time to entertain unwanted and in fact, rude visitors who are only interested in identifying real estate opportunities. You should contact an agent. There are two in the village. They can show you properties that are available! But for now, get out. Leave. Go away!"

"I just thought—" Matt began defensively. Then he muttered something. Olivia didn't catch the whole thing but she heard the word "coffee."

"There's a bistro in town," Olivia yelled. "I don't offer free coffee to people who arrive without an appointment. This is not a guesthouse, it's a working farm!"

Swathed in her robe, Olivia advanced, pleased to see that Matt was now backing away from the house and retreating to his car.

From her flattened position against the wall, Xanthe made a dash for the passenger side, reaching it just before Erba.

"Go! Now! Get out and never come back!" Olivia yelled, feeling a sense of release at being able to scream out her frustrations at top volume. Who cared what they thought of her? Let their last impression be of a maddened, mussy-haired woman shrieking at them. She didn't care. Anything that put them off coming back was good in her books.

"We're going."

Matt returned to the driver's side, quickening his pace as Erba trotted inquiringly around.

The car started and reversed carefully, detouring to avoid the rock that had nearly annihilated the undercarriage on the way in.

And then they were gone. Olivia heaved a sigh of relief. Good riddance. She fervently hoped this would be the last time she saw either of them.

"Erba, you—" she began, uncertain whether to praise or reprimand her wayward goat. But the words froze on her lips, as she saw a large white minivan cruising purposefully up the dirt road, slowing as it reached her farmhouse.

She wasn't out of danger yet. Now, more trouble was heading her way.

CHAPTER TWENTY FOUR

Olivia watched the van nervously as it stopped on the road outside the farmhouse.

Looking at how large it was, she wondered briefly if Detective Caputi was picking up a number of suspects en route to the prison cells. Or perhaps she'd brought a team of investigators with her to conduct the search.

Olivia bit her icy lip. Why did all of this have to happen on the one morning that she had ventured out of doors in her sleepwear? Would the police let her change into normal clothes before they locked her into the van?

But then the driver's window buzzed down and a British man called out to her.

"Yoo-hoo! Excuse me, could you possibly help us? We seem to be lost."

To her surprise, Olivia recognized him. This was Barry, the designated driver of the group that she'd met outside Quercia Winery. Now, here they were, outside her farm.

She sighed. They needed help. There wasn't time to change clothes. She'd just have to give the unwanted impression of an eccentric local, and be thankful that it wasn't the detective arriving at her gate.

Stepping carefully in her thick slippers, Olivia padded along the sandy driveway to the car.

"How can I help?" she asked.

Another window opened, and the pink-spectacled woman peered out.

"My goodness, I remember you. We met you outside that winery the other day!"

"Yes, that's right," Olivia said.

She felt worried that these British tourists had recognized her so easily. Did that mean that she'd appeared just as batty and disheveled when they'd met her outside Quercia? Even though she'd believed she was well groomed and in charge of the situation?

It was a worrying concept.

Olivia didn't have time to think about it, though. She needed to help these people and make sure they got on their way.

"We should have stayed at Quercia. The vintner at that highly recommended winery, Boschetto di Querce, was very arrogant. It wasn't a pleasant experience to be served by him, although the wines were good," the pink-spectacled woman shared.

"Perhaps you can go back to Quercia today. Their wines are top quality and they're also very friendly to visitors," Olivia said. Remembering what Raffaele had written in the notebook, she added, "The Sangiovese blend is wonderfully easy drinking, while the Merlot-Montepulciano has great character, and is a very fine wine."

"We'll definitely go there today," she promised.

Another window rolled down.

"We'd have been back there already if our driver didn't keep getting us lost," the red-jacketed woman observed.

There was general laughter from the bus. Barry's already florid face turned a deeper shade.

"This time, the satnav malfunctioned."

"A likely story," someone in the back chortled. "Too much grappa last night, I believe."

"Where do you want to be?" Olivia asked.

"We want to go into the village of Collina," the red-jacketed woman explained. "There's supposed to be a magnificent ruined castle at its entrance, and we've also heard that there are two rival bakeries in town whose owners fight with each other all day. We're keen to buy some pastries and breadsticks for the road, and we wouldn't be offended if any harsh words were spoken. In fact, a few of us already have our phone cameras ready."

From the back of the van, Olivia heard a familiar voice addressing her phone in piercing tones.

"Siri, turn on my camera. Now!"

Olivia concealed a smile. She didn't know how many people in the village were aware that the supposed feud between the owners of the two bakeries across the street from each other was nothing more than an elaborate act. They had started it as a joke and continued when they saw how it drew visitors to the town and increased their sales. In reality, the owners of Mazetti's and Forno Collina were the closest of friends.

Since wine tourism in the area had nosedived sharply, Olivia was glad to see that bread tourism was keeping the local economy turning over.

"Of course I can help." She smiled. "You rejoin the main road, turn left, and then take the next turn right a half mile later. It's a narrow tar road so look out for it."

"Excellent. That sounds simple enough. Do you know about the rivalry? It sounds like quite a thing! Which bakery should we buy from?" Barry asked.

"It's very bitter and long-standing," Olivia explained. "I would definitely recommend buying equal quantities from both stores, to avoid making things worse. The prices are always exactly the same."

From the back of the van came another plaintive appeal, "Are you there, Siri?"

"They also have excellent coffee—to-go, as well as ground and beans," Olivia added.

"That'll be just the thing to take back home to Deans Bottom after our vacation," the red-jacketed woman agreed. "Now, Barry, you'd better turn the car around before we all forget the directions. And somebody help Shirley with her phone camera, because it doesn't look as if Siri is listening."

The minivan headed back the way it had come. Olivia felt pleased to think of the tourists experiencing the scenic village of Collina for the first time. Even though it was her local town, she never grew tired of seeing it, and always felt the same thrill of wonderment as she passed that ruined castle with its crumbling stone and ancient battlements.

She was sure that the bakery owners would be on good form. They always put on a special show for tourists who arrived with cameras.

As Olivia headed back to the house, she had a brainwave about the critic's notebook.

She would take it with her to work, and as soon as she had time, she would go to the local police station and hand it in as evidence. She could explain to Detective Caputi where she had gotten it from and why she'd grabbed it and run.

Handing it over would prove her innocence, and show she was acting with the best intentions. Hopefully it would also mean Silvano could be arrested before he could commit any other crimes.

Pleased that she'd thought of a solution for the incriminating book which would land a suspect safely behind bars, Olivia headed to work with Erba on foot, since a fine day was forecast.

At the winery, Olivia's spirits sank again. It was obvious how badly sales had been affected. No tourists were waiting—none at all. The parking lot was empty and Marcello and Nadia were ensconced in a meeting in his office.

They were speaking in hushed voices, and on the hour, every hour, Gabriella took in a fresh round of espressos, looking as if the world had ended. Olivia felt sure that they were trying to stem the flow of canceled orders from restaurants around the country.

Jean-Pierre stared at her helplessly.

"What shall we do?" he asked.

Olivia couldn't even suggest a stocktake. They had done that already.

"I will train you on new wines," she decided. "Go to the storage room and bring out one of the recent Sangiovese, Miracolo, white blends, and Vermentino. We will do a tasting session to fine-tune your palate. Then I have to go to the police station for a short meeting, so if you don't mind loaning me your car, I will leave you in charge here for the morning."

Looking encouraged, Jean-Pierre fetched the bottles.

Olivia wrote all of them down on the day's sales list. She was going to buy every one! She could invite friends around to help finish them. Well, one friend. Danilo would be an enthusiastic companion in drinking these fine bottles.

She opened the two white wines first and poured them into glasses.

"You must close your eyes now," she told Jean-Pierre. "I am going to swap these glasses around, so that you will have to assess which is the pure vermentino, and which the white blend. You need to remain alert to the characteristics of the wine you are drinking, and then compare it with the other. Here's some water to clean your palate."

To ensure Jean-Pierre remained honest, Olivia turned her back as she switched the glasses from hand to hand. Then she turned back to the young trainee.

"Here is your first wine," she said.

"I don't have to spit, do I?" Jean-Pierre asked anxiously. "Because watching that the other day made me nauseous."

"We are only tasting a few, so you may drink the wine normally," Olivia reassured him.

The image of the critic spitting the wine out loomed in her mind. She also felt queasy thinking about it. The tension of the moment, plus the spitting, hadn't made for a comfortable stomach, that was for sure.

And as Olivia's thoughts turned back toward the unlikeable deceased critic, she heard footsteps outside the winery. She almost dropped the tasting glasses as she saw who was walking in. It was Silvano, the editor.

Clearly, he had come to see her. As his gaze fell on her, it sharpened, and he headed purposefully toward her.

Olivia was starting to hyperventilate. Jean-Pierre sensed her tension and opened his eyes.

"Is everything okay?" he asked. "That was the vermentino, I think. Who is this person?"

"Olivia," Silvano said. "May I speak with you in private?"

Olivia felt her blood pressure spike. What would happen in private? What was this murderous man planning now? What other sharp-pointed stationery items did he have secreted on his person?

An idea occurred to Olivia.

"Jean-Pierre, please wait outside the tasting room. If you hear any shouts or commotion, come back immediately." Remembering her duties as a mentor she added, quickly, "And you are right. It was the vermentino."

"I will remain alert," Jean-Pierre said in a firm voice. He marched out, casting a distrustful glance at Silvano as he left.

She hoped that if Silvano had any dastardly plans, her assistant's watchful presence outside the door would scupper them.

She poured two glasses of the white blend and took them to a table at the far side of the room.

Silvano sat opposite her. As she looked more closely, Olivia realized that the editor seemed rattled. He appeared deeply uneasy, in fact fearful, as if he had lost control of the situation.

That suited her fine. She didn't have control of it either, but at least it meant they were on an equal footing. Plus, her temperamental French bodyguard was ready to burst in at a moment's notice and come to her rescue.

Silvano sipped nervously at his wine.

"I know you took Raffaele's notebook," he said. "When I finished my phone call and saw you had gone, I realized that you must have seen it in my bag and assumed the worst. I should have hidden it," he said in sorrowful tones. "Or, at least, I should have been brave enough to tell you I had taken it, when you mentioned the book."

"You—you—" Olivia began. It felt difficult to get out that crucial word "killed."

"I promise you I didn't." Silvano stared into her eyes, his gaze wide and anxious. "I will explain what happened. Please believe me. It is the truth, every word. I swear it. The only reason I did not tell you yesterday is that I feared you had already made up your mind that the killer and the thief were the same person."

"All right," Olivia said. She sipped her wine, trying to channel Detective Caputi. If she could get the same level of intimidation into her stare, she was sure that the editor wouldn't dare to lie.

"Like I told you at my house, I was worried about what Raffaele was doing. The inaccuracy of his reviews which were based on his personal likes and dislikes and not about the wine at all, his arrogance, the certainty he had about his own power. So I decided this was my only chance to fix it. I went to the Gardens of Florence hotel in the afternoon after Raffaele was murdered, and sat in the bar until I was sure the police had left and there was nobody in sight. Then I sneaked into his room and took the book. I intended to change all the reviews immediately, but the police froze the website. As soon as they catch the killer and unfreeze it, I will correct them."

Olivia sipped her wine again, buying herself some time as she frantically puzzled over what Silvano was telling her.

From one angle, it sounded true and plausible, and his actions made sense and were, in fact, heroic. From another angle, this could all be an elaborate, cleverly crafted lie.

"Who do you think did it?" she asked.

He shook his head, looking helpless. "If I knew, I would tell the police immediately. It could be any of the winemakers who suffered from the viciousness of Raffaele's pen." Silvano winced as he said the word "pen," clearly remembering what its final use had been. "Please, return the book to me. I am desperate to make amends. If that book falls into the wrong hands, the damage can never be corrected. Many of the winemakers have become my personal friends. I know what they are going through!" he begged.

Olivia took yet another sip of wine as she agonized over the choice she had to make. She'd been so sure Silvano was guilty, but thinking it over, she wondered what she would have done in his shoes.

Would she also have stolen the book to try and save the wineries Raffaele had treated so badly?

Olivia shook her head. She had no idea—about Silvano's guilt, or her own instincts! Now she had to make the right call, whatever it might be.

"All right," she heard herself saying. "I'll give it back to you if you promise to change the reviews as soon as possible."

"Of course I will!" Silvano looked relieved.

Olivia's mind was in turmoil. As soon as the words were out of her mouth, she started regretting them. She didn't know if she had made the right decision or a terrible mistake.

She got up and walked over to the tasting counter. She reached behind it, to the shelf where she kept her purse, and drew the book out.

Before she could change her mind, she strode back to the table and handed it to him.

"There you are," she said.

"Thank you, thank you!" Silvano clutched the book, his voice filled with gratitude. "I promise you that at the soonest opportunity, I will—"

He never got a chance to finish what he was saying.

From outside, Olivia heard the tramp of approaching footsteps. Jean-Pierre shouted in warning. A moment later, the tasting room door burst open.

CHAPTER TWENTY FIVE

"There he is! There is Maestro Raffaele's killer."

Olivia stared in shock as Brigitta led the way into the tasting room, pointing triumphantly to Silvano.

Detective Caputi, flanked by two uniformed officers, followed close behind.

"See? Look, the stolen notebook is in his very hands." Brigitta gesticulated dramatically. "It is as I suspected, Detective. My investigation work was correct."

"I didn't—" Silvano tried in a trembling voice, but the words petered out and he stared down at the book with a defeated expression. He'd knocked his wineglass over as the police arrived, and it was lying on its side on the polished wooden table. Fortunately, it was already empty.

Olivia's mind was spinning. Was he really guilty? Or was this strong circumstantial evidence simply pointing toward him?

At any rate, there was nothing she could do now. The two uniformed police officers were already flanking Silvano and helping him, none too gently, to his feet.

"Give that to me!" Detective Caputi tugged the leather-bound book from Silvano's grasp and slipped it into an evidence bag. As she did so, Silvano groaned in despair.

Olivia barely managed to stop herself from groaning, too. The notebook was now in the hands of the police. It could stay locked in an evidence room for months. The chances of the winery's salvation were looking increasingly remote. In fact, Olivia decided, they might be nonexistent.

"I have nothing to say," Silvano murmured as the handcuffs clicked around his wrists. "I know how this must seem. I will cooperate with you fully." He turned back to Olivia. "Please, I must implore you, can you ask my neighbor to take care of Garibaldi until I am back?"

"Of—of course," Olivia said, and Silvano nodded in relief before bowing his head again.

Brigitta folded her arms, smiling in satisfaction as she watched Silvano stumble toward the door, with Detective Caputi following behind, barking instructions into her walkie-talkie.

Jean-Pierre moved aside to let them pass, frowning as if he was perplexed by the speedy turn events had taken.

"Was this a trap?" he asked, treading cautiously back into the tasting room. "A setup?"

Brigitta looked even more pleased with herself.

"I tailed him the whole way to your winery," she said. "I had a feeling he was going to try and plant the book elsewhere. Luckily, the police arrived while it was still in his possession."

That wasn't what had happened at all! Olivia felt she should set the record straight, but didn't know where to start. Explaining she'd stolen the book and then given it back would only complicate things.

"That was very clever of you," Olivia praised Brigitta as the assistant turned and headed for the door, clearly not wanting to miss the moment when the man she'd hunted down was loaded into a police van.

Deep down, Olivia had to admit to that she felt slightly miffed by the speed and sheer style with which the assistant had acted. She had tailed the suspect, summoned the police to the scene, and implemented decisive action to get a result.

Olivia felt ashamed of her subtle questioning techniques, which had ended up being completely useless. Now, it looked as if the case was closed, and that meant Olivia had made the wrong decision in trusting Silvano.

She propped her elbows on the tasting room counter with a sigh, staring down at the polished wood while fretting over her own recent actions. She had felt torn as she'd sat opposite the editor. It had been almost fifty-fifty which call she had made, but in the end it had been fifty-one, forty-nine in favor of believing him. Now, Olivia was starting to doubt herself. Her investigative instincts had failed her.

Then Olivia drew in a sharp breath as a warm hand touched her back, its presence lifting her mood immediately.

"Olivia, I am shocked by what has just happened," Marcello said, gently massaging her shoulders. "I saw the police leaving. Detective Caputi said that the website editor was arrested here, while in possession of important evidence."

Olivia nodded. "It was the book Raffaele wrote his reviews in."

Marcello's eyes narrowed and his handsome face grew stern.

"I am sure there were truths in the book that never made it onto the website," he said.

Olivia could only admire his perceptiveness.

"I had a glimpse of it," she admitted. "Raffaele thought our wines were wonderful. Silvano said that fame had gone to his head, and that he was letting his own personal prejudices influence his reviews."

Marcello nodded sadly. "And now, the book is in the hands of the police, the editor is in custody, and the website cannot be altered."

He leaned forward and brushed a stray lock of hair away from Olivia's face.

"I think you must take the day off, after the stress of this morning. We are not likely to get many visitors today. Rest while you have the chance," he told her gently.

Olivia looked up at him gratefully.

With her sleepless night and frost-struck grapevines and Matt's arrival at her place, she had more than enough to cope with even before Silvano had arrived. Worse still, Marcello's kindness was making her emotional. If she didn't go home immediately, she was liable to fling herself, sobbing, into his arms. Right now, that would be an unwise idea.

Tempting, but unwise.

"Thank you," she said. "It's been very stressful and I'm going to take your advice. Tomorrow, I'll be rested and ready to lead the charge as we regroup!"

She didn't miss the flash of admiration in Marcello's eyes as he heard her fighting talk. It made the grim day seem brighter.

"Hold the fort, Jean-Pierre," she called, as she grabbed her purse from the shelf and marched out with her head high.

As she headed down the service road that led past the goat dairy, her shoulders slumped again and the bravado she'd summoned up evaporated.

"Erba, I don't know what to do!" she confided to the goat as Erba spied her and gamboled toward her. She felt jealous of her goat. Her adopted animal had enjoyed a fantastic morning, filled with interesting visitors who'd fallen into flower beds when she'd butted them. Olivia thought that this day, one of her darkest, had been a highlight in the goat's life. Perhaps that was a lesson, she pondered. It was all about perspective.

"Are you coming home with me, Erba?" Olivia asked. The goat was hesitating, clearly aware it was the wrong time of day, and she'd miss out on playtime with her friends.

Deciding to abandon Olivia, Erba scampered back toward the dairy, leaping clear over a medium-sized rock by the side of the road.

"You're way too playful," Olivia chastised her. She wondered briefly if the nutritious alfalfa might be giving Erba an excess of energy. Perhaps that explained her too-spirited behavior and the incidents of head butting. After all, her ancestors had lived on nothing but mountain herbs and probably the occasional washing line.

She decided to reduce the goat's ration and see if she calmed down. She could always increase it again if Erba seemed tired.

Seeing Erba was on an alfalfa-induced energy high, it would be better for the goat to stay at the winery the full day. Olivia decided to collect her later. In the meantime, she hoped the walk home would give her some time to settle her thoughts.

As she strode out of the winery, goatless and alone, Olivia wondered whether she was seeing this case from the wrong perspective.

What if she'd gotten the entire situation as upside down as—as Xanthe had ended up after Erba's impromptu game?

What if there was another way of looking at things?

CHAPTER TWENTY SIX

As Olivia headed up the sand road to her farmhouse, she noticed yet another car parked in her driveway.

She hurried up to the gate, feeling nervous about who it might be.

As she drew closer, Olivia saw to her relief that the visitor was Danilo. Finally, somebody whose company she was happy to have.

He hurried to her, looking concerned.

"Is everything okay? I came to work in your barn, and hoped I could surprise you by finding an unbroken bottle by the time you got back! But I noticed you have been affected by the cold weather. I see your young vines are frost-damaged."

Olivia felt touched. It was so kind of him. It wasn't his farm, or his vines, and here he was, helping her.

"Do you think they will survive?" she asked anxiously.

"If the temperature did not drop too low, they may be all right. You should know in a day or two. In the meantime I have collected some of the straw from your barn and placed it among the rows. The loose straw will help to hold heat in during the night, and this will mean that they do not suffer any further damage, and have the best chance to recover."

"Thank you," Olivia said, feeling grateful. "That's one less worry. But there are others, and important ones."

"Are you worried about the murder?" Danilo asked. "This is why you have arrived back early and are looking upset?"

"Yes. There was a new development in the case today. Someone was arrested at the winery, after being caught with incriminating evidence."

Danilo's eyes widened. "Who? Not one of the Vescovis, surely?"

"No, no. The man who's now in custody is the website's editor, Silvano. He had the notebook on his person."

Danilo's eyebrows shot up. "The notebook with the reviews? Where the truth was written? So the police believe that the editor killed him and stole it?"

Olivia nodded.

"Brigitta, his assistant, is certain of it, and the police think so, too."

"But you do not?"

Olivia decided she needed to tell him everything.

"Do you feel like going for a drive to the coast? I promised Silvano that I would ask his neighbor to look after his dog while he's in jail. While we're in the car, I can tell you everything, as it's more complicated than it seems."

"Great idea!" Danilo's face brightened. "I was looking forward to a morning's work in the barn, but when the other choice is to take a drive in your company—well, there is no choice! Shall we take my car?"

Olivia felt her heart give a skip of happiness at his words. Danilo enjoyed her company? How lovely of him to say so.

He was a kind person and a true friend, she thought, scrambling eagerly into the pickup's passenger seat. Perhaps, during this drive, she could find out about his romantic situation. She'd have to wait for the right moment, as she didn't want to ask a personal question like that at the wrong time. In fact, for some reason, Olivia found she was feeling more and more hesitant about asking at all.

By the time they pulled up outside Silvano's cottage, Olivia had updated Danilo on every detail of her investigation, including her interviews with the winery owners and vintners, as well as her eventful visit to this very cottage, and how she'd snatched the book and run.

"Now he's been arrested, and I still don't know if he's guilty or not," Olivia explained. "Should I have given the book back to him? Is he the real murderer? I feel frustrated that I got it wrong! And I can't understand why I feel so bad about suspecting Gianfranco when he has a clear motive, went to the hotel, got angry there, and even destroyed the camera on his way out!"

They climbed out of the car and Olivia turned to face the sea. It was calmer than it had been the last time she was here, and sunshine sparkled off the waves. She breathed in the heady fragrance of salty air.

"Olivia, your instincts are very good," Danilo said, shading his eyes with his hand as he joined her to admire the view. "It could have been somebody completely different, and both Silvano and Gianfranco could be innocent."

"I feel as if I need to make a leap of logic," Olivia confessed. "I can't help thinking I'm missing something important that's waiting just out of my reach."

Danilo nodded understandingly.

Reluctantly, Olivia turned away from the hypnotic view to face the house where the first part of this drama had played out.

When Silvano had said "ask the neighbor," Olivia had wondered which neighbor it would be, but looking again at the houses, she saw Silvano only had one neighbor. On his other side was an empty plot of land. Perhaps some lucky person would buy it one day and build a house. For now, it made her job easier.

They headed up to the small, weathered cottage which looked to be almost identical to Silvano's, except that the door was freshly painted in an attractive bright blue, with two colorful pots of pink geraniums on either side. The effect was Instagram-worthy, and Olivia decided then and there to adopt the idea for her own farmhouse. To her, those flowers flanking the front door personified Italy. Quickly, she took out her phone and snapped a shot of it, with Danilo watching in evident amusement, before lifting the small brass knocker and knocking politely on the door.

A round-faced woman with graying hair and a welcoming smile opened it. She was holding a pink leash, and on the other end of the leash was a small, fine-coated dog that Olivia thought might be part Italian greyhound. The dog wagged its tail when it caught sight of Olivia and Danilo.

"*Buon giorno*. How can I help?" the woman asked.

"Silvano from next door asked me if you might be able to look after Garibaldi for a while. I'm not sure how long. Maybe a day or two, perhaps more. He's—er—"

Olivia found herself at a loss for words in explaining Silvano's predicament, but luckily the other woman picked up the reins of the conversation.

"Ah, out of town again?" she said. "He told me he might be traveling at short notice, as he has had a lot of inquiries for his website services."

Olivia wished she was the type of person who could simply nod in agreement; however, this pleasant-faced woman deserved to know the truth.

"He's actually been taken into police custody. Very briefly, I hope," Olivia added hastily as she saw the woman's smile vanish, to be replaced by a shocked expression. "I'm sure it will be sorted out in no time at all."

As she spoke, Olivia's resolve to hunt down an alternative suspect became even stronger. The consternation in this good neighbor's eyes was surely proof that Silvano was not the killer.

"This is terrible! How can the police have made such a mistake?" the woman asked, echoing Olivia's thoughts. "I heard about the murder, of course. Silvano could never have been guilty of such an action. It was obviously a *crimine di passione*—a murder committed in the heat of the moment. Silvano has a cool head and an even temperament. The police should be looking for that person who can be easily pushed to the edge, and who will explode into violence. I hope they release my innocent friend soon."

"I hope so, too," Olivia agreed. "Thank you so much for helping with Garibaldi. Silvano was so worried about him."

"I have a key and will fetch him straight away. My little Tortellini will be delighted to have her fluffy companion to stay again." She bent and patted the dog's head. "Quite often, when I am walking her, I pass by Silvano's house and take Garibaldi along, too. In fact, I was intending to knock on his door now, as I am going out with Tortellini."

Olivia felt relieved that Garibaldi would clearly be in the most caring of hands until his owner returned.

Olivia and Danilo stepped back from the quaint, colorful porch as the neighbor headed out, with her tan-colored dog gamboling eagerly alongside her, and went straight to Silvano's house. A minute later, she walked the happy pair of dogs across the road and along the sandy seaside path.

"You are thinking hard," Danilo observed, as they strolled back to his car. "You are looking worried. Now that you have shared your suspicions, I am feeling that way, too. I feel something is not adding together."

"Silvano's neighbor reminded me what I've been puzzling over all along. It was the way she said that word 'innocent.' Danilo, it means more than not being guilty. It's about who a person is! Silvano is a gentle individual. So are the vintners from those other wineries. They're reasonable people who love and care for their wineries and families. Yes, everyone has their breaking point, but a normal person wouldn't be provoked into such extreme action just because of a bad review."

As Danilo nodded in agreement, Olivia had a brainwave. In fact, a breakthrough! Finally, she realized where she'd been going wrong.

She'd been investigating methodically, looking for people with a reason to kill Raffaele, and the opportunity to do so. She'd been exploring timeframes and analyzing alibis, just the same way Detective Caputi must have been doing, too.

The problem was that methodical research worked fine on paper, but as Silvano's neighbor had pointed out and Olivia herself felt deep down, this wasn't about paper.

It was about people.

No matter how desperate they were, none of the people she had interviewed so far could possibly have acted in this irrational way. It would take a flawed personality type, with an unstable temperament, to commit such a murder in anger.

She needed to hunt for the character who possessed those qualities. Then the motive would reveal itself.

As this truth occurred to her, Olivia thought again of that notebook, and the content she'd read inside.

With a flash of insight, she realized what the missing step in her investigation had been.

"I know where we need to go!" she exclaimed. "Danilo, do you feel like tasting some wine?"

CHAPTER TWENTY SEVEN

Shortly before lunch time, Olivia and Danilo drove through the imposing gateway of Boschetto di Querce. This winery, Oak Grove, was the
one that had received the glowing review on the critic's site.

Olivia felt so nervous she had to bunch up her hands to stop herself
from biting her nails. She had no idea what would play out at this magnificent winery, but she knew this visit was her last hope of solving the case.

She'd been so sure about her intuition when they'd left Silvano's
house, but doubts had crept in during the drive and now she felt uncertain again. Olivia firmly told herself to have faith. Her instincts had to be
correct. Didn't they?

"Look how lush these fields are," Danilo observed as they headed up
the long driveway. She could tell he'd sensed how nervous she was and
was doing his best to distract her. "Being on a level plain between a river
and a range of hills, this winery must be the most fertile in Tuscany."

"No wonder they're such a major producer," Olivia agreed.

"Quality and quantity," Danilo said.

The quality of the wine, Olivia knew, was not simply a product of their
geography but the result of specialized knowledge, care, and planting.

"*Mio Dio*, but it is busy!" Danilo exclaimed, as they turned into the
parking lot.

It was bursting at the seams with tour buses and private cars. There
were even a few bicycles chained to trees. No matter what it took, the
public was flocking to this winery to taste the offerings that Raffaele had
graded so highly.

The tasting room was sumptuously furnished, with wingback chairs,
leather couches, and dark wooden tables. Olivia felt as if she was enter-
ing an exclusive home, and noticed that a lot of the décor looked antique.

Equipping this tasting room with its furniture, wall coverings, ornaments, and lighting must have been an expensive exercise.

Olivia's hands felt cold. She wished this setting was not as intimidating or glamorous. The enormous room was buzzing with tourists, even though in the elegant environment, conversation was muted.

A waitress in a smart black skirt and jacket showed them to the only empty table in the room, which had just been vacated by a group of tourists.

"Will you be enjoying our full tasting menu?" she asked.

"Yes," Olivia said. It was time to start playing her role. Could she set events into motion the way she had planned? Her stomach felt taut with tension as she continued. "We've heard so much about this place. I'd love to speak to the vintner who made the wines when we try them. Will that be possible?"

"Oh, yes," the waitress said. "The head vintner always insists on introducing his new wine to guests, so he will serve the first wine to you. Please relax for a few minutes, as we are rather busy."

"With pleasure. What's the vintner's name?"

"Gino Galletti."

Olivia jumped. The name was familiar. She had heard it before, but where?

Frantically, she racked her brain as the waitress set a plate of snacks down. This information could be crucial. Gino Galletti. Who was he, and why did she know about him?

Then, with a rush of footsteps, a harassed-looking man arrived at their table. He was tall and lean, with an expression that looked set in a permanent sneer. He was carrying a tray with a bottle and two glasses.

"Welcome to Boschetto di Querce. I am head winemaker Gino Galletti. I am sure you are eager to experience the top quality wines that I have created, which are the best in Tuscany," he announced.

"Of course," Olivia said with a tight, false smile.

As he spoke, in a flash of insight, she realized where she'd heard his name before.

Jean-Pierre had shouted it out as an insult, while kicking Matt and Xanthe out of the tasting room. Afterward, Jean-Pierre had said that

Gino used to work at a neighbor's winery but was asked to leave due to his arrogant behavior.

This was another piece of the puzzle, and an important one. Olivia could hardly breathe as she realized what it might mean.

Gino poured the tasting portions.

"Our Sangiovese. It is so subtle and finely made that by comparison, its competitors from other estates taste like cough mixture," he proclaimed.

Olivia swirled the wine and sipped.

"It's lovely. Very pleasant," she complimented him, choosing her words carefully because she didn't want to praise it too highly.

Danilo nodded. "Great quality," he agreed.

"That is all you can say?"

Gino was frowning darkly at them, as if their positive comments were degrading to this fine wine.

"I cannot believe the insults I am hearing from you. Do you have any palate for wine at all? Any knowledge?" His dark gaze drilled into her and Olivia decided it would be strategic to respond with the truth.

"Actually, I do have some wine knowledge. I'm the sommelier at La Leggenda."

"You are?" The other man looked briefly taken aback. Then he regrouped swiftly. "I think they had a moment of fame a while back. I believe they are third-rate at present."

As obnoxious as this man was, Olivia was encouraged by the direction the conversation was taking. It was time to amp up the pressure and see if she could trigger the explosion she needed.

"La Leggenda makes great wines. You have heard of the Miracolo, haven't you? It's probably the most famous red blend in the whole of Tuscany," she shot back.

Gino's frown deepened.

"I believe your most recent vintage is very disappointing."

"The blend is extremely consistent. So if previous years were lauded by many, and this recent vintage was criticized by only one person, it would surely mean that the one person was wrong?" she said pointedly.

Gino shrugged. "You cannot let your entire reputation hinge on that wine alone. This Sangiovese that received the recent review was a brand new creation. We used three different types of Sangiovese grapes to blend it."

Olivia was expecting him to smile smugly as he mentioned the review. Instead, he grimaced in a sour way.

"A brand new creation that has so far been underestimated. That, one day, will win worldwide acclaim."

"My rosé is also a brand new creation," she argued, letting the defensiveness come through in her tone.

The man's eyebrows shot up.

"The rosé received dreadful reviews. Clearly an inferior wine," he spat.

Even though the insults burned Olivia, she felt encouraged. She had arrived here hoping to prove her hunch was correct and so far, she thought it was. Gino seemed volatile, and the type who could commit a crime in anger. But had he? How could she find out?

Gino continued, punching the air as he spoke.

"I am playing in a different league from you, with your sour and badly made beginner's rosé. This wine of mine was reviewed as incredible, but even that was unfair and insulting to it. If that stupid critic had written fair reviews, then everyone would know it was acclaimed as the best wine in Tuscany!"

Olivia felt goose bumps prickle up and down her spine.

She had made a breakthrough! But what to do next? She had to get more proof. How could she obtain it?

She needed to set a trap so subtle that her target didn't even notice it until he stepped inside.

Olivia racked her brain over what to say, hoping Gino wouldn't pick up that her hands were suddenly trembling. This was a pressured situation. If she didn't choose exactly the right words, her chance might be lost forever.

"I will tell you what," she suggested to Gino. She made sure to keep sounding defensive, so that he would think he'd pushed her buttons. "Come to our winery and try the new rosé. Then you'll see for yourself how good it is. In fact, I challenge you that my wine is better than yours. I believe you are wrong!"

She raised her voice to a shout as she said the final words, and saw Danilo's eyebrows shoot up. He was worried Olivia was spoiling for a fight. That was good, as it meant her performance was convincing.

Gino frowned. Olivia could see he didn't like the invitation and thought it would be a waste of time. In fact, he looked insulted by the very idea of a challenge.

He shook his head firmly. He was going to say no. In fact, he was opening his mouth to rudely decline her invite, when Danilo realized what Olivia was hoping to achieve.

Danilo cleared his throat and spoke in a teasing way.

"I am sure that this vintner will refuse your challenge, because deep down, he is scared to lose—especially to a woman," he said, grinning as he nudged her with his elbow.

That was enough to push Gino over the edge, and relief surged through Olivia as she saw him change his mind at the last possible moment.

"I am not afraid! And yes, I accept!" he snapped.

CHAPTER TWENTY EIGHT

Olivia's head was spinning with excitement as she arrived back at La Leggenda. She scrambled out of Danilo's car and rushed into the winery. She'd been on the phone the whole way back, putting her plans into place, but she had no idea whether her cunning scheme would succeed.

"So, we wait in the tasting room?" Danilo asked. "It is a long time since I have been here! What a fine place it is. Magnifico."

As they headed into the tasting room, Marcello walked down the corridor from his office.

He hesitated, his eyes widening in surprise as he saw Olivia.

"You are back?" he asked.

Then he stopped in his tracks, and his gaze became even more astonished as he saw Danilo following her in.

Olivia realized that the atmosphere in the winery suddenly felt strangely uneasy. Glancing around, she saw that Danilo and Marcello were regarding each other with the same wary expressions. Danilo was noting Marcello's commanding height and his classically handsome good looks with a hint of consternation in his eyes, while Marcello's gaze rested, with an almost imperceptible frown, on Danilo's broad and well-defined shoulders before moving up to take in his chiseled cheekbones and purple hair.

"Um," Olivia said, hoping to break the odd tension that filled the air. "Marcello, this is Danilo, a good friend of mine who lives near my farm. We decided to—er—to come back and meet someone here."

There hadn't been time to call Marcello and brief him on all the facts in the short, speedy drive back to the winery, and there definitely wasn't time now, with Gino arriving any minute.

"And Danilo, this is my boss, Marcello, who's given me all these wonderful career opportunities," Olivia further enthused, hoping that enough sparkling conversation from herself might dissolve the awkward silence that had descended.

"*Buon giorno*. Welcome, Danilo." Marcello stepped forward, and although he gave his trademark smile as he extended his hand, Olivia thought it looked forced.

"*Buon giorno*, Marcello. What a beautiful winery you have," Danilo said, extending his hand in turn. He gave a friendly nod as he clasped the other man's hand—but for some reason, Olivia thought, not as friendly as she had expected.

"Well, I can't wait for you to taste my new rosé," Olivia said to Danilo. "Shall we sit down?"

"I hope you enjoy our wines," Marcello said.

He turned and strode back down the corridor to his office as if Danilo's arrival had caused him to rethink his plans for the afternoon—or else, perhaps, he'd forgotten what he'd been heading out for, Olivia wondered, feeling confused.

In any case, the strained atmosphere in the room seemed to have eased with Marcello's departure, although Olivia felt tenser than ever as she worried about how the next few minutes would play out. She hurried over to the tasting counter where Jean-Pierre—who was a conspirator in the upcoming drama and had been hastily briefed—was busy pouring wine for another guest, a woman on her own, who was sitting nearby.

They had barely had time to sit down before Gino arrived.

He marched into the winery with his chin in the air, and unlike most visitors, did not even pause to admire the stunning backdrop of wooden barrels that Olivia always thought felt like the heart of the spacious room.

"I do not have much time," he greeted them without preamble. "As I explained earlier, I was heading out to the shops anyway. That is the only reason I agreed to comply with your ridiculous request."

Olivia gave him her sweetest smile.

"It's so kind of you. Naturally, you are our guest here today and we will pay your tasting fee. Jean-Pierre will pour you the rosé immediately."

With his lips tightened in concentration, aware of the critical role he was playing, Jean-Pierre poured a tasting portion of Olivia's new rosé and handed it to Gino.

Olivia picked up her own glass. While she was too nervous to appreciate her wine at this moment, it warmed her heart to see that Danilo was staring at it in admiration.

Danilo sipped the wine and although he made no comment on it, his eyes widened and he quirked an eyebrow at Olivia. The message was clear. Danilo thought her wine was amazing.

Gino was a tougher critic. He was staring at the wine intently, as if disappointed by its vivid, jewel-like color. She was sure he was desperate to find fault with it, and sensed that he was frustrated he hadn't been able to immediately write it off as hopeless.

He swirled, breathed in the bouquet, and finally tasted the wine.

There was a long pause.

"It is not as bad as I was led to believe," he said grudgingly, sounding disappointed. "A well-made wine. Certainly a good effort, but far from the quality of my own creation."

The other customer at the counter set her glass down with an audible clink.

"Your own creation?" she asked innocently. "Are you a winemaker, too?"

Gino turned to stare at this stranger in surprise, as if she should have asked permission before speaking to him. His disdainful gaze traveled from her dark hair, held back with five glittery pink hairclips, over her bright lilac jacket emblazoned with turquoise unicorns, and finally rested, with an expression of astonishment, on her cerise, sequined boots.

"I am the top winemaker in the area. In the country, even. I lead the team at Boschetto di Querce, and my new Sangiovese is a triumph of winemaking," he sneered.

The other woman's eyes widened.

"But I was there yesterday!" she exclaimed. "I tasted that wine."

Olivia felt a thrill of admiration. Brigitta was performing her role with total authenticity, despite the mad rush she'd had to arrive here in time.

"So you will agree with me then." Gino stated this as if it was inarguable fact.

Brigitta frowned. "Well, no. I liked your wine, of course. It was really nice tasting."

Olivia heard Gino's hiss of indrawn breath at the insulting use of the word "nice," but Brigitta was steaming ahead.

"Yes, it was really pleasant. Easy drinking. But this rosé is unique. I mean, have you ever seen this color before? I have to say, it's my favorite."

She lifted up one of her boots and wiggled it from side to side, placing her glass close to it as if to compare how similar the two bright pinks were.

Gino gave a choking sound.

Since he was at a loss for words, Olivia continued moving the conversation along.

"So, there you go! Two against one, I'm afraid!"

Danilo cleared his throat. "Three against one. The rosé is spectacular. Without a doubt, it is the winner in my mind."

Now Olivia was alarmed to see that the formerly sallow-cheeked Gino had turned the same color as her rosé. In fact, his burning cheeks were giving Brigitta's boots a run for their money.

"You are all ignoramuses! How can you possibly prefer this wine over my phenomenal Sangiovese red? Did you not see what it said on Tuscany's leading wine site? My wine was reviewed as incredible. Yours received the worst possible ranking. Mine is the best in Tuscany."

Olivia raised an eyebrow.

"But the website didn't say that. It just said 'incredible.' It didn't say incredibly what. It could have meant, incredibly average. I don't think that write-up was very well edited."

"Exactly. Incredibly average is probably what he meant," Danilo agreed.

"It is the top wine in the area!" Gino spluttered.

"Not according to the site," Olivia insisted. "Maybe it meant incredibly sour?" she added thoughtfully. "I did find it a little bitter, especially the aftertaste."

"Yes, I agree with you. Bitter," Brigitta said. "I felt like it needed some sugar. I am sure that's what the writer meant to say. An incredibly bitter wine that was, however, not a bad attempt at winemaking."

"Well, I'm glad we've sorted that out and clearly, with a three against one vote, it's pretty much a runaway victory for the rosé," Olivia said with a satisfied smile. "It's a pity your website review wasn't more positive, but at least it was accurate."

"Not so!" Gino slammed his empty glass down on the counter and scrambled off his stool. "You do not understand, you imbeciles! Raffaele di Maggio himself believed my wine to be the best in Tuscany and the finest new wine he had experienced that year."

Olivia stared at him disbelievingly.

"Well, anyone can say that. But it's not what he wrote."

"It is, it is, it is! It is exactly what he wrote and those were his words that he spoke to me. I saw them myself, in his own notebook where he jotted down the impressions of his wines. That stupid, unfair man did not grade my superb wine accurately. His review was pathetic, insulting! Why did he not write the truth on the site, which is that my wine was the best he had ever tasted? He even refused to change it when I arrived at his hotel—"

The vintner stopped abruptly, as if realizing that his infuriated outburst had caused him to say too much.

"You murdered Raffaele di Maggio," Olivia stated. "You couldn't bear the fact that the review was not as good as his original comments to you were. Raffaele might have had a big ego, but yours is even bigger, and it's no wonder they talk about it all over Tuscany! In fact, I'm not surprised you couldn't hold down a job at the winery down the road. You're very rude."

"I left that place voluntarily. I desired to work for a bigger winery to showcase my talent," Gino spluttered. "And how can you say I committed a murder? I did no such thing!"

"Oh yes, you did!" Olivia was terrified her strategy hadn't worked. Gino was denying everything—even having been fired! As well as being arrogant, he was a serial liar. What could she do to obtain a confession? And where were the police? She'd expected them to be here by now. Had Detective Caputi not understood, or worse still, not believed her?

Olivia was starting to fear she'd been thrown to the wolves!

"You stormed into Raffaele's hotel room and demanded he change the words because you thought the review was insulting. Then you grabbed the envelope opener from his desk because you were so angry he wouldn't acknowledge your winemaking greatness. And then you stabbed him with it," Olivia declared, hoping she sounded more confident than she felt.

"I did no such thing!" Gino was screaming now, his eyes wide. Olivia thought his hair might be standing on end. "Why would I use an envelope opener, when that pen was right there? That nice sharp pen that he used to write the real truth? Isn't it fitting that I arrived at the hotel to confront him and when he refused to change his words, used his own weapon to punish him?"

Silence descended on the winery. The air seemed to ring with the residue of Gino's furious words.

Then, realizing what he'd said, Gino leaped into action.

"You tricked me!"

In a flash, he was on his feet. Olivia had expected that he might make a run for it, but she hadn't anticipated what he would do next.

The angry vintner shoved Danilo violently, sending him and his chair tumbling backward. And then he fled—but not in the direction of the tasting room entrance, where Jean-Pierre was already waiting.

Instead, Gino bolted toward the restaurant.

"Stop! Come back!" Olivia yelled. Her plans had fallen apart! Her suspect was escaping.

She powered after Gino, pursuing him as fast as she could run.

The dark-haired man ducked left and right, swerving past a group of departing customers. Olivia swerved the other way and found she'd gained some ground.

Glancing back, Gino saw she was hot on his heels. He grabbed a dessert trolley and shoved it onto its side.

Plates of tiramisu and panna cotta, slices of polenta cake, and tubs of gelato packed in ice scattered across Olivia's path, as Gabriella's furious shriek rang across the room.

Olivia made a desperate leap. She cleared the mess of spilled desserts, landed on a stray ice cube, and only just kept her footing as she slithered over the polished tiles.

Then she was racing behind him, out the side door.

Gino was heading at a frantic pace toward the service road. He was taller than Olivia, his legs were longer, and, she had to admit, he was clearly fitter. With every stride, he was gaining ground and she was starting to flag. Her lungs were burning. She'd never been a sprinter. Or a long-distance runner either, to be truthful. Really, she was more of a walker.

The road wound up a hill—Olivia's trembling legs were protesting the incline—and past the goat dairy. That gave her one last, desperate idea.

"Erba!" she yelled at the top of her voice, slowing to a jog. She had no option. All her running reserves were spent.

As Gino crested the hill, Olivia saw a familiar silhouette appear.

There was Erba, brimming with her alfalfa-induced energy.

She'd seen Olivia—and she'd also spied a new, interesting person who looked like he might be ready for a game.

Looking purposeful, Erba gamboled in the direction of the running man.

"Butt!" Olivia gasped.

Behind her, she heard footsteps. Glancing around, she was encouraged to see Danilo catching up fast.

"Butt, Erba," Olivia pleaded. "Just this once! After that, it's officially a bad habit and you're never to do it again!"

To Olivia's relief, Erba picked up on her instructions. She cantered playfully toward Gino.

At the last minute, he saw Erba approaching from the side and made a desperate leap to avoid her, but Erba was too fast for him. With a prance, she cannoned her head into Gino's thigh, skipping away in satisfaction as the vintner cartwheeled to the ground.

In a flash, Danilo whooshed past her. Before Gino had a chance to pick himself up, Danilo leaped onto him, knocking the wind out of him completely.

And then Olivia heard the tinny roar of a Fiat engine.

The car accelerated up the service road and screeched to a stop alongside them.

Detective Caputi jumped out of the driver's side, as a uniformed officer emerged from the passenger seat. Jean-Pierre and Brigitta spilled out of the back, together with an anxious-looking Marcello.

The steely-haired detective gave her a cool glance.

"We were held up in traffic," she explained. "The bakers in town were throwing ciabatta rolls at each other and the entire street was at a standstill, with five tour buses blocking the way. We had to backtrack and take another route."

Olivia could see that if she'd had more time, Detective Caputi would happily have arrested both the bakers, and all the tourists!

The policewoman turned to Gino and her gaze became icy.

"Signor Galletti," she greeted him coldly. "You confessed to a crime in front of four witnesses, and a fifth heard you shouting from his office down the corridor." She glanced at Marcello. "We request your presence at the police station. You have the right to remain silent, but it may harm your defence if you do not mention when questioned something which you later rely on in court."

Still gasping like a fish out of water, Gino was cuffed. The uniformed officer helped him to his feet and a moment later, to Olivia's relief, Raffaele's murderer was firmly locked in the back of the police car.

CHAPTER TWENTY NINE

The next morning, when Olivia arrived at work, she was astonished to see several vehicles heading into the parking lot, as well as a small tour bus.

Over the past few days, she'd become careless. In view of the non-existent tourist traffic, she'd taken to arriving only five minutes before opening time. She'd have to hustle, now, to prepare for these crowds.

She ran to the entrance, arriving at the same time as Jean-Pierre.

"Quick," Olivia called to him. "We need to prepare."

She hurried into the tasting room, arranging the tasting sheets and glasses on the counter just before the first of the tourists filtered in.

"What a lovely place." The couple who led the way into the tasting room sounded Canadian. "I'm thrilled we found it before we flew back home. Talk about a hidden gem," the vivacious, dark-haired woman said to her partner.

"My wife is hoping that your new rosé is available for tasting," the blond man addressed her, pulling out two chairs and staring admiringly at the arrangement of wine barrels behind Olivia.

"I—yes, yes it is, of course." She hadn't added it to the menu yet. How had these tourists even heard about it?

She would have to reprint her tasting sheets to include the rosé.

"Jean-Pierre, our assistant sommelier, will serve you and start with the white wines," Olivia said hastily. "We are busy printing a new run of tasting sheets. They will be ready in fifteen minutes."

"Great. We'll gladly start with a white wine."

Thankfully, neither this couple, nor the next, nor the tour group who followed, seemed unhappy to wait.

Leaving Jean-Pierre to serve the vermentino and white blend to all of them, Olivia fled to the back office. Right now, she was thanking her lucky stars she was used to writing copy at short notice, and hadn't lost any of her speed typing skills.

In fifteen minutes, the new sheets were ready.

She ran to Marcello's office, where the laser printer was, to collect her print run. Olivia was hoping to have a word with him, but Marcello was too busy on the phone to do more than give her a warm smile and conspiratorial wink.

"Yes, we can double the order, no problem," he was saying. "You want to add the rosé? There has been such a demand for it in recent hours, that we are stipulating a minimum order of five cases." He paused. "Ten cases? Yes, that we can deliver for you."

Olivia grabbed the sheets and practically danced out of the office.

She'd only just finished presenting the updated wine list to the waiting groups, before new visitors entered.

Olivia caught a glimpse of flashing cerise out of the corner of her eye, and swiveled around to face the new arrivals.

This astonishing morning was producing still more surprises.

Brigitta and Silvano walked in, wreathed in smiles, their arms linked in a friendly way.

The last time Olivia had seen them together, Brigitta had been directing the police to arrest Silvano. Now, they seemed to be the best of friends.

"Hello," Brigitta greeted her cheerfully. "We've come to taste your wonderful wines together, and then we're having lunch in the restaurant. I'm buying, as I owe Silvano an apology. Thanks to me, he had to spend an afternoon in a prison cell." She laughed merrily. "They released him last night and gave him the book back."

"Oh, I'm so glad you were able to go home," Olivia said, relieved that the likeable editor hadn't had to suffer too long for the good deed he'd attempted.

Although he had done more than attempt it, she realized, as Silvano smiled warmly.

"My first actions, after collecting Garibaldi, were to update all the reviews on Raffaele's website," he explained.

Olivia's mouth fell open. What a wonderful and generous act.

"Your review was the first one I edited and I gave all your wines top grading. As a result, La Leggenda now heads the list of Wineries in Tuscany to Visit. I was also glad to be able to correct the reviews of other excellent wineries. Quercia, Cantina Carducci, and Vino Sul Mare are all now on the first page, together with a number of other great vineyards in this area. No wineries have a poor grading, as none deserved it. Every one of them should now attract tourists, visitors, and buyers."

Olivia's heart soared. This was wonderful news for the whole of Tuscany.

"Thank you so much, from all of us. You've been a hero."

He shook his head modestly. "My pleasure," he said.

Brigitta tugged his arm.

"Come on, we need to sit down or we won't get a seat at all," she said. "This place is becoming very full. I want to get a good lunch table, too, with a view."

To Olivia's amazement, the next visitor into the winery wasn't a tourist, but a delivery person. She could barely see the short, sturdy man behind the enormous arrangement of colorful blooms he was carrying.

"Er, can I help you?" She hurried over, peering around the fragrant bouquet to locate his face.

"Thank you, yes. These are for Olivia Glass. Where should I put them?"

"For me?" Olivia stepped back in confusion. It wasn't her birthday—was it? Had she forgotten this auspicious day in all the craziness that recent events had brought?

Nope, definitely not. Her birthday was months away. What, then, was this floral arrangement doing here, and who on earth could it be from?

With some difficulty, she and the delivery person wove their way in between the groups of tourists and placed the flowers on a table at the back of the tasting room.

Only then did Olivia have a chance to read the card.

"Dear Olivia—We understand through the grapevine—haha—that your tireless efforts have resulted in an arrest, and also repaired the damage done to our winery. This is a small token of our enduring gratitude. You are our heroine. And we will never forget that you personally bought wine and supported us during these past dark days. With grateful thanks—Gianfranco and the team at Quercia Winery."

"Oh, my goodness," Olivia felt her eyes welling up. The flowers were beautiful, and all the more special for being such a surprise.

As the delivery driver left, he nearly collided with another arrival.

This courier was carrying a massive wooden box piled high with fruit, chocolates, cookies, and a bottle of pink champagne.

"Who is that for?" Jean-Pierre asked curiously. "I have never seen so many Ferrero Rocher chocolates in one hamper before."

Directing the delivery person to the table next to the flowers, Olivia read the message.

"Dear Olivia—Gianfranco just told me you are responsible for the poor reviews being reversed. In fact, we have received additional orders this morning from our supporting restaurants. Thank you so much for this incredible outcome, not to mention your loyal purchasing of our wines in difficult times. You are welcome any time as an honored guest at our winery. From Mr. Carducci and all at Cantina Carducci, we wish you long life and happiness."

"It's for me again!" she exclaimed. "I'll never eat all of these. I think this wonderful gift must remain here, for all of us to enjoy."

As she removed the printed message, which she intended to keep forever as it was so touching and special, Olivia heard her assistant call her name again.

Another delivery? Surely not.

She turned around to see Jean-Pierre's demeanor had changed. His suave, smiling attitude had vanished. He was frowning, his jaw jutted, his shoulders tensed—in fact, he looked like a charging bull. And as she watched, he started behaving like one, accelerating toward the doorway with his head lowered.

A moment later, Olivia realized why.

Matt was walking into the winery.

CHAPTER THIRTY

Upon seeing her ex walk in, Olivia bristled. Now she knew how Pirate had felt the first time she'd tried to pick him up. If she had black, shiny fur, it would be standing on end like a scrubbing brush, looking spiky and threatening.

Xanthe wasn't with Matt this time. Or, more likely, she'd found a selfie opportunity in the parking lot, Olivia thought unforgivingly.

"Leave, now!" Jean-Pierre shouted. "We are too busy for you today. You must come back another time. Maybe next year!"

Matt stared nervously at Jean-Pierre.

"Please?" he asked, giving him an appeasing smile. "I was hoping for a quick word with Olivia. Then I'll leave. I promise not to taste any wine."

Jean-Pierre hesitated and glanced at Olivia.

With a sigh, she walked over. She hadn't expected Matt to be polite. In fact, she didn't know what to make of it, and clearly, nor did Jean-Pierre. Matt's tone seemed sincere. It wasn't filled with the ringing self-importance that had characterized every other word she'd heard him utter thus far.

"What do you want? We're very busy this morning." She gestured expansively at the rapidly filling room.

"I see that. Could we—could we talk in the foyer for a moment?"

Olivia decided that she would give Matt one moment, and no more than that.

"I won't be long," she promised Jean-Pierre.

She followed Matt to the entrance hall, where they flattened themselves against the wall as another tour group filed in. Olivia heard familiar voices passing her by.

"Well, Barry, I can't believe you didn't tell us about this winery before now. It looks incredible."

"It wasn't on the site at all before last night."

Raucous laughter erupted.

"A likely story. You didn't look properly. It must have been there. Too much of that Metodo Classico at lunchtime, I believe."

"I'm excited to taste their rosé, I must say. A brand new first-ever release, which is a sure award winner. What dinner parties we'll host once our cases of it have been delivered back in Deans Bottom."

Olivia turned back to Matt, feeling impatient. She was eager to get back to her British acquaintances and introduce them personally to her rosé.

"I can see you're busy," Matt gabbled. "I don't want to waste any of your time. But I—I sneaked away from our hotel this morning—we've just moved to the Gardens of Florence. I'm not sure if you've heard of it? It's top class."

Olivia's eyes narrowed, recognizing a return to Matt's old persona. He was bragging about staying in the best place. She should have known his new apologetic veneer would wear off soon.

"Never heard of it," she snapped.

"Oh." Matt looked taken aback. "Oh. Well, anyway, it's very nice. We're in their presidential suite and they said we're the first guests since it's been newly refurbished. I decided I wanted to stay at a hotel with a gym. Fitness has become very important to me recently, Olivia. I want to use this vacation to get into shape." He ran a hand over his head. "I was also thinking of adding a few purple highlights to my style. What do you think?"

Olivia felt her patience evaporating.

"I have no idea about your hair. Did you come here to ask me that?" she said.

"No, no. I came to chat with you alone, because Xanthe is meeting an old friend for breakfast in Florence. Things—things haven't been so great between us. Even before our vacation. You know, I have been thinking Xanthe is very narcissistic. She never seems to pay me enough attention."

Olivia's eyes widened. If only Matt took this line of reasoning further, he could have an important insight about himself as well.

Matt didn't wait for her to comment, but plowed on.

"I've realized what I lost with you. I saw that even before coming
here. It was why I chose Tuscany. I was sort of hoping that if I arrived in a
mysterious way and surprised you by being in your life again, you might
also realize what you had lost when we split up."

Olivia stared at him incredulously.

"But we didn't split up. You dumped me because you said it wasn't
working out, and you were cheating on me in the meantime. That's actually the main reason I ended up here, in Tuscany. That bust-up was the
starting point for my new life adventure."

Matt shuffled his feet.

"I recall it was more of a mutual decision. I mean, you have to admit,
passion had cooled on both sides. In any case, I thought by coming here,
perhaps we could reignite it."

"Matt, you haven't said or done a single thing that would make me
consider starting over with you. All you've done is interfere in my life,
stalk me, and brag about earning pots of cash. When was money ever a
huge priority for me anyway?"

"Ah, yes, you see, that's what I really appreciate about you, Olivia.
You're not a materialistic person at all. Even so, my recent bonus was
phenomenal, so I thought it was worth mentioning."

Olivia shook her head. This conversation was absolutely surreal.

"Spending truckloads of cash on your girlfriend and then rubbing it
in my face is not the way to endear yourself to me again. I don't think
there is a way. I'm sorry, Matt, but I've moved on. We didn't part on
good terms and I don't even regard you as a friend anymore. You're an
ex. That's all. Just an ex. One of the mistakes I made on the great learning curve of life!" Channeling her inner Italian, Olivia waved her arms,
nearly knocking the beret off a passing French tourist.

"Oh," Matt said. He seemed deflated. "So there's no chance you'll
change your mind?"

Olivia rolled her eyes. "There is no chance whatsoever. Matt, I don't
even think this is about me. It's about you. You're never going to be

happy with anyone until you're happy with yourself, and clearly you're not. Xanthe doesn't seem like a bad person, and think how rich and full your Instagram pages will be. You've been behaving horribly by using her to try and make me jealous, and she actually doesn't deserve you. If I were you, I'd have a deep think about your behavior, and go back and apologize to her."

Matt's eyes were like saucers. Clearly, Olivia's insight had not been what he expected.

"Please don't contact me again. And try to be a better person for the rest of your vacation. And your life," Olivia said, feeling a flicker of spiteful glee that Matt was finally being forced to confront the real problem in his relationships.

She didn't have anything more to say, so she turned and walked back into the winery, heading straight for the British tour group with a smile. She was sure they'd be excited to find out she worked here.

It was after five p.m. when the last of the tourists left. Olivia had been so energized by the busy day and the buzz of nonstop visitors, she hadn't had a chance to think about how sore her feet were, or how hungry she was. As she closed the tasting room door, both these realities came home to her in a flash. She was starving.

Checking her phone, she saw that Danilo had left a message.

"I hear you have been very busy at the winery today. How about a vine inspection at seven p.m.? I can bring pizza."

"It's a—" Olivia almost typed back "date." Just in time, she stopped herself, and substituted the word "deal," along with a string of smiley emojis. Knowing that pizza and wine-growing advice would be waiting back at the farmhouse made her feel motivated all over again. It was time to head home.

She rummaged in her purse for her comfortable walking shoes, transferring her smart high-heeled dress shoes to the carrier bag.

As she slipped the flat shoes on, Marcello walked out of the winery.

He headed straight over to her, smiling.

"I have not had a chance to congratulate you today. I have been tied to the office all day, with orders streaming in. Only now has the phone stopped ringing," he said.

"I'm so glad," Olivia said.

She smiled at Marcello, seeing her delight reflected in his expression. And something else—something that made her heart hop, skip, and jump.

Marcello took a deep breath.

"I have been waiting for the right moment to talk to you, Olivia—not about work, but personal matters. About my feelings."

Now Olivia's heart had leaped into her mouth. She couldn't believe this was happening. He was about to voice his thoughts and make real what, until now, had been an unspoken truth between them.

She felt as if she couldn't breathe as she waited for Marcello to tell her what was in his heart.

Chapter Thirty One

After a pause that felt like an eternity to Olivia, Marcello continued speaking. His blue gaze didn't leave hers. She felt hypnotized by it.

"Olivia, ever since you arrived at La Leggenda, I confess, I have had feelings for you." He spread his arms. "At the same time, I have been torn. My last relationship was a bad one, I promised myself I would never be involved with an employee again. Then I told myself I could break the promise for you, but the time never seemed right. Always, it was too important that things remained as they were."

Olivia swallowed.

"I understand," she said.

She wasn't sure if she did understand. Marcello sounded regretful. This conversation wasn't going how she'd hoped it would. And yet—deep down, she thought perhaps it was. That she'd been expecting this, in a way.

"I have battled with myself for many weeks about it. And I have decided I cannot let this continue without making a decision and giving you an explanation. The truth is, Olivia, you are too valuable to me now as you are. As our head sommelier, our marketing guru, one of our biggest assets. The person who saves our winery and the whole of Tuscany from a catastrophe." He smiled, and she found herself smiling again, too. "I cannot afford to lose you. Thus, I cannot allow my romantic heart to prevail in this matter, but must force myself to be guided by my logical reasoning. So, instead of inviting you to my cottage for wine and pasta as I have dreamed of doing, I must tell you with the greatest reluctance that for now, I feel we should remain as friends."

Olivia felt pummeled by an avalanche of colliding emotions. The hope she'd felt as he started speaking lay crushed at the bottom of the pile. She felt raw shock at his words, but also pride at how highly he thought of her. Then along came disappointment, thundering down the slope and obliterating everything else, so that she thought she might burst into tears.

Except, right at the end, in the last flurries of the fall, she felt something entirely unexpected.

Relief.

To her amazement, Olivia realized that was the emotion that remained after the maelstrom had passed. She felt relieved that things wouldn't change, that there wouldn't be any of the complications that romance would bring, that her job was steady and secure and that the working relationship she had with Marcello, which she treasured and valued, would continue to be stable.

She found herself nodding.

"It's weird and confusing, but I feel exactly the same," she confessed. "What I have—with you, with La Leggenda—is too precious at the moment to want to change it."

As she spoke, she wasn't sure if her words were altogether true. But they were partly true.

"I'm glad that you think the same, and that we have had this chance to speak. Sad, but glad."

"That's me, too. Sad, but glad." Olivia nodded bravely at him.

Marcello kissed her cheek.

"Have a good evening," he said, before turning and walking swiftly toward his house, as if wanting to put distance between them in case he was tempted to say anything else, or perhaps change his mind.

"Come, Erba," Olivia called.

Her small goat capered loyally up to her and it was only then that Olivia felt tears prickle her eyes for regret at what might have been.

Or maybe it was just that her eyes were watering in the chilly breeze.

"Home time," she told the goat.

The walk back to the farmhouse passed in no time. It felt like only a few minutes later that she was heading up the sandy driveway.

Olivia went straight to the barn. There was half an hour of daylight left, and she planned to use it to continue clearing the pile of rubble. She hoped that a session of hard and honest effort would stop her from agonizing over what had just happened between her and Marcello.

To her amazement, when she walked into the barn, she realized that for the first time, the pile looked smaller!

It no longer looked like an immovable mountain, but rather a manageable size that could be easily cleared with a little more effort. Her hard labor, and Danilo's tireless help, had whittled it down to a point where she could gauge how many barrow loads were left to remove. Fifteen trips, or twenty at the most, and the pile would be history!

Excitement flared inside her as she remembered the locked storeroom on the hill. Surely a small metal key would have fallen all the way down to the bottom of a heap like this, if it was here at all? Perhaps finding it would be her final reward.

As Olivia filled her third barrow load, she heard a shouted "hello" from the almost-dark doorway.

Danilo had arrived.

Olivia hurried to the door to greet him, smiling in delight as she dusted off her hands.

"Italian or American hello?" he asked her, his hands outspread.

"Both," Olivia said.

He enfolded her in a warm embrace, and as she wrapped her arms around him, Olivia felt a thrill of warmth. One last rock from her emotional avalanche bounced down the slope and hit her sharply on the head.

She realized, to her astonishment, that she had developed feelings for this charming, generous-hearted man that went beyond the relaxed, platonic friendship she'd thought they had.

Somewhere between clearing out the barn and the trip to Florence and the evening they'd spent discussing the case, Danilo had become more to her.

Well, this is complicated, Olivia thought—or maybe not so much. She didn't know. She felt totally confused about what was playing out between them. Just as she'd thought her heart was bruised by Marcello's charming and honest rejection, she'd discovered it hadn't sustained any serious damage and, in fact, had already been exploring a new romantic direction of its own.

At any rate, now was not the time to think about this surprising discovery, and she didn't feel ready to share her feelings with Danilo, who was already heading over to the vine plantation to assess the condition of her frostbitten grapevines.

He had parked his pickup so that the headlights shone on the nearest vines, and he detoured to the car to take out a heavy-duty flashlight. He trained the beam on the dark stems and brown, withered leaves, now cocooned in protective swaths of golden straw.

Although, Olivia thought, maybe they didn't look quite as withered as they had. The leaves looked springier and not all of them appeared to be completely dead. In fact, she thought one or two vines might have shot up since yesterday.

"I think they will survive this," Danilo said. "They seem to be doing well. Sangiovese are very tough and weather resistant, and it takes a lot to kill them. I think we will have to try harder," he joked, putting his arm around her shoulder in a friendly way. Or was it simple friendship? she wondered, feeling her heart start to skip again.

"I hope these vines will produce extra-special grapes, since they're resilient enough to survive being iced over." She smiled.

As she said that, the words reminded Olivia of something.

Several years ago, when she and Charlotte had eaten at a fancy restaurant in Chicago, there had been a unique dessert wine on the menu that she'd never heard of before. She and her best friend had both been intrigued by it and had ordered the wine to enjoy with their coffee and cake, even though it had been outside of their usual price bracket. Olivia still remembered the description, and how refreshingly sweet, yet acidic, it had been.

Californian Ice Wine—Made from Grapes Frozen on the Vines.

The wild vines dotted around her property, laden with grapes, were not ruined after the freezing weather. Instead, the iced-over grapes would give her a unique opportunity to bring something brand new to the market.

She was going to make what would hopefully be Tuscany's first ice wine.

Now Available for Pre-Order!

AGED FOR SEDUCTION
(A Tuscan Vineyard Cozy Mystery—Book 4)

"Very entertaining. I highly recommend this book to the permanent library of any reader that appreciates a very well written mystery, with some twists and an intelligent plot. You will not be disappointed. Excellent way to spend a cold weekend!"

—Books and Movie Reviews, Roberto Mattos
(regarding *Murder in the Manor*)

AGED FOR SEDUCTION (A TUSCAN VINEYARD COZY MYSTERY) is book #4 in a charming new cozy mystery series by #1 bestselling author Fiona Grace, author of Murder in the Manor (Book #1), a #1 Bestseller with over 100 five-star reviews—and a free download!

Olivia Glass, 34, turns her back on her life as a high-powered executive in Chicago and relocates to Tuscany, determined to start a new, simpler life—and to grow her own vineyard.

When a bachelorette party comes to the winery, Olivia is hard at work to accommodate the wedding party—when a shocking murder leaves the wedding in shambles—and Olivia in the spotlight. Will she find the murderer and clear her name?

Hilarious, packed with travel, food, wine, twists and turns, romance and her newfound animal friend—and centering around a baffling small-town murder that Olivia must solve—the TUSCAN VINEYARD is an un-putdownable mystery series that will keep you laughing late into the night.

Book #5 in the series will be available soon.

AGED FOR SEDUCTION
(A Tuscan Vineyard Cozy Mystery—Book 4)

ALSO NOW AVAILABLE FOR PRE-ORDER! A NEW SERIES!

BEACHFRONT BAKERY: A KILLER CUPCAKE
(A Beachfront Bakery Cozy Mystery—Book 1)

"Very entertaining. I highly recommend this book to the permanent library of any reader that appreciates a very well written mystery, with some twists and an intelligent plot. You will not be disappointed. Excellent way to spend a cold weekend!"

—Books and Movie Reviews, Roberto Mattos
(regarding Murder in the Manor)

BEACHFRONT BAKERY: A KILLER CUPCAKE is the debut novel in a charming and hilarious new cozy mystery series by #1 bestselling author Fiona Grace, whose bestselling Murder in the Manor (A Lacey Doyle Cozy Mystery) has nearly 200 five star reviews.

Allison Sweet, 34, a sous chef in Los Angeles, has had it up to here with demeaning customers, her demanding boss, and her failed love life. After a shocking incident, she realizes the time has come to start life fresh and follow her lifelong dream of moving to a small town and opening a bakery of her own.

When Allison spots a charming, vacant storefront on the boardwalk near Venice, she wonders if she could really start life anew. Feeling like it's a sign, and a time to take a chance in life, she goes for it.

Yet Allison did not anticipate the wild ride ahead of her: the boardwalk, filled with fun and outrageous characters, is pulsing with life, from the Italian pizzeria owners on either side of her who vie for her affection, to the fortune tellers and scheming rival bakery owner nearby. Allison yearns to just focus on her delicious new pastry recipes and keep her struggling bakery afloat—but when a murder occurs right near her shop, everything changes.

Implicated, her entire future at stake, Allison has no choice but to investigate to clear her name. As an orphaned dog wanders into her life, a devoted new sidekick with a knack for solving mysteries, she starts her search.

Will they find the killer? And can her struggling bakery survive?

A hilarious cozy mystery series, packed with twists, turns, romance, travel, food and unexpected adventure, the BEACHFRONT BAKERY series will keep you laughing and turning pages late into the night as you fall in love with an endearing new character who will capture your heart.

Book #2 in the series—A MURDEROUS MACARON—is also available!

BEACHFRONT BAKERY: A KILLER CUPCAKE
(A Beachfront Bakery Cozy Mystery—Book 1)

ALSO NOW AVAILABLE FOR PRE-ORDER!
A NEW SERIES!

SKEPTIC IN SALEM: AN EPISODE OF MURDER
(A Dubious Witch Cozy Mystery—Book 1)

"Very entertaining. Highly recommended for the permanent library of any reader who appreciates a well-written mystery with twists and an intelligent plot. You will not be disappointed. Excellent way to spend a cold weekend!"

—Books and Movie Reviews (regarding Murder in the Manor)

SKEPTIC IN SALEM: AN EPISODE OF MURDER is the debut novel in a charming new cozy mystery series by bestselling author Fiona Grace, author of Murder in the Manor, a #1 Bestseller with over 100 five-star reviews (and a free download)!

When Mia Bold, 30, learns that the pharmaceutical company she works for only cares about money, she quits on the spot, walking away from a high-powered career. Worse, her long-time boyfriend, instead of proposing as she expected, decides to break up with her.

Mia's true passion lies in her own podcast, devoted to debunking the occult and shining light on the truth. The daughter of a con-man father, Mia feels a moral responsibility to the truth, and to spare others from being conned.

When Mia, at a crossroads, receives an invitation from a famous supernatural podcast inviting her to move to Salem and join their podcast as the skeptic-in-residence, Mia sees a chance to start her life over again and to pursue her life's mission.

But things in Salem do not go as planned. When an unexpected death happens—in the midst of Mia trying to debunk a haunted inn—she realizes she may be in over her head. With her own future now at stake, can she really prove that witches and ghosts do not exist?

A mesmerizing page-turner, packed with intrigue, mystery, romance, pets, food—and most of all, the supernatural—SKEPTIC IN SALEM is a cozy with a twist, one you will cherish as it has you fall in love with its main character and as it keeps you glued (and laughing) throughout the night.

Book #2 in the series—AN EPISODE OF CRIME—is also available!

"The book had heart and the entire story worked together seamlessly that didn't sacrifice either intrigue or personality. I loved the characters – so many great characters! I can't wait to read whatever Fiona Grace writes next!"

—Amazon reviewer (regarding Murder in the Manor)

"Wow, this book takes off & never stops! I couldn't put it down! Highly recommended for those who love a great mystery with twists, turns, romance, and a long lost family member! I am reading the next book right now!"

—Amazon reviewer (regarding Murder in the Manor)

"This book is rather fast paced. It has the right blend of characters, place, and emotions. It was hard to put down and I hope to read the next book in the series."

SKEPTIC IN SALEM: AN EPISODE OF MURDER
(A Dubious Witch Cozy Mystery—Book 1)

Made in the USA
Las Vegas, NV
29 September 2022

56205354R00129